CLAN SLUAGH NA MARA
MARA
DOCK
TO MARA
OIRE COELLE
CLAN TRIACT
CLAN CHERYIC
MAGNAR'S FIRST
HIDEOUT
MAGNAR'S SECOND
HIDEOUT
CHERYIC CITY
CHERYIC DOCK
TO BELFAST
CEARTAS
CLAN GRAOTIC
BEOFADA
CLAN DUCHANNON

THE MIRACLE

OF BROKEN ENDINGS

A Novel by

Talia Martini

TO DAD

In hope that this helps make your
fiftieth birthday a little better.

Prologue

It was a time long before the one you know that The Battle of Culloden occurred, and the clans of Scotland were destroyed by the British. It took no more than an hour. This is the tale you are told over and over because no one has the means to describe the actual events at hand. All it took was one single clan to go, hide, and forge a life in the mountains, never detected by the British, who did not know the terrain like the Scotts.

It was in a time not so later than the one you know that the World War began. The war took ten years, and when peace was finally declared, the United Kingdom, which had long been evacuated, was declared unfit to live in. In fact, half of the United States was unfit to live in as well, and a famine befell the nations. As a result of the devastation that the famine had caused on the dwindling life on earth, an international committee was formed. The committee felt it was forced to instill a ban on all explosive and nuclear weapons. Every nation, both experiencing the famine and the aftermath of the war, agreed to this. The treaty was signed, and guns and explosives were outlawed everywhere.

When Owen Cheryic heard the news that the Outsiders had fled Scotland, and his clan, the only surviving one in Scotland could be free at last, he stayed inside the mountain. The city under Ben Nevis had grown prosperous, if somewhat dark and damp. It was all the clan knew, to live beneath the mountain during the day and travel by night. Hundreds of spies had been sent out during the war to update Owen on how the world had fared. Only four had returned: Kin Sluagh na Mara, Jaxon Duchannon, Harris Craotic and Aklen Triact.

Kin Sluagh na Mara fell in love with the sea. After he returned, he took three ships to explore it. He eventually settled on a mesh of islands off the coast of Scotland, drawn to their danger and rigor. Jaxon Duchannon had lost many friends during the war and wished to begin a farm so that he could quietly live out his days in memory of his companions. But he was so popular, his family and friends insisted upon going south with him. Three hundred people accompanied him. Aklen Triact was one of those who followed him, but he was no southerner. The Highlands were his passion, so he rode north and chose to remain there, with many of his loved ones. Harris Craotic remained with Owen Cheryic for ten years, until a boy was caught stealing from him. He chose to cut the boy's hand off as justice. Owen Cheryic grew angry that Harris had performed such an unjustified act behind his back and sent Harris away to exile. Harris would not accept this and convinced Owen Cheryic's son to stab him in his sleep. The boy did so and then rode north with Harris Craotic and two hundred men.

In his dying words, Owen Cheryic passed on his city to his second son, Broden. Under Broden Cheryic, the clan prospered, rising above ground when all threat of Outside danger was perceived gone. But Broden remained haunted by the prospect of the Outsiders returning to Scotland. He met with the five new clans and devised a treaty, which kept the clans united against Outside threat, but separate within the barriers of Scotland.

the greatest adventure

Three red deer ambled in and out of columns of their castle of trees. Their eyes glistened to form silver specks beneath the shadows of the firs and pines. The trickle of a small brook was enough to cover the sound of Eason Rankin's movement as he crouched behind the bushes and placed an arrow on his bow. He positioned two others at the ready by his side. If he could kill all of them, he could provide the people with an abundant feast for *L'anaman* and the innocent creatures would not have to live without one another's company.

As they trotted, one stopped idly to graze on a green patch, not ten feet from Eason. Another ventured farther ahead, leading with its nose. The third, with immense branching antlers, stopped and perked its head up. Eason drew his arrow, aiming at the farthest deer and released. The arrow passed through its eye before it had a clue of what was happening. Quicker than thought, Eason drew another arrow back into his bow and released, puncturing the grazing deer in the stomach. He hastily grabbed at his third arrow, but it was too late. The buck had scrambled away, condemned to a lonely life.

Eason approached the deer. The first had been killed at contact, but the second drew short, vigorous breaths, kicking its hooves slightly. Eason drew his sword and slit the animal's throat, waiting patiently for it to bleed out and muttering under his breath calming words in Gaelic. Then, one at a time, he lifted them carefully onto his horse, grunting with exertion. Upon finishing this task, he stretched out his arms and led the horse home.

Eason's nephew, Magnar, had been the designated hunter for the night. However, the boy hadn't come home from his trip through Ben Nevis yet, and the feast *L'anaman* would not wait for the boy. In Eason's mind, Magnar was too young to go out into the mountains without an adult. But the clan had its ways which Eason still had not grown used to. They did not mind their children risking their necks if it was in the name of the spirits or to provide food for the table. So Eason had permitted the boy to leave.

It was an hour's walk to the outer gates of the city, during which he thanked the spirits for the moon's light. Without the moon, he was unsure how his failing eyes would lead him home in the pitch black. But the moon was there in full and lit up the tall grasses of rare highland farmlands surrounding him. Something inside of Eason was warning him not to return. He shrugged it off as wariness of the usual annoyances that he endured: the laziness of the boys or the small chittering gossip of the people. He would have preferred to live in solitary in the woods, with only the company of badgers and eagles. But, responsibility took hold of him, as per usual.

When he arrived at the gates of the city, which the guard courteously opened for him, he passed old stone buildings of all shapes and sizes. The city was quiet at night, aside from soldiers taking a jog and a tavern that shook with obnoxious laughter. Eason despised going out during the day when everyone was bustling around and trying to mingle with their Chief.

"Tis a bonnie[1] day, Gliocas.[2]" Some would say.

"Aye, the grass is green enough." He would respond and walk away before a villager could say another word.

Or it would be, "are your nephews well, Gliocas?"

"Unfortunately," he would grumble in response.

He continued his way down the dirt road into Town Square. Across the square was his own home and quarters. Upon his arrival, he tied the horse off, allowing it some fresh hay. A man would come later to run it in a nearby pasture. He threw his deer in the meat cooler below the front stairs, wiped his feet off onto the woven straw mat, and slammed open the rotting wooden door.

"Caiden skin the d-"

Three figures stood inside: a small, blond ten-year-old with hair past his shoulders and a thin yet strong form, and a shorter, weaker, tanned seven-year-old with puppy dog eyes and chocolate hair down to his shoulders. But the one who formed a lump in Eason's throat was a woman in her mid-thirties with curly, dark brown hair, bright eyes, a complexion like the older boy's, yet a reckless, stubborn aura much like the younger boy's. She wore clothes that sent a chill of nostalgia across Eason's body. He believed the breeks had

---

[1] Beautiful

[2] Your Majesty

once been called “jeans” and the shirt with a soft, brightly colored fabric was a “t-shirt”.

Caiden, the smaller boy, ran his wooden horse across the carpet, oblivious to the woman, making “nay” noises as his little horse trotted.

Magnar, the older, blond boy, stood rigid with his arms crossed. His tunic had been soaked with mud, then dried again. Little crusts of dirt flew off of him when he moved. The boy glared at Helen, unable to remove his eyes from her nonchalant stance.

"What are you doing here?" Eason asked, none too politely.

Helen smiled a knowing, devious smile.

Eason shuddered. His sister appeared to have become even more deranged than when he last saw her. Her eyes seemed so feverish and bright; she could hardly focus them on one single individual. They flew around wildly, from person to person.

"Is that the way you now greet family here? Aw…pity…I thought you and your little crew would be more welcoming than that." She made a mock pity face that closely resembled Caiden’s pouts.

"What do you want, Helen?" Eason’s voice was dangerously quiet. Everyone in the clan knew to fear his tone. But Helen didn’t live with the clan. Her smile widened, and she let out a high-pitched giggle. In a sudden jolted movement, she straightened up and placed her hands on her hips.

“You remember that girl?” She asked with a smirk.

“It depends what girl we are talking about, sister. Stop this nonsense,” Eason replied impatiently.

"Tall. Chestnut hair. Paler than the moon. You used to say that her brown eyes were so huge that they could replace a mirror for anyone who wanted to see their reflection."

"Our sister, Christine?" Eason asked, quickly gaining interest in the conversation. Even saying her name seemed like a distant memory, for he had not heard it in so many years.

"Mhm." Helen smiled cruelly.

"Well, what of her? Is she well?" Eason asked.

"Not really."

"Do I need to go to her?" Eason asked, panic rising within him.

"Nope. The funeral is over."

Eason's breath seemed to stop.

"She is dead?" He asked, dreading the answer.

"Yes. *She is dead.*" She said in a tone that mocked Eason's official vocal pattern. For the first time, she noticed the boys and waved at them.

Eason's vision blurred as he found his way to a chair. I cannot cry, he thought, not in front of them, not in front of her.

"I had an aunt?" Eason heard Magnar ask. "How'd she die?"

"Um...well...the thing about that…" Helen began, "boys can I talk to your uncle alone? Oh, and by the way, her daughter is still alive."

"Wait!" Magnar interrupted. "You canna just kick us out, we're part of this family too!"

"Magnar and Caiden go to your room," Eason commanded hoarsely. "And I already told you, canna is no word for an heir."

Magnar just stared, wide-eyed at Eason's betrayal. But Caiden dragged him with one hand and his wooden horse with the other to their room.

***

"They can't just kick us out like that; it isn't right." Magnar crossed his arms angrily, his back pressed against the old chipped bedroom door. He turned his ear against it, trying to make out what the muffled voices were saying.

Caiden plopped onto his bed, which produced a loud CREAK.

Magnar scowled.

"Sorry." Caiden giggled, struggling to light a candle.

"I can't believe that witch is our maw," Magnar grumbled.

"Why no?" Caiden asked, running the wooden horse across his knee.

"Because she's...you know...a fanny," Magnar whispered, now bending down on his knees, attempting to peep at the crack below the door.

"Uncle said not to use that word!" Caiden shouted, nearly dropping his lit candle in one hand, while still racing his horse with the other. "He'll skelp[3] ya for sure!"

"Aw don't be a wee clipe.[4] The point is, she's not well."

"So? Maybe Uncle can help her." Caiden said, making a toy soldier stab his horse in the gut.

"You're too young to understand." Magnar sighed.

Caiden dropped his toys. The candle fell to the ground as well, but the boy stomped on it before it could make a fuss.

"I turn eight in a few months!"

"Exactly. I turn ten in a few months."

---

[3] Spank

[4] Tattle tale

"Not until November."

"And?"

"I understand. Uncle can help maw." Caiden went back to his toys.

"You cannot help someone who is completely evil." Magnar scowled again, peering below the crack, yet only seeing the legs of chairs and foundation of a countertop.

"Maw is not evil," Caiden mumbled.

Magnar sighed and continued trying to make out what the voices were saying.

"Why did maw give us to Uncle?" Caiden asked.

Magnar rolled his eyes.

"Because she's evil."

"But Uncle is nice. Most of the time."

"Well, Uncle isn't her. Can I listen to them now?" Magnar asked annoyedly.

"But why did she give us up?"

Magnar just ignored him, his ear to the door.

"Why? Why? Why?" Caiden got off the bed now, approaching Magnar. "Why Magnar, why?!"

"Haud yer wheesht will ya?![5]" Magnar shouted back.

"Boys, be quiet!" Eason's muffled, but distinct voice shouted angrily.

The boys remained quiet for a full ten seconds.

"She gave us up, Caiden, because she hates us," Magnar whispered, sensing the truth in his statement.

"Wheesht,[6]" Caiden said, laying his ear against the door. "I'm tryna listen."

---

[5] Be quiet!

[6] Quiet!

Magnar rolled his eyes. They managed to crack the door open without attracting any attention.

"There's another thing, Eason." Helen's voice could be heard saying.

"What?" Eason asked, sounding quite exasperated.

"Christi had a brat."

"A child? Aye, you told me."

"Mhm. A girl. Most annoying damn thing you'll ever come across. Although, I imagine you're used to it with those brats running around."

"Are you referring to your sons?" Eason challenged.

"I guess. Anyway, the girl is going to be staying with daddy."

"What?" The boys practically could feel the heat radiating from Eason, as he sneered that word through his teeth.

"What's the matter, don't like that? Oh wait, I forgot about your strained relationship with him. Hm. Well, it's not your problem, is it?"

There was a long pause, during which, Magnar felt a bead of summer sweat trickle down his head. Or was it a nervous sweat? He could not tell.

"Was this in Christine's will?"

"She didn't have a will."

Eason sighed. "Why not just bring the girl here. Even with a dying mind, Christine wouldn't want her daughter to live five minutes with that wretched man."

"I thought you might say that!"

A few seconds passed, and a door creaked open.

"Rose, this is your Uncle Eason. He kind of ran away from home, and your grandfather hated him, but don't worry about that, you'll have fun! Ok goodbye!" Helen could be heard saying.

The door slammed shut and there was nothing but silence. Caiden couldn't seem to take it anymore; the boy was shaking with excitement. He opened the door and ran outside.

what lies ahead

Helen was gone. A tiny girl stood in front of the door with Magnar's green eyes. Yet that was the only physical similarity she had to Magnar, for it was Caiden who matched her appearance the most. She shared his dark brown locks, which ran down just past her shoulders, and her thick lips were pushed together by giant chubby cheeks, just like his.

She just stood there, not looking at anyone, letting a clunky pillowcase fall to her side as she stared at the ground with an expressionless face.

Magnar and Eason peeked behind the door with unblinking eyes at this...*Sassenach* girl.

Swiftly, Caiden ran from the door and gave the girl the biggest hug he possibly could. She wasn't much of a hugger; she did not reciprocate at all, perhaps because Caiden was squeezing nearly all of the Oxygen from her tiny bones. He broke away, noticing that the girl was exactly his height. She said nothing, but gaped at him shyly with sizable green eyes.

Eason stared with amazement: It was as if the two were looking in the mirror. They easily could have been twins, but for the girl's bright eyes.

Caiden smiled.

"Welcome to the family, cousin."

The girl stood rigid, not replying.

"We are gonna have sooo much fun! I can show you the river, you can join our manhunt games, wrestle, play catch the chicken, fling stones, play knucklebones and Niddy noddy..."

Even Eason was beginning to feel dizzy amidst the overwhelming list of activities that Caiden had already planned within the last minute and a half.

"Enough Caiden, give the lass some room." Eason interrupted, lifting the boy away from her.

The over-excited boy nodded, possessing a smile that easily reached from ear to ear. Yet he never slowed his tongue. He went on about all the adventures they would have together, the monsters they would slay, the camping trips to the forest they would take, etc.

After about an hour, he looked back at Eason.

"Does she talk?"

Such a question was rewarded with a slap in the back of the head from Eason.

"She's only quiet, lad. Be polite." Eason said softly. His expressions seemed to soften as he faced the girl, dragging a hand across his dark beard. "Are you hungry? The meat I got needs preparing, but we can get you some porridge and seeds if you'd like."

The girl slowly nodded, not daring to part her eyes from the ground.

Eason smiled sadly. “Caiden and Magnar,” he ordered, “go get some oats from the cellar. I need to talk with our new family.”

Caiden and Magnar trudged out the door, slowly at first, and then subconsciously decided to race each other as they both broke into a full sprint out the door. Eason took a seat in a large cushioned chair by the fireside. The living room of the humble house was small, but comfortable, with merely Eason’s chair and a couch across from the fireplace, both sitting on top of a dusty, red, woven rug.

Eason gestured for Rose to take a seat.

She did so on the couch.

“How long ago was it that your parents passed?” Eason asked quietly.

“About a week ago.” The girl said softly.

Eason nodded, fighting back the compelling wave of tears behind his eyes. He could not cry. Not in front of the girl, even for his own sister.

“I am so sorry for your loss. I loved your mother also; she was my sister.”

Rose nodded.

“Have you been staying with your aunt?”

She nodded again.

“Well, hopefully living here will be much better.”

Rose fixed her eyes on the neatly compacted dirt floor.

“Do you even know who I am, my dear?” Eason asked, it suddenly occurring to him that Helen wouldn’t have told her.

“My uncle?”

“Aye. I am your mother’s brother. Yes, I ran away from home when I was young, came here, and ended up living with my Uncle. Where you are now is Scotland.”

Rose scrunched her brow.

"What is Scotland?"

"Tis a land abandoned by industrialized men, who were threatened by warfare. The ancient clans however, had no warning of war, and so stayed in the mountains, ignorant and blissful. Here we have thrived since the industrialized man left. I, my dear, am the Chief of the Cheryic Clan, a humble yet tightly bound clan which is envied by even the wealthier clans of Scotland."

Rose's mouth hung open, and Eason realized that he had failed to imagine how many times the earth had turned for this girl today. The news of Christine had been difficult for him, but this child had no idea what life had in store for her now. Eason hung his head, embarrassed that he had been so ignorant.

"I'll give you a whole history lesson one day, but for tonight, you can sleep in my room, and I will stay on the couch. For now, just know you'll stay here from this day forward. We'll decide what else to do with you later. Now let's see what's taking the boys so long down there."

***

The boys hadn't even reached the bag of porridge. After all that time, they had been fighting over who would carry the bag upstairs, hastily throwing the sac back and forth until a hole had ruptured in the bottom and oats showered out of the sack. Eason smacked the backs of each of their heads and sent them off to bed. He scooped what he could from the sack and took it upstairs to cook for Rose, vowing to clean the mess when she had gone to bed. When she had settled, he forgot all about the spill and passed out on his couch.

today and tomorrow

When Rose awoke the next morning, she briefly forgot where she was. Her arm brushed across scratchy sheets, so rough it felt as if they were made of straw. She rubbed open her eyes to see the splintered planks of wood that made up the ceiling. She searched for a light switch but found that the only light source was a small window, shedding streams of the rising sun above her bed.

Tap. Tap.

The door creaked open and a small person poked their head through it.

It all flooded back to her: Her parents were gone, and she was in this strange, scary house in a distant land.

"Rose! Rose! Do you wanna play!?" Caiden asked, his head bobbing up and down through the cracked-open door.

Rose shrugged.

Caiden darted inside, jumping up and down on the bed.

"We can catch chickens with Evander!" Caiden shouted.

"Caiden, I told you to let her rest!" Eason's voice could be heard shouting from the kitchen.

"Sorry Uncle," Caiden called apologetically, yet the enthusiasm never left his voice and he continued bouncing.

Eason appeared in the room, holding some berries in a clay bowl. He wore a worn brown kilt with faded tartan lines of pale blue over a silky white tunic. His giant black boots boomed with every step he took.

"Caiden, get off of there now!" He ordered. The man's voice reminded Rose of a thunderstorm, low and loud enough to rattle the house as he raised it.

Caiden jumped down, darted out of the room, and shouted for Magnar, all in a split second.

"Here my dear, keep up your strength," Eason said quietly, handing Rose the berries.

Rose began eating some in Eason's presence, but as soon as he left, she threw them out the window. She couldn't eat. Not now.

For the next few days, the same routine followed. Caiden would run into Rose's makeshift room in the morning, begging Rose to play, but she would just sit by the window, picking at Eason's food. Eason was patient...for once. He told Caiden to give the girl time, that she'd come around. Eventually, Eason had a bed put in his own office and declared that his old room was now Rose's. She remained in that room, staring out the window. By the end of the week, Magnar made his first appearance in the girl's room.

"Rose?" He said.

She glanced over from her perch on the windowsill, but her eyes were still distant.

"I made this for you." He said, taking an interest in the loose dirt in the floor. He handed her a wooden amulet, which had a rose etched into the tiny pendant.

Rose hesitated, but let him drop the amulet in her tiny palm. She idly pressed her thumb against the design. Simple, yet beautiful.

"I like your name." Magnar said, "Roses are nice flowers, but when you try to pick them, well, your fingers regret it. Here."

Magnar draped the amulet over Rose's head, and after studying it on her, he gave a nod of approval and left the room. As if on command, Caiden bolted inside.

"Rose, please please please please please play with me!" He begged, literally falling onto his knees.

Rose pressed her thumb into the amulet, stood up, and followed Caiden out the door. Caiden squealed, jumping up and down, overjoyed at the prospect of a new friendship. Millions of thoughts flooded over him at once, as he went over all of the things they could do and debated both internally and externally about where to go first.

Caiden placed his hand on the doorknob, but hesitated, shooting a quizzical look back at the girl.

"Stop." He ordered, shooting his hand in front of Rose's face, nearly slapping her in the process. She obeyed. He quickly turned around and scooted Rose away from the door.

Caiden proceeded to plod back into his room, dragging Rose by the hand. He opened the wardrobe near the door. The wardrobe, like many things in this house, had seen too many years. He fumbled through some clothes in it for a few moments, then seemed to find what he was looking for. He glanced back at Rose and handed her a blue tunic, loose breeks, and leather boots.

"Tell me if these don't fit." He commanded, then left her to change. "This way, you don't look like a sassenach.[7]"

When Rose appeared again, looking very much like a highlander boy, Caiden squealed with glee. Rose was beginning to become used to the boy's high-pitched squeals, only grimacing slightly when he did them now. Everything fit perfectly, although the city would definitely think she was a boy. Caiden didn't mind this aspect, though; it meant she could play even more games with his friends.

Caiden and Rose ran straight to the door. Although Caiden bolted ahead of her, Rose froze upon meeting the outside.

She had never seen the city in broad daylight, it felt like she had fallen into a medieval movie of some sort. The house was directly in front of a town square, the size of a football field from Rose's old world. In the center of the square, sat an old stone well, and among the outskirts, there were shops and stands with people of all ages selling everything imaginable! A frail old man in a dirty coif was storing fish in a cooler he had built by digging a hole underground and placing a stone overtop. Another man, this one large around the middle, with a braid tied down his back stood behind a stand with glimmering metallic armor, nearly blinding to look at in the sun.

A young man with a light brown cloak sold beautiful bows engraved with such delicate designs that Rose doubted that the bows could ever actually be used...they must have been for wall decorations.

---

[7] Outsider

A baker sold rolls, bread, muffins, and biscuits. A blacksmith had an array of weapons on his table that he let neither Rose nor Caiden go near. There were stands selling deer skins, deer meat, goat meat, goat milk, bird meat, bird feathers, cowhides and dairy, jewelry made of solid gold or diamonds, cloaks, gowns, tunics, kilts, pots, books, maps, even things as simple as locks, bottles, candles, wood, etc. She even observed a man selling horse manure!

Surrounding this square of shops, shabby old stone and wooden buildings huddled together, creating alleys just big enough for dirt roads, wagons and horses. Of course, above all of this, Ben Nevis towered behind them, creating a chill which ran down Rose's spine when she craned her neck up to behold it.

In the middle of the square, men were building. They were stacking wood the size of small trees, creating some sort of pyre four times Rose's height.

"What are they building?" Rose asked. It was the most words that she had spoken together since she arrived.

Caiden laughed. "A firepit for *L'anaman* of course! Didn't ya realize what day it was?"

Rose stared at him, blankly.

Caiden gasped. "You don't have *L'anaman* where you come from, do ya?"

She shook her head.

Caiden squeezed her hand so hard it turned purple, and before she could say a single word, he was dragging Rose toward the mountain.

They were sprinting through the North Road. Caiden was attempting to explain the nature of L'anaman through breaths. Poor Rose, trying to take in her environment and decipher

Caiden's short-breathed accent at the same time, struggled to keep up.

"The spirits see...our ancestors..." *Gasp. Gasp.* "They protect us through the mountain." *Gasp.* "They protect us in death and we protect them in life." *Inhale.* "That's the deal, though I dunno who struck that one up." *Exhale. Inhale.* "But we pick the fruit, see, as a reminder of their gifts to us." *Exhale. Gasp.* "And then we sing and dance and celebrate by the fire. Like a birthday!"

They passed by many families also heading toward the mountain. Caiden explained that he never goes to the mountain so early in the day during L'anaman, but it was probably best to beat the crowds to the fruit anyhow. That way, they'd get the best ones.

They reached the base in twenty minutes; they had flown north so quickly. It had been an uphill run, so both children threw themselves to the ground, exhausted. When Rose's wheezing subsided, however, she examined her new environment.

They were surrounded by trees and bushes of fruit, all full and ready to be picked. Apple trees with red, green, and golden apples weighing the branches down, some, with branches so heavy, Rose was afraid they would snap. But they were low enough so she could reach her little hand up and pluck one. Bushes of blackberries and raspberries grew all around as well. Cherry trees wove between bushes and apple trees. Rose even saw a few pear trees.

She scrunched her nose.

"But apples grow in the fall. It's June."

Caiden grinned and patted her back. "The spirits are good to us."

He tossed Rose a pear so green and shiny that she could see the reflection of her eyes in it. She took a bite. Juice drizzled down her chin, but she didn't care. She closed her eyes and took another bite. When she opened her eyes again, she saw that Caiden was already on his fourth apple, surrounded by three cores bitten down to the seed, lying idol on the ground around him.

He grinned, licking each of his fingers, one at a time. "Wanna meet my friend, Evander?"

Rose shrugged, not ready to leave the fruit yet but not comfortable enough to protest.

Caiden grabbed her by the hand once again and dragged the poor girl back downhill.

The children ran back to the city, through town square to the bakery. Inside the bakery, there was a glow from the fireplace that lit the room with warm lighting. The smell of bread made Rose's stomach growl. The room was small and there was a counter with muffins, bread and other delicious treats sitting on glass platters with floral designs. A woman in her early thirties stood behind the counter, kneading dough. Her sight took Rose's breath away. She was exceedingly lovely, with blond locks flowing down her back, flawless pale skin, a warm smile, and deep blue eyes.

"Why Òganach[8], Caiden, how lovely it is to see ya today." She put her hand to her heart and bowed her head slightly, a small break from the dough she was kneading. "Who is this wee lad you've brought with ya? I've not seen him before. Is he Triact?"

Caiden and Rose giggled simultaneously.

---

[8] My Lord

"This is my cousin, Rosalind Martelli. She's a Sassenach." Caiden stated.

"Ooo ma dear, forgive me, but yer in a man's clothing!" The woman apologized.

Rose giggled some more.

"Rosalind, welcome to the Cheryic Clan." The woman bowed her head. "Ma name is Lilias O'Connor, and ma husband, Andrew, unfortunately, is away in the square. What brings ye to our land?"

"Uncle Eason is taking care of me while my parents are away." Rose replied timidly.

"I thought your parents were dead?" Caiden asked, raising a brow to the girl.

Rose blushed and looked to the ground. The room went silent.

"Oh, ma dear," Lilias gasped softly, "I am very sorry."

Rose didn't reply.

"Weel," Lilias sighed, "both of ya must be famished. Take a muffin, ma treat."

Caiden squealed with excitement. Rose smiled and took one. It was still warm from the oven, cinnamon and raisin: her mother's favorite. She ate it in one bite.

"Is Evander here?" Caiden's muffled voice asked through a mouthful of muffin.

Lilias disappeared through a door behind the counter.

"Hawl! Evander! Caiden is here!" She could be heard calling.

THUMP THUMP THUMPETY THUMP THUMP THUMP!

A little boy's big booted feet scrambled down the stairs and a blond figure erupted through the door.

"Caiden!" Evander greeted. "You shoulda seen the monster bear my da and I ran into this morning. It woulda swallowed us whole if da hadna[9] been so quick with his bow!"

"Really?!" Caiden's eyes nearly bulged right out of his head. "How big was it?!"

"Weel," Evander began thinking to himself, "'Bout the size of…two of these houses. Like really big."

"Evander," Lilias scolded, smacking the dough with her forearms. "What did yer da tell ya 'bout exaggeratin'?"

"But it's true!" The boy whined. Suddenly he caught himself, realizing there was a third presence in the room. He stepped back shyly behind the counter. "Hi."

Rose couldn't help noticing how much like his mother the boy looked. They had the same wide smile, golden locks, and deep blue eyes. The only difference was their skin. The boy's skin possessed redder, tanner tones that had seen many more days in the sun than this woman, who looked as if she had never seen the outside in her life.

"Who's yer friend?" Evander asked genuinely.

"This is my cousin, Rose. She's a sassenach." Caiden replied.

Rose rolled her eyes, wishing he would stop saying that.

Evander assessed her, eyeing her up and down as if she was some sort of alien.

"Ooooo...I never seen an outsider before. Do they always go 'round wearin' man's clothing?"

"Evander!" His mother shot him a warning look.

"Sorry," Evander looked sheepishly at the compact dirt floor. "Hi."

---

[9] Hadn't

"Hi." Rose replied shyly.

"What do you wanna play?" Evander had already turned back to Caiden.

"Let's play manhunt in the fields."

"Aye." Evander replied.

"Stay out of trouble, children." Lilias warned them. "Or I'll skelp all yer wee bums!"

"Trouble? Us? Never." Caiden replied with a wide, mischievous grin, and they darted out the door. For the rest of the day, they played tag, chased fish in rivers, and sword-fought with sticks.

Rose was getting whacked in her side by Caiden's stick sword when bagpipes played a lively tune in the distance. As soon as they began, Caiden did his usual yanking Rose's wrist so hard that her hand nearly came clean off, and shouted, "We're late! Uncle's gonna skin me!" The three darted back through the city gates toward town square.

Town square had changed drastically from how Rose had seen it that morning. There were no more market stands; they had all disappeared. But people were crowding inside the square, many already seated on the ground. Rose and Caiden parted from Evander hesitantly. They pushed and shoved through many people to get to the center and sat next to a large stone in front of the woodpile. Magnar had already taken his seat at the stone's right hand.

"You're late." He said.

"You're early." Caiden snapped back.

Magnar grinned, setting his eye on the woodpile before him. "You get the fruit of your maw, Rose?" He asked, still staring ahead.

"Huh?"

Magnar smiled. Rose couldn't help noticing how mature he looked for his age. He was ten and already had worry lines above his brows. He sat too still, too peacefully with his legs crossed and his back arched perfectly.

"Your maw gave you the fruit you ate today."

"She's dead."

He shook his head. His eyes twinkled slightly, resembling Eason's as he turned to Rose.

"She made such an impact on this earth that without her, the fruit would not be possible. The seeds would not be nurtured. Uncle says the ripples of her life led to the fruit's upkeeping. And even now, she's maintaining soil, as her ancestors have for thousands of years."

Rose turned back to the wood. "Huh."

"Show-off." Caiden whispered into her ear.

She giggled, but did not mean it. She secretly hoped Magnar was right.

The drums sounded, and as if on command, everyone took a seat. They all turned to face the house, where that same rickety door that the children had flown out of in the morning creaked open and Eason stepped out. He wore his simplest clothes: this time a dark blue tunic with his worn kilt and some boots. He carried a flaming torch. He marched through the path that the crowd had parted for him, until he halted at the stone next to the children.

He paused for a moment.

He turned to the crowds, who were seated silently. The anticipation was so apparent that Rose felt her muscles tense up, one by one. The crowd held their palms to their Chief, even Caiden and Magnar joined. Rose, feeling quite awkward, did the same. Eason bowed for what seemed like ages, and when he finally rose again, he looked to the people.

"We ask one thing from the spirits." His voice boomed so loud, that Rose was sure even the farthest child would hear it. "That we may dwell in their home for all the days of our lives. They give us this. And they love us and protect us so much that they allow us more. The fruit is merely excess love, more than we require, a symbol of their generosity. Though outwardly, we may be wasting away to corpses. Inwardly, by our ancestors, we are renewed day by day. We are one with them. We are one with their world and together they are one." He paused for another moment. "My sister is one with them now. They took her, but always what they take is for a purpose. Now my niece may live with us and be one with us." He paused again.

Far in the back, an elderly man struggled to push himself from the ground onto his feet. It was such a clumsy, awkward movement that a younger family member was forced to help him. When he stood, he stared with such intensity at Rose that she squirmed and looked away. When she looked back, his hands were held out to her as if to embrace her from far away. Another man with a long beard and barely any teeth stood as well and made the same gesture. Then they began rising, dozens at a time, until women joined in, and children.

Rose sat awkwardly, hoping it would stop, unsure of who to look at. She eventually settled her gaze on a pebble in the dirt.

Magnar leaned over. "They're showing they're open to you. They welcome you."

She didn't know what that meant but didn't want to question it in front of all these people. So Rose nodded silently, having no idea how to respond.

After what seemed like hours, they sat back down and Eason resumed.

"A cosmic connection. And what is more cosmic than the love of the people and the fire of their souls, spreading rapidly, but still together?"

He threw the torch into the wood and it lit immediately, Eason's face glowing in the dark.

"Let us sing and dance with the spirits tonight! *Gabhamaid gaol dhuinn!"*

Everyone stood at once so suddenly that Rose jumped as she realized she was the only one still sitting.

"*Gabhamaid gaol dhuinn*!" The people replied in unison, Caiden's voice ringing over them.

Immediately a violin played in the background, as well as drums and something that looked like a guitar. Eventually, the bagpipes joined in as well, creating a loud, chaotic, but beautiful tune for the sun to set to. Everyone grabbed a partner. Caiden practically carried Rose around the square for the rest of the night, yanking her through dances and shouting songs at the top of his lungs.

In the middle of the fifth song, however, Rose was yanked from Caiden by a middle-aged woman with dark eyes and ginger hair. Her lips drew downward to a sulk so permanent that frown lines appeared below her lips. She wore a ramshorn headdress and a silk gown with overbearing sleeves.

"Lassie, what are ya wearing?" She asked through lips painted red.

Rose looked down at her outfit and shrugged.

"This will not do. Where is your uncle? Eason! Eason!"

She screeched and carried Rose by her shirt through the dancing crowds until finally she found the Chief holding a mug of ale, laughing with a man whose mustache was so long, it touched his chest.

"Eason!" The woman scoffed. "This your niece? She looks like a common street lad! What have you done to her!"

The mustache man quickly disappeared in the crowd and Eason drew his lips into an amused grin.

"Relax Chelinda. It is *L'anaman.* A day for simplicity."

"But not a day for ridiculousness!" Chelinda spat back, still gripping Rose's tunic.

Eason laughed heartily. "You may measure her for a fitting tomorrow." He gently grabbed her hand and moved it off of Rose's tunic. "Can I interest you in some ale?"

Chelinda scoffed and bustled away, her nose high in the air.

Eason laughed again and took Rose by the hand. "A dance, princess?"

And she danced with her uncle until the fire burned low, for *L'anaman* is not over until the last spark has been extinguished by the earth.

yet to be said

A woman with long chestnut hair stood in the midst of a field. She looked timidly side to side, thin and weak with exhaustion. As Rose approached her, the woman backed further and further away, until out of nowhere, the woman's back was against a wall.

Rose hesitated. She was causing fear in this woman's eyes, though she did not know why.

The piercing screams came out of nowhere. Rose whirled around and noticed the pack of dogs running full speed toward them. She instinctively crawled into a ball, covering her head. But the dogs darted past her. Rose lifted her head in time to see the dogs pile on top of the woman.

"Eason!" was the final word that escaped the woman's lips, but it was too late. Faceless men in long black suits approached to observe the scene, muttering indistinguishable words of approval to one another. Rose grabbed a sword and lunged toward the faceless people around her as they spat at the corpse of the woman.

A low booming voice from a towering faceless man seemed to give orders, rewarded with shrieking laughter from another. Dogs and men alike, all closed in on Rose.

***

"Aaaaaaaaaah!"

Caiden darted up at the sound. He looked over at Magnar's bed to find him sitting upright, his ears perked up and eyes locked on the door.

"Rose's room." Magnar said, and the brothers tumbled out of their beds.

As soon as they entered the room, they saw Rose lying in a fetal position on the bed; her face drowned in rivers of tears. She clutched herself and rocked back and forth.

"Rose!" Caiden called, as he quickly approached the bed. Rose jumped at the sound so hard that she tumbled right onto the floor. She scrambled away from Caiden and into the corner of the room, breathing heavily.

Caiden hesitated.

"Rose, it's me." He said, tears threatening to escape from his enormous eyes. "It's Caiden. Are you okay?"

Rose stared blankly at him. Fear contorted her eyes, giving her whole complexion a disconcertingly weak look.

"Rose." Caiden tried again softly.

Magnar placed a hand on his brother's back. He too tried.

"Rose, it's Magnar." He called slowly in a hushed tone. He pushed his messy, dirty-blond hair away from his eyes and took a step closer so she could see him clearly. Rose opened her mouth as if to say something and then closed it, swallowing deeply.

"Get Uncle." Magnar ordered, his eyes fixed on Rose's crumpled figure.

Caiden leapt out of the room.

Magnar slowly shifted himself closer to Rose, leaving only a meter between them. They faced each other wordlessly until Rose sighed deeply and finally looked him in the eyes.

"There you are." Magnar smiled, yet his heart ached.

With a sob, her head collapsed back into her knees. Magnar quickly knelt beside her and embraced her.

He nodded and held her closely. "It's okay. Don't worry. It's just me. I'm not going to hurt you."

"Promise?" Rose asked.

Magnar gave a sad grin.

"I'm the eldest, Rose, and the heir to the Chieftain. It's literally my job to protect you and Caiden."

"I'm only your cousin." Rose whimpered.

Magnar sighed. "So? Eason's only my uncle, yet he protects me like a son. You may be a cousin by blood, but you are my sister."

Rose sniffled.

"I will be Chief one day. You will be my royal family. I promise, I will do whatever it takes to protect you."

Rose's sobs subsided and she fell into a peaceful sleep in her new brother's arms. She was so tiny, that dark-haired girl, so weak. He quietly placed her on the bed. With good grace, he kissed her head before leaving the room.

Waiting beside the doorway was a stout shadow of a man, towering over the young prince, his arms crossed.

Magnar's ears momentarily turned red and he dared not look Eason in the eyes. Eason allowed a small smirk to show on his lips as he looked over his heir from head to toe.

"How much of that were you there for?" Magnar asked sheepishly.

Eason grinned.

"You shall be a great Chief, my son," he said and tousled his son's hair. Magnar turned to leave, but Eason grabbed the boy's arm.

"But a warning to you," he began, "Such promises should rarely be made. Especially to your family."

Magnar puzzled at this. "Forgive me Uncle, but shouldn't such promises be left for family?"

Eason grunted. "You are an honorable little man. But you have much to learn about Chieftain."

***

"What happened?" Eason asked.

Rose sat facing the desk in Eason's room-office, taking interest in the arm of the chair. Eason was still in his morning robes. Dark circles had formed under his eyes from a restless night, and his usual neat locks which fell to his chest were tousled and knotted.

Rose shrugged.

"Rose," Eason said impatiently. "Tell me what you dreamed."

Rose shook her head.

"How can you expect me to help you if I don't even know what you are upset about?" Eason's voice deepened.

"I don't care if you help me," Rose replied defiantly. She refused to meet his gaze, fixing her eyes angrily at a small clump of dirt on the floor.

Eason stood up from behind his desk and turned the chair next to Rose's to face her. He sat down in it.

Tears welled up in the girl's eyes as she struggled to keep her composure.

This time in a patient and quiet tone, he spoke to Rose, "Please tell me what happened. This is important."

Rose's eyes drifted toward the window. Shades of purple, pink and blue lit the sky, and though the window was not to the east, she knew the sun was rising. Her eyes were a dark color, barely green anymore, nearly black. Eason recalled Christine's eyes displaying a similar miracle: They changed with her mood, growing darker as she withdrew into herself and brighter when her mood would lift.

Rose explained the dream, hesitating during some moments, receiving many inward winces from Eason throughout.

"These people, did they look like anyone you know?" Eason asked, his mind spinning.

Rose scrunched her brows. "No, I don't think so. Why?" Rose asked, drawing her brows together, puzzled.

Eason gave a small pitiful smile. "What happened that day? The day of the accident, I mean."

"I dunno." Rose shrugged. "I was with my nanny. Mommy was at work. Ummm this lady came and told me to call her Auntie. She...she asked for a *Christine* at first. And then she asked if my mommy was home."

"You don't know your mommy's name?" Eason asked.

"Of course, I do," she responded, "Arwen."

Eason puzzled over this, but just for a few moments. "What happened then?"

"She took me on a plane. She didn't even let me take my stuffed animals. She said we'd miss the plane. She didn't say that mommy was…gone…until we were off the plane. Then I was here."

"Your…errr, Auntie has always been a handful," Eason said, "Well, go play. I know an eager, impatient little boy who is most definitely waiting for you outside."

"That's all?" Rose asked, her mouth hung open. "You're not gonna say anything else?"

"Oh…aye, what else is there to say?" Eason replied, the expression on his face carefully hidden.

Rose shrugged and trudged to the door slowly, but turned back to her uncle before walking out.

"What was my mommy like?" She asked. She looked so little in the frame of the door. Her arms were skinny twigs, yet her cheeks were chubby and round, her head could have been a perfect sphere.

"You know perfectly well what your mother was like. You lived with her for almost the same amount of time I did." Eason replied, dismissing her question with a wave of his hand as he hastily read over the documents on his desk.

Rose remained glued to the doorway. "I knew her as my mommy, someone who made me dinner and sang me songs. You...you knew her as a sister."

Eason smiled and shook his head, as if humored by the thought of his sister being so motherly.

"Sang you songs." He murmured to himself, removing his pipe from his pocket. Eason laughed softly and for a few minutes, appeared to have forgotten that Rose was still standing in front of him. Finally, he glanced up and noticed her tiny, stubborn figure in the doorway. He sighed.

"I suppose she sang you The 'Greatest Adventure'?" He began, his face pensive at first, until he chuckled.

Rose's eyes widened. "How did you know? She'd sing it to me every night. She also told me it was the most important song ever made."

Eason chuckled a little more, the crinkles in his eyes deepening as he did.

"We'd watch that movie as much as we possibly could. It was our favorite, as ancient as it was…she always brought the strangest boys home too. Most of the boys she brought were terrible." He chuckled. "She had boys chasing her everywhere she went. She rejected many as if it were a game to her." He gave a dry laugh at the thought. "But she was also kind. She never said a word against anybody, not even my father."

"Grandpa? I never met him." Rose noted.

"Good. I was sad to hear the old bawbag is still alive. Go play."

***

Eason was amazed at the rapidness that Rose adapted to her new climate. He had always heard of the versatility of children. He'd seen children, whose parents had passed on, acclimate quickly to their new lives with other relatives. But he had not expected a change this drastic to be normalized so quickly with Rose. The summer days passed, one after another, with the children doing who-knows-what outside all day and coming in only at the hour of their curfew. Finally, Rose had been in their keeping for nearly two months. This was when they discovered Rose's birthday, only after Magnar had politely inquired, of course.

It was the same day and same year as Caiden's. August 7th. When the Cheryic people realized this, they named the two, "The Twins." This was partially because they easily could have been twins with their features and birthday, but also because the two were together so often, it was just easier to call them by a single name.

Of course, Caiden jumped up and down upon hearing the news. The two would be celebrating their birthdays together! How wonderful this would be!

In the week that followed, the two received gifts from all over the city, varying from muffins from Evander's family to a gown from Chelinda. In fact, a festival was held in the town square to celebrate the prince and the princess's birthday. Even people from outside of the city came to give the children gifts. Musicians played music they had written primarily for the children, painters gave portraits they had painted of The Twins, and everyone welcomed Rose into the clan. Eason forced Rose to wear the dress Chelinda had given her, to show how grateful she was. It was an elegant dress, made of golden velvet with a skirt that puffed out just enough to be noticed.

Rose detested it. She couldn't move, run, or play in it. What was the point of clothing you could not move in?

Caiden was not so fond of his matching velvet vest and breeches either. He could move more easily in a kilt. Not only that, but he was forced to wear stockings and dress shoes that were so stiff, blisters had formed within his first few steps. Halfway through the festival, he threw them off. Chelinda scoffed at this, but Eason chose to ignore it.

Eight years old. Eason remembered when Helen had first brought Caiden and Magnar to his home, eight years ago. She was crying about how she just couldn't do it, and then she just dropped them off. What was Eason to do? Reject the children? No, he had cared for them like one of his own. He hoped he had done enough.

After the party, Eason called Rose into his room-office, while Evander, Caiden, and Magnar all waited in the living room, playing cards.

Eason strode behind his desk, pulling a long and wide package from underneath. He handed it to Rose, who gaped at it with wide eyes as she fumbled to unwrap the parchment.

"Magnar! Caiden! Evander! Look what Uncle gave me!" Rose jumped up and down, resembling Caiden's usual elation.

The boys marveled at the bow and became almost as excited as Rose was. It was made from light-colored wood, etched with intricate designs, which Rose could not help but to run her fingers over.

"I don't know how to shoot," Rose noted. "Can someone teach me?"

Caiden and Magnar stepped back. Magnar detested hunting. He hated the idea of sitting and waiting to kill something. Caiden played with swords, and occasionally went on hunts with Uncle, but had never actually hit his targets in archery.

Evander stood up. "I can teach ya! I hunt all the time with my da!"

Rose made no reply. She merely grabbed him by the arm and yanked him out the door.

Caiden and Magnar, in their spare time, would play sword fighting in the schoolyard. The ground was about 100 meters long and 50 meters wide, with targets on the first half, then a sword-fighting range on the second. Behind that was an obstacle course used for soldier training. For the first ten minutes of practice, Caiden observed with interest as Rose attempted to shoot. But Caiden's patience only went so far, so he soon challenged Magnar to a brawl at the other end of the field.

"Stick that nook in the arrow on the string, on top of the gold." Evander smiled as Rose fumbled with the arrow. "Aye, that's it."

Rose had begun to take Evander's good nature for granted. He was often helpful with the things necessary for survival that Eason had been too busy to teach the boys about. His father had taught him all the practical dos and don'ts of survival in the highlands, from hunting to finding fresh herbs in the wild. He could be quiet at times, but there couldn't possibly be a more patient child than him on this earth.

She drew the bow back and tried to aim.

"Wait," Evander commanded. His voice startled Rose so much that she jumped and released the arrow. It whizzed past the target and into the hill. Evander giggled as Rose let out a grunt of frustration.

"You scared me!" Rose scolded, her eyes still fixed on the arrow stuck in the hill.

Evander giggled some more and shook his head.

"Sorry. I just wanted to say that yer hand should be at yer chin." Evander explained.

Rose merely replied with an *I have no idea what you are talking about* look.

Evander sighed. "Pull the string back but dinna[10] shoot." Rose did as he said. Evander moved her hand to the corner of her mouth. "Dinna bend the elbow of that arm so much." He gestured toward the arm that was holding the bow.

Rose straightened it.

---

[10] Do not

"Mind[11] to aim with two eyes." Rose looked at him questioningly. Evander smiled. "Just do it."

She shot.

She missed the target yet again.

"Ah!" Rose stomped her foot.

Evander laughed. "It's ok. I couldna[12] hit the target at first either. Now I can almost even hit the bull's eye." He grinned proudly and patted Rose on the back, who was already fumbling with another arrow.

***

Magnar felt guilty that he could not teach Rose how to shoot a bow, for he had had little training with the weapon himself. He vowed to make up for it to Rose as soon as he could. He realized the very next day that the opportunity had presented itself.

“I’m riding to the mines today to see how they are faring. Would any of you wish to come with me?” Uncle asked us.

“I’ll come!” Caiden replied excitedly.

“Do we have to ride our own horses?” Rose asked sheepishly.

Eason looked puzzled.

“Why yes, I want to ride swiftly and lightly so that we can be home by tomorrow,” Eason replied.

Rose sighed. “No, thank you. I’ll stay.”

Eason nodded and turned to Magnar, who sat with his brows creased, and his eyes fixed on Rose.

“You should come with me. You will, in fact, be Chief someday. You must see how I do my work.” Eason reasoned.

---

[11] Remember

[12] Could not

“I have more important things to do here, Uncle. But thank you. I will learn next time.” The boy replied.

Eason raised a brow. “More important? A ten-year-old lad such as yourself?”

“Aye,” Magnar replied.

Eason grunted disapprovingly. “If you insist.”

When Caiden and Eason left, Magnar approached Rose in the living room-kitchen.

“You’ve never ridden a horse, have you?” He asked Rose, who was searching in the nut jar for a few peanuts to snack on.

“That’s not true; I took riding lessons once last year. But I fell off the horse, so I stopped.”

“Are you afraid?” Magnar asked, not meaning to be rude, simply curious.

“No.” Rose pouted. She found four peanuts and plopped them in her mouth.

“Come with me.” Magnar smiled.

Within the Cheryic boundaries, there is very little farmland. However, on the outskirts of the city, right on the edge of the forest was the most fertile farmland that could be found in the highlands. It stretched to the Southern boundary of the Cheryic lands. There, horses, goats, sheep, pigs, and chickens were raised; potatoes, peas, turnips, cabbages, broccoli and brussel sprouts were grown on some farms; and blueberries, strawberries, raspberries, brambles, and apples were grown on others.

Magnar had no doubt in his mind where he would go. He guided Rose to Old Farmer McHenry’s. The man never fell idle of his generosity and manners, not to mention the complete loyalty and respect he possessed for the Chieftain.

Furthermore, the old man was known to have the most well-bred horses in the Cheryic land.

When they finally arrived at Farm McHenry's little wooden hut, they knocked on the door, dust flying in the air with each knock upon it. A few seconds later, a man with a scruffy, rapidly graying black beard appeared. He bowed his head.

"Òganach! Àille! How can I help you two?"

Magnar hesitated to see how Rose would react with being called by a political endearment for the first time. She looked slightly puzzled, yet said nothing.

"Good sir, would there be any horses that you can allow me to borrow so I can teach my cousin to ride on this bonnie afternoon?" Magnar asked, placing his right hand on his heart as Eason had taught him.

Farmer McHenry nodded, grinning. "Indeed, it'd be ma pleasure. Feel free to ride them 'round my corral as well, but no in it. Just dinna scare the others off. Allow me to show ye to them."

They followed him around to the back of his humble cabin. He stopped, put two fingers in his mouth, and whistled one simple melody, which reminded Magnar of a lullaby that Eason used to play on the violin. On cue, two beautiful horses, already saddled, galloped up to them. One was chestnut and the other, black as coal.

Farmer McHenry laughed and patted the dark one's back.

"Here y'are, these bonnie ones are called Righ and Anam. Good luck to ye both."

And with that, the jubilant man hobbled back inside his hut. Magnar turned to Rose. "You get Anam. Now mount the horse."

Rose did as he said and struggled to push her little legs up and over the saddle. She failed the first few times: jumping and falling, climbing and falling, but she eventually managed to hoist herself upon it.

"Good. Now, do you know how to gallop?" Magnar allowed himself to feel a hint of mischief, a feeling he was used to rationing as the heir.

"Yes but-"

"Then let's go!" He whacked her horse in the butt, then kicked his own, racing Rose's horse as she grasped onto it for dear life. Magnar chuckled as she squealed.

"MAGNAR!" She yelled after him. "I don't like this!"

"Don't panic, or you'll fall!" He laughed. They rode in such a fashion for ten minutes until finally, Rose regained her confidence and began to giggle. Bit by bit, she loosened her grip on the horse itself, and grabbed the reins, steering the horse where she wanted it. Eventually, she even kicked the horse to go faster, challenging him to a race.

Magnar grinned. "You're ready now."

Rose perked up. "Ready for what?"

Magnar clicked his mouth twice and the horse galloped North, toward Ben Nevis.

They took the main road to the mountain's base, then began up a rocky path leading around the mountain. At some points, Rose became afraid the path was too narrow, and the horse would slip and fall into the trees below. She didn't dare to look down, or sideways for that matter, because the entire city could be viewed next to her, so tiny from her advanced position. Eventually, they came to a flat, spacey landing where Magnar dismounted his horse and tied it off to a nearby tree branch. Rose did the same.

He reached for his pack and handed her a leather jacket and some rope.

"Better tie yourself with this. My feet are more sure."

Rose hesitated She peered up the steep ledge, but she gulped and did as she was told.

Magnar wrapped his satchel around his back and smirked.

"You ready?"

Before she could say another word, he had jumped on the rocks like a cat, gracefully balanced. She awkwardly climbed behind him. But before she knew it, the cliff was getting so steep, that she felt herself leaning backward. She looked at the ground. The city looked like tiny stones in a vast green land. She began breathing heavily, tears welling up in her puppy-dog eyes as she looked up, trying to assess how far she had to go.

"Magnar!" She called. He was a few steps above her.

He looked down at her and noticed the tears streaming down her face.

"Do you feel the breeze, Rose?" He asked.

Not only did she feel a breeze, she felt a cold chill at the back of her neck, tossing her frizzy hair all over her face.

"It's the spirits." Magnar called over the wind, "nobody in the clan has ever fallen from this mountain. The spirits are the wind in our back. Your maw's probably tossing your hair around right now."

Rose bit her lip and carried on, unsure of whether to believe him or not. Would her mother have believed Magnar? As she climbed, Rose debated the notion in her head. Her mother either would have laughed and said it was all nonsense or believed him wholeheartedly. No in-between. Rose sighed and tried to embrace the wind on her back. She may as well believe Magnar if she was stuck here. She took a deep breath and reached for another rock. Magnar's thin figure loomed over her. His blond braids drooped down; sometimes their silver bands clapped on a rock.

Then he was gone.

Rose looked wildly above her, but could not see him. She scrambled faster, shouting, "Magnar!"

His head appeared grinning over her.

"It's the peak!" He held his hand out.

Rose let out a sigh of relief as he pulled her up and over, surprisingly strong for his size. They sat for a moment together, Rose attempting to catch her breath when she looked onto the horizon. The city was but a tiny thumbprint in the body of the world below. Even the farmland looked small. The forest...that was endless. It was the flesh and blood of the world, it seemed to her. Pine trees overshadowed the rest, although she could see a few alterations in the gymnosperms, from light blues to sprayed needles. Back in her home, she had never once seen so much green in one place. All of this would be covered in cars, roads, houses and mud. She didn't think it had been possible that any earth was left. At least, she hadn't tried to imagine it.

"They say when you first climb the mountain, you become a man." Magnar said softly. "I suppose it's probably the same for girls, although it's not the tradition. So today, you are a woman."

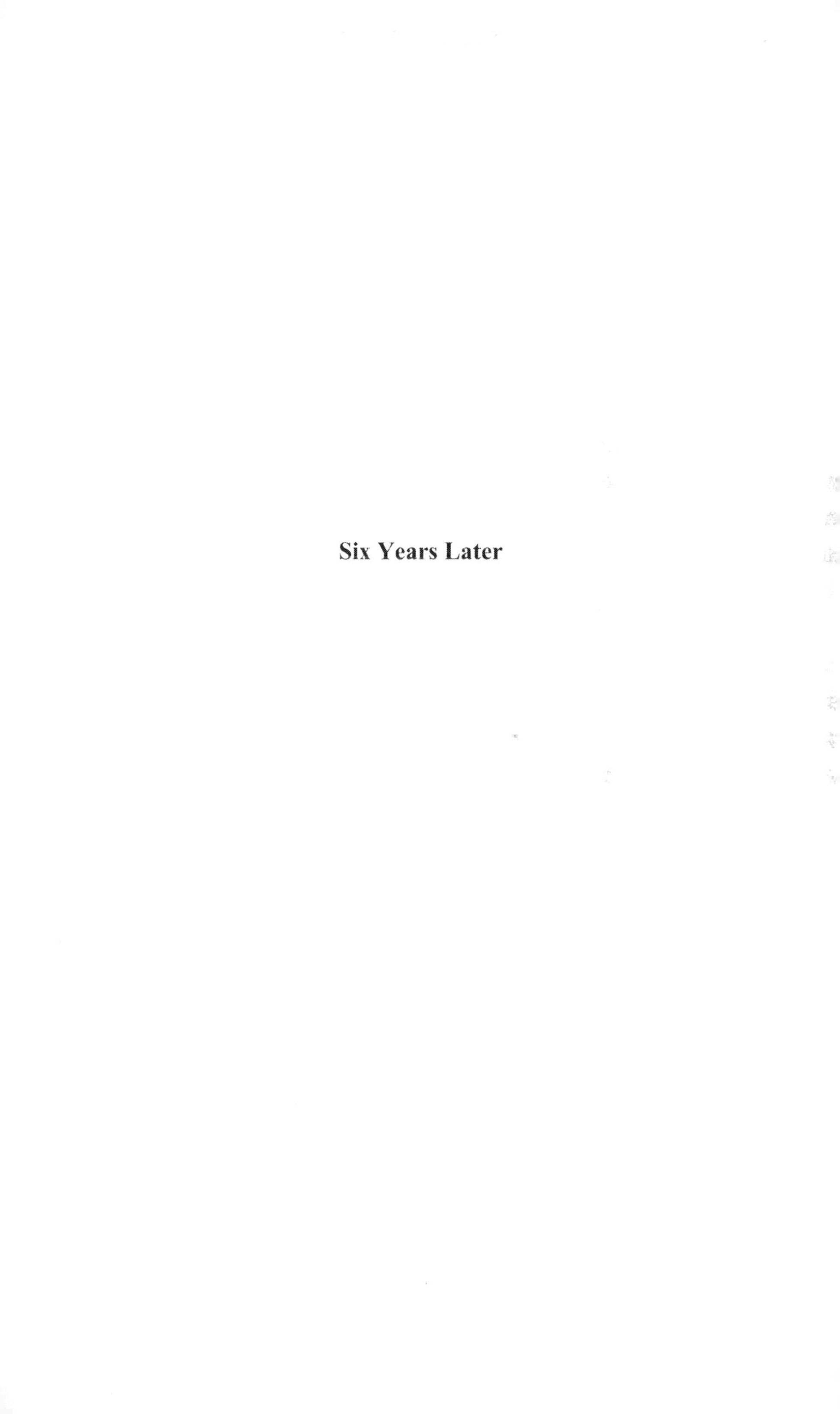

Six Years Later

the chances and changes

"IT'S LATH AONACHD! IT'S LATH AONACHD!" Caiden shouted. He pounced on Rose's bed, who lay on her side with a giant matt of frizzy hair in her face.

"Huh?"

"ROSE! IT'S UNITY DAY! COME ON!"

Rose rubbed her eyes and blew some strands of hair from her mouth. She sat up rigidly and smiled. Caiden had a habit, which unfortunately for Magnar and her, he had refused to outgrow, of announcing to the world what day it was before the sun had even risen, as if they didn't already know.

"It's Lath Aonachd!"

It was her sixth annual Lath Aonachd since she had come to the clans. It had been...utterly dull and interminable. Sure the princes and eligible young men entered into tournaments and fought for prizes such as weapons, gold, or exotic animals. But as a princess, she sat upright through all the festivities, clapping as the boys had their fun.

This time, however, she had a plan.

Eason had already been up, and Rose's favorite breakfast was ready for her on the table: Cold Salmon on poached eggs and toast, along with a glass of fresh warm milk.

She gulped these down, giggling at the new No Weapons on the Table note, which Eason had freshly pasted onto the corner of the table. The boys had their fun the night before, nearly destroying the whole kitchen during a table sword fight over the last oatcake. Eason, apparently, had enough.

Caiden scrambled to the table as well and devoured everything, giving Rose the illusion that he was drinking his food with one gulp.

"Are you gonna finish that?" He asked Rose as he pointed to her bread crust.

She playfully punched his side and returned to her room to dress.

***

The sight of other clans surprised Rose every year in the same way. It shocked her to leave the bubble of the city, usually for a random spot of flat land somewhere in the highlands. She supposed she should be used to the different people, this being her seventh year. But they made her uncomfortable. She didn't know where to put her hands as she walked through the crowds with Caiden.

Caiden, at the age of fifteen, still acted exactly like the seven-year-old she had first met. The two were inseparable these days, as he dragged her from place to place. The two wove in and out of the tents, which had been set up for multiple festivities. Most were large enough to fit the crowds, although a select few were small, likely just so officials and Chiefs could have their meetings.

Highlanders everywhere were drinking various forms of ale and whiskey, the men of all ages finding various women to flirt with from other clans. If they chose to wed outside the clan, this time of year likely was their only opportunity. But most chose to wed within their clans. It was easier than the daunting prospect of warring with your in-laws across Scotland. Even so, the ale had quickly gone to the people's brains and promoted a looser behavior.

The Twins sat in the grass, observing the people who walked by, playing the little game they did every year. The object was to pick a man or woman who walked by and to guess their clan. The men were easy. Triact men wore green and blue kilts; the Fisher People wore navy and gray kilts; Craotics wore Red and navy, and the Farmers wore garnet and black.

(Rose, upon arriving, had wondered why the names of the clans were names as unique as Craotic, Triact, Cheryic, and then as basic as Farmer and Fisher. There were two reasons for this phenomenon. 1) The Fisher people were technically called Clan Sluagh na Mara. Nobody wanted to say this mouthful, so the nickname was adapted centuries ago: Fisherpeople. 2) As for the Farmerpeople, the nickname was a sort of mockery. Clan Duchannon was the real name, but everyone in the clan had a farm. Hence, the rather new nickname: The Farmerpeople.)

The Cheryic men, of course, wore brown and pale blue kilts, but the Twins could generally recognize the faces of all of their people, if not the names.

The women were always more difficult to figure out. Some bore traces of tartan that gave them away. The thin, sickly-looking women tended to be Farmers. Those with sour looks to their faces, arguing angrily with their husbands, usually were Craotics. Triact women typically wore bright, flamboyant colors with make-up caking their faces. Fisherwomen rarely appeared at the festival, most of their men forced them to stay home.

When the time was drawing near to the first event, Caiden dragged Rose by the hand to a giant tent, which the crowds were beginning to flock toward, giddy with more anticipation than usual.

Inside of the tent, the Twins took a seat on the grass outskirts of a small arena. Five empty thrones of stone faced the middle, forming a lump in Rose's throat as she thought of her uncle.

"You remember the plan?" Rose asked Caiden.

He smiled and shifted impatiently in his seat. "OF COURSE!" He squealed.

"Wheesht! You want the five clans to be in on our secret too?"

Caiden shook his head rapidly and then bounded toward the sign-up stands in the corner of the tent. Rose stood, cloaked, facing the center of the arena.

***

"I am tryna tell ya that they're invading our lands!"

Chief Duchannon, more commonly known as The Farmer Chief, had been ranting all day in the private tent. It was tradition for all five chiefs to discuss affairs of state at this time. This meant that Eason was forced to sit through the endless speeches of four different men, as well as the bickering. He drew his hand to his brow, smoothing it and rubbing his temple simultaneously. The sooner they could get to the events, the better.

"What do I care what happens to the farmlands?" The Fisher Chief replied. "These peasants can damn well try and get north to Sluagh Na Mara. If they do, my ships will catch them."

The Farmer Chief hunched over, dragging his hands over his old worn face. His remaining thin strands of gray hair stuck to his sweaty skin.

"These were no peasants." The Farmer Chief said almost in a whisper. "Their clothing was strange. Unkempt. And their weapons…sharper than any I've ever seen."

Eason looked up from the table, meeting the Farmer Chief's eyes.

"Naw," the Farmer Chief continued. "These were Outsiders."

A series of murmurs erupted in the little tent. The Farmer Chief ignored them.

"If ye think this will not affect the whole land, all of ya are wrong. We will not trade ya our crops if we have no enough for ourselves. And the Outside *wants* our crops. But I think they want more...*our land*."

Eason puzzled over this and glanced over at the Triact and Craotic Chiefs. The Craotics had long been the Cheryic's enemies and rivals, so whatever Eason declared here was sure to be countered by the Craotic's words. The Triact Chief, however, was young. Very young. New. Impressionable.

"We must aid the Farmspeople all we can," Eason declared. "If the Outside wants their land back, however, they will take it back. They outnumber us and although they no longer have weapons more powerful than us, their armies are more disciplined. They don't fight like we do."

The Triact Chief nodded. "What do you suppose we do?"

Eason shrugged. "Start by learning about them. Where they are from. What they want. Then we unite under The Treaty of *Còig Cinnidhean*. 'Upon the impending date of the Outer World's reunification with our land, let the warring brothers and sisters of the sons and daughters of Owen Cheryic join again as their ancestors in the Ben. Only when bloodlust is set aside between the brother and sister will they maintain their land against the odds before them.'"

The Craotic Chief scoffed, the lines of his face stretching as he did.

"How are we supposed to learn about them?"

Eason reached into the folds of his kilt and brought out a paper whiter than any he had seen in nearly 30 years. He threw it to the Triact Chief, who opened the folds.

The young Chief puzzled over it for a moment, moving his lips slightly as his dark eyes glided over the words. Then he cleared his throat.

To Eason Rankin of Clan Cheryic,

We hope this letter finds you in good health and is delivered quickly. We understand that your people do not know the ways of helicopters or such machinery, so we chose to respect this by sending a rider. Congratulations! Your father has won the recent presidential election of the United States of America. As his secretary of state, I would like to offer an invitation to meet. We understand that transportation is difficult for you and will be happy to meet you in Cheryic City on July 14th.

As preparation for this meeting, I will brief you on the topic of discussion: We wish to form an alliance between

our two great nations and offer you our protection. There is no cost. Your father simply wants to restore a bond both nationally and personally.

We look forward to hearing from you!

Sincerely,
John Clancy
Secretary of State

The room fell silent as the words from the letter sunk in.

"This is good though, isn't it?" The young Triact Chief asked, waving the letter in his hand.

"That is what they want you to believe." Eason said softly, "but in truth, I was once an American. They do not simply form alliances. They take and take and conquer."

"But they will protect my people from the invaders, will they not?" The Farmer Chief asked, leaning forward.

Eason shook his head.

"Try to understand," he said, "they *are* the invaders."

The room grew so silent that the tension it had formed was nearly palpable.

Eason screeched his chair back from the table and stood. "I brought this to the clans because this is not simply a Cheryic matter. What I do or say at this meeting will affect the whole of Scotland. As we know, there is an international ban on explosive and nuclear weapons. So any guns or bombs are no longer a threat to our people. But their army is still powerful. And they are natural conquerors, always have been and always will be. It is written in the creation of their nation. I advise us to keep as distant from a relationship with them as possible without going to war."

The Craotic Chief rolled his eyes and slammed his hands to the table, raising himself to Eason's level.

"This will only anger them!" The Craotic Chief said, "I say befriend them. Use their protection for good! We need to remain the clans, and it will not be long before people see how inhabitable this land is, and nations draw closer to our borders. We don't want to be pushed back to the mountains again!"

"This is what the Americans are trying to do at this very moment." Eason said through his teeth. He could feel his face getting warm. "Trust me. I have lived among them-"

"When you were a child!" The Craotic Chief interrupted. "We all know the tale of the young lad who ran away from his father. Tell me, are you trying to run from him again?"

Eason felt all eyes in the room turning to him. He gripped the table so hard, the whites of his knuckles showed.

"You ignorant bawbag," Eason seethed. "You'd rather use the Americans for power than maintain the great nation our ancestors have created for us. This is what the Americans do! My father does not want to visit to chat about old times. He wants this land. And they will get it if we are not harsh."

"They will get it if we are too harsh as well," the Triact Chief interjected. It was the first time the boy had talked in a long while. "I say we take it to a vote."

Eason did not want to take it to a vote. It was too soon. He had not fully made his point. But he knew in his heart that if he continued ranting like this before the tournament, the men would grow impatient and surely not be in his favor.

"I will sit this vote out," said the Fisher Chief, "since this does not concern Sluagh na Mara."

The Craotic Chief narrowed his eyes at the Fisher Chief.

"Are ye daft?" he asked. "Do ye think the Americans can't attack ya just because you're on an island? How do ya think they're getting to Scotland in the first place?"

The Fisher Chief grumbled a few swears below his breath, but then sat upright in his seat.

"All who are not in favor of this alliance?" The Craotic Chief called.

Eason and The Triact Chief raised their hands.

The Craotic Chief smirked as Eason rubbed his head in his palms.

"All who are in favor."

The Fisher Chief, The Craotic Chief, and The Farmer Chief raised their hands.

***

"Are you ready?" Caiden whispered to Rose.

Her palms were shaking slightly, but she ignored them. She was meant for this; she could feel it inside of her, welling up like a swollen balloon ready to pop at any moment.

A crowd had formed around the arena. They were shouting profanities and cheers all at the same time, canceling out each other's voices to form one roar. Magnar had won the last sword-fighting tournament for his age group. He had won a prize falcon, and the nearby girls were fawning over both it and him.

Caiden handed Rose his sword. It felt heavy in her hands, but this wasn't the first time she had picked it up. She had practiced a few times before with the boys at home, mostly serving as a dummy to do drills on.

A stout man entered the center of the arena, holding a white scroll. "William of Clan Duchannon, you have the floor." He projected throughout the giant tent.

A tall, chunky boy with what must have been a thousand orange braids hanging down his back hobbled to the floor, grasping his sword readily.

"Caiden of Clan Cheryic, you are the challenger," the stout man called.

Caiden strode to the center of the floor and patted the stout man on his back. "I'm feeling a bit peely wally[13], I'm afraid," Caiden yelled for the arena to hear. "Rosalind Tyra Rankin of Clan Cheryic will fight in my stead."

The room fell silent.

The stout man reddened in the face a bit and opened his mouth as if to interject, but then thought better than to protest a prince.

Rose trudged to the center of the floor, feeling like each of her feet were dragging through quicksand. She clenched her fists around Caiden's sword to cease the shaking. In the corner of her eyes, she could see Eason sitting like a statue on one of the thrones. She could feel him seething, but didn't dare look over at him.

Rose bent her knee to the initial fighting stance, facing the boy who must have been twice her height.

"Do not go easy on me." She told him, "or I'll remove your head from its shoulders."

The boy shrugged and nodded quickly as if he'd known this from the very beginning.

"Ready!" The stout man called, "And fight!"

Rose lunged at the big boy, but he sidestepped and-

---

[13] Sick

She awoke a few hours later alone in a dark tent with a horrible ache in the side of her head. She attempted to sit up, but the room became dizzy, so she lay back down.

"You fool!" She could hear her uncle's voice booming in the background. "Going in there without warning anybody but…Caiden? As if he knows anything about fighting or responsibility at all!"

"I'm sorry." She whispered. But the only response she was given were his heavy footsteps stomping away.

***

Magnar sat alone at a campfire near Rose's tent. Well, perhaps not alone. The falcon he had won as a prize that day kept him good company. He sat stroking its head, nose in a book, constantly glancing at Rose's tent. He was told over and over again that she would be fine, but still, he worried. Of course he had not been told of her plans. The Twins were constantly plotting new schemes without him. It was the downside to being obedient, he supposed. Disobedience was a luxury given to those who are not first in line to rule an entire people. At least that's what Eason would always tell him.

He eyed Rose's tent warily. The sun had nearly set, so he had to squint and tilt his novel, The Kings Below the Ben, toward the fire to make out the writing.

"Magnar."

Magnar jumped so hard, he nearly fell from the tree stump he had perched on. He whirled around.

"Cinnie!"

Cinnie Mabuz was the physician's daughter. Her long blonde locks fell down to her hips and she often wore a sky-blue gown to compliment her eyes. Magnar had always been friends with her, but only through a few boys he knew from school. They rarely had exchanged more than a few "hellos" and "goodbyes" in the past.

"You have a friend," she said, gesturing her head to the bird. She stood awkwardly rigid with her hands clasped in front of her.

"Aye." Magnar replied. "I'm gonna wait for Rose to wake up to name it. She's always good at this creative stuff, whereas when I attempt to think of a name, all I think of is Falcon or…on my more innovative days...Chief Falcon."

Cinnie giggled.

In the distance, men could be heard shouting Gaelic instructions at one another, while concurrently making dirty jokes and engaging in small fistfights. Triact men, likely, loading tents onto carts to take home.

Magnar added another log to the fire.

"Would you like to sit?" He asked.

She nodded and took a seat beside him.

The log crackled a bit, sending sparks into the air and Magnar added bits of straw. Cinnie occupied herself by tracing random lines in the dirt with her finger.

"You were very brave today," she said after a long while.

"Well, thank you," Magnar replied.

Cinnie nodded and glanced around, looking for something to take interest in. She found nothing.

"Well," she said, "see you at home, Òganach."

Magnar nodded and as she walked away from the fire, he winced so hard, he accidentally ripped out a page of his book.

***

Rose awoke again to high-pitched whispers.

"Jean, I dinna ken[14] if we should even be here."

---

[14] Know

"Ah Gwen, what do ye ken? She's the first lassie to enter a tournament. Sure she got knocked 'round a bit, but still. We owe her these."

"Da would skelp us should he find out."

"Will he find out?"

"noo."

"Well then tis no concern of ours, is it?"

"Wheesht! She's wakin'!"

Two heads blurred into vision above Rose: One with a round face and curly brown hair. The other so thin and frail that her cheekbones were perfectly arched and defined in the candlelight. Straight, bright hair fell down her back and nearly to her knees. The curly-haired girl assisted Rose as she scooted herself up. The blond one graciously scooched a pillow behind her to prop herself up on.

"What happened?" Rose asked.

"Yer the first lassie to enter a tournament, ever," The blond girl said, her eyes wavering to the other girl, "Ne'er mind the rest."

"Here," the curly one said, "we picked those for ya today."

She placed a bouquet of evening blue wildflowers on Rose's chest. Rose reached for them in a slow, muddled movement and awkwardly smelled them. She hated flowers (as ironic as her name allowed it to be). She never knew what to do with them.

"No, no, ye dinna smell 'em," the blond said, ignoring her giggling friend.

"Here."

She placed the flowers in a bowl on the side table and threw a pot of scalding water over them. Rose found herself wondering whether she'd been holding the pot the whole time, but decided she did not care enough to ask.

"Ye drink it. Helps with the pain." The blond smiled.

The curly girl leaned over to Rose and whispered. "We give it to my da when Daisy's kicked 'em in the face too hard. Which happens more often than natural."

Rose grinned the best she could and reached the bowl to her face but hesitated. "You haven't told me who you are, or what clan you're from?"

The girls glanced at each other and chuckled. The blonde one even snorted a few times. "We're not Craotics if that's what yer worried about." The blond said, "We're farm girls from Clan Cheryic. Ah'm Jean and this here's my sister Gwen."

Rose held the bowl to her mouth and took a sip.

"OUT!"

Eason stood in the door, pointing a finger toward the outside, which was now pitch black. The girls glanced at each other, and Jean squeezed Rose's hand quickly before they scurried out like mice from a cat.

Eason stormed toward Rose so rapidly, she flinched and nearly spilled the hot water. But he stopped dead in his tracks before reaching her side. He shook his head, pouring himself some hot water in a cup and sipping at it.

"I should've known you'd be reckless. Your mother was the same exact way."

Rose suddenly took a deep interest in the weaving of the fabrics of her blankets.

"In all of your years here, have you not grasped the fact that I am Chief and I rule an entire clan and city?"

She shrugged, avoiding his eyes at all costs.

"Answer me, lass. You have the audacity to go behind my back, why not do it to my face like a real warrior?"

Rose met Eason's piercing green eyes with her own. Neither Magnar or Caiden had managed to achieve this yet, for they thought it equal to meeting the eyes of an aggressive dog. While Eason had never laid a hand on them, he had this look about him when he became cross, which yielded all of Cheryic City to its knees. Now Rose stared at him directly.

"Would you have said 'yes' if I asked you?" Rose asked.

Eason scoffed. "Of course not. These people are not Americans. All is not equal here. An Outsider cannot just come and rule and change a culture without consequences."

"So, you're a coward?"

Eason groaned. "You've grown far too comfortable, child."

"You are?"

"Do not insult your Chief one more time." Eason growled through closed teeth.

Rose sighed, scooted herself slowly from the bed, wincing as her headache grew strong, took her Uncle's hand, and met his eyes again.

"I want to be a warrior, Uncle," She said softly, "w ith Caiden."

Eason stood silent for a moment, opened his mouth as if to respond with something witty, but closed it and stormed out of the tent.

all yours to make

The Cheryic Clan returned home with the children trudging along with them. The long journey and Eason's snubbing gave Rose the time to think of a name for Magnar's falcon: *Valar*. It was a reminder of her mother, her old life, and a damned good name, so she thought. Magnar began training the bird to hunt, send messages, and steal from the Twins.

When the Twins had been home for a few days, and Caiden learned that Rose wanted to train to be a soldier with him, he was ecstatic. The first thing he said to her was: "A real soldier needs a good sword." He then approached Eason, who was skinning a deer in the living room-kitchen.

"Did Magnar leave?" Caiden asked, the corners of his lips drooping into a perplexed frown.

Eason shook his head, not looking up from his work.

"I didn't see him go."

Caiden creaked open the door to the boys' room and squeezed his head inside. He leaned on the door until it was wide open, revealing the inside. No one. Just an open window behind an empty bed.

"He's up to something." Caiden declared to Rose.

She just shook her head, “tsk tsk.”

"I have an adventure for you." Caiden exclaimed, tiptoeing discreetly through the living room-kitchen. “We hunt through perilous alleyways and forests, slaying beasts and saving…”

Caiden hesitated at Rose, who stood crossing her arms, awaiting his next word.

“…babies…” Caiden continued, “We are saving babies. I wasn’t going to say damsels, but *you’re* sexist to assume so.” Rose rolled her eyes. “Anyway, the ultimate quest is to find Magnar and save him from whatever evil witch has him under her spell.”

This time, Rose yanked Caiden. “Come on.”

Magnar wouldn't be hard to find. Caiden and Rose knew all of the places he liked to go to, and the forest was first on that list. It was a breezy day, already showing signs of early autumn in the leaves. Rose clung to her cloak as she ran, after all this time, still unused to the highland chill. Caiden, however, was sweating profusely through his loose linen tunic as he ran. Rose recalled the moment that Eason first told the children that in America, the temperature would range from 0 to 35 degrees Celsius. Caiden and Magnar refused to believe it was true, concluding that Eason was making one of his very rare jokes. Rose, however, had known for a fact that it was true and missed the days of the heat.

They ran past town-square, where little children waved at the young royals of the Cheryic clan. They would have run all the way to the forest if they hadn't passed the smithy. But ideas sprung into Caiden's mind so fast, he could not control the impulse to change his course. He halted so suddenly that Rose ran straight through him, causing both of the Twins to tumble down the hill to the smithy's entrance.

Within this smithy stood a young apprentice called Burgard McCaig. He was about the age of Magnar. The boy had a permanent scowl glued to his face and sharp features, including a cleft chin. His dirty blond hair had been cut short in such a way that was menacing as he stared through the Twins with murderous neon eyes.

Caiden charged inside the smithy as quickly as he could, and Rose, having no idea what the plan was, jogged close behind.

The children slowed to a walk when they had arrived inside of the smithy. (Running through the fire and weapons of the smithy had proved to cause many accidents in the past. This was, of course, how Caiden explained it to Rose. There had been four deaths in the past twenty years as well has one kid who had been turned dumb after a hammer had whacked his head in.)

The smithy was a room about the size of a gymnasium. It made a person feel as if they were being boiled in a large, dark pot. The heat was scorching, and all around, there were giant glowing fireplaces in the darkness and about two-dozen blacksmiths all working in unity. Hammers were clinking in every direction. Rose and Caiden both resisted the impulse to cover their ears with their palms.

Caiden poked the side of Burgard McCaig, who shot a glance down at The Twins. McCaig probably was about three heads taller than the both of them. He must have stood seven feet off the ground, with muscles ripping through his arms, easily visible through his rolled-up sleeves.

"Hi Burgard McCray!" Caiden smiled enthusiastically, "How are you on this bonnie afternoon?"

The boy didn't smile; he just narrowed his green eyes at Caiden and slightly bowed his head. "It's McCaig, and what do you want, Òganach?"

Caiden's smile never dimmed.

"Well McCray, you see, this is my cousin. She's been staying with us for a while and hey she'll probably keep staying with us for forever. You know, it's her choice when she's of age. And…well…Rose, flex those muscles."

Rose grinned, flexing her muscles, which truthfully, were quite strong at the biceps, likely from the summers of assisting fishermen. Caiden squeezed her arm, and Rose bit down a bubble of laughter that threatened to expose her amusement.

"See these arms, McCray? Feel them," Caiden held out Rose's arm for McCaig to feel.

McCaig did not feel them. He crossed his arms, staring the two of them down, as if willing them to burst into flames.

"Alright, don't feel them then. But you can take my word that these are some strong arms. Right Rose?"

Rose raised her brows.

Caiden pushed her arms down.

"I need you to make a sword, a good one, for this lassie."

McCaig crossed his arms and laughed. "Me. Make a sword. For a lassie." He practically spat out the words.

Caiden's smile faded as Rose clenched her fists at her side, struggling to bite her tongue before she said something Eason would reprimand her for later.

"Aye." Caiden's voice was so tense, both Rose and McCaig jumped. "Yes, you will."

McCaig laughed and turned back to his work. "I dinna think so."

"Why?"

McCaig turned back around. "Because," he pointed a finger at Rose, "Lassies," he sneered, "dinna fight. They canna even pick up a sword. They'd be nothing but a bunch of jessies[15] in battle, that's for sure. I'll no be the start of the Cheryic army going to pish."

Every word McCaig spat out sounded like a challenge, and Caiden had trained for his whole life to take on a challenge such as this one.

"Burgard McCaig!" He boomed, attempting to sound like Eason. "You're gonna make my cousin a sword, and it'll be a damn good one, ya ned! "

McCaig grabbed Caiden by the ear and dragged him outside the smithy. Rose scurried behind.

"Call me a ned, do ya? Well, here's what I say to you, prince!" McCaig spat into Caiden's ear before punching him hard in the face. Caiden's vision blurred as he was overwhelmed with a quick wave of nausea. His nose throbbed, sending agonizing waves throughout his entire forehead. He couldn't see anything, but he heard a yell, a man's cry of pain, then a girl's. When his sight was restored, he saw a girl beside him struggling to get up. A man with a bloody nose was hunched over her, laughing. He kicked her in the ribs.

Caiden growled. He managed to push himself up, then tackled McCaig from behind. As McCaig struggled to punch

---

[15] Cowards

Caiden, but could not reach him, for the boy was hanging onto his back like a squirrel, Rose pushed herself up as well. She managed to punch McCaig in the ribs, a pitiful attempt at making any impact on this giant boy. With a swift movement, McCaig grabbed hold of Caiden's thighs and threw him to the wall. Caiden hit so hard, his head split on the clay wall and he groaned. His vision turned red, and as much as he willed himself, he could not get up. He heard a loud wail from the man, then another, and finally silence.

***

Magnar pranced home from the forest with rosy cheeks and a smile he could not seem to hide. But the smile faded as soon as he heard the wail of a boy.

His head jerked toward the smithy, where he saw the distant figure of a giant holding his hands in the air in surrender, while a girl held out a glowing red sword in her hands. She turned as if to walk away, but first, smacked the hilt of the sword against the boy's head. The boy fell to the ground. Magnar bolted toward the smithy.

"Hawl! What in Owen's name is going on here?!" He shouted. He continued running until he was close enough to see the features of bloody Burgard McCaig. Rose stood over him, clutching her ribs. She had dropped the sword on the ground. Her lips were swollen, and the rim of one of her eyes was turning a hideous shade of blue.

"Rose. You beat up McCaig? You can't just go around beating up people Caiden doesn't like! Where is Caiden?" Magnar asked, but his question was answered as soon as the words escaped his lips.

Caiden lay sprawled out against the smithy.

“Aw shite.” Magnar murmured, sprinting toward the boy. He let out a sigh of relief as soon as he realized that Caiden was still breathing.

McCaig was unconscious on the ground. Yet Magnar knew he wouldn't be for long. He hated to leave the kids alone with McCaig, but he had no choice. He dashed inside the smithy toward an old man who was carrying packages to different blacksmiths: Gilbert Stowe, the man Caiden should have consulted with for whatever he wanted. The noise within smithy had been so loud that none of the blacksmiths had noticed the commotion occurring outside.

"Gilbert!" Magnar shouted.

Gilbert turned toward the prince and smiled.

"Òganach! What c-"

"Come with me." Magnar interrupted, such a quick reaction set a worried look on the man's worn leather face.

They both came outdoors to the scene. Caiden and McCaig still lay unconscious on the ground. Rose remained in the same frigid position that Magnar had left her in, unmoving. Gilbert's mouth opened ever so slightly with astonishment; his wrinkled arms shook as he dropped the weapons he had been carrying.

"I need you to fetch a doctor while I carry my brother home." Magnar said. The old man nodded, a worried grimace fixed on his face. He hurried off as fast as a man of his age could run, surprisingly quick, in Magnar’s opinion.

Magnar tensed as he carefully lifted his little brother, afraid of dropping him on his head again.

"Let’s go, Rose." He commanded.

She stirred, wide-eyed, and slowly followed them.

"Yeah. Ok. I’m fine." She murmured, clearing her throat.

Magnar shook his head. The Twins had always been impulsive, but never as reckless as this. He prayed silently to the spirits that he would not die before he produced an heir. If either of The Twins ruled, a war would surely follow.

Eason sat in the bedroom-office, reading through endless documents of proposed laws. He thought the day would be peaceful and quiet since Rose and Caiden had run off. Lord only knew what Magnar had been doing, but at least he was out of the way as well. Days like these made the little house feel so huge. Each time a wall creaked or Eason's pen scratched the parchment, it created an echo throughout the house.

This tranquility lasted for a full thirty minutes.

Gilbert knocked on the door with Mabuz Reid and his daughter, Cinnie. Mabuz was the most renowned physician in the city, and thanks to Rose and Caiden's foolhardiness, he was all too familiar with the Chief's home. When Eason opened the door, poor Gilbert began babbling about Magnar dragging a crippled Caiden home, but the children had not arrived yet.

Eason sighed. "Make sure they're alright."

Gilbert began to hobble off. As soon as he reached the door, however, it slammed open. The man leapt in his shoes. Magnar carried Caiden inside and in his shadow, Rose shuffled as well. Her usual olive face displayed the color of cow's milk.

Eason darted up as Magnar lowered Caiden down on the couch and slowly helped Rose into his chair. Cinnie, seeing Rose as the easier patient, immediately began tending to her, leaving Mabuz to care for Caiden.

"What happened?" Eason asked Magnar.

"I don't know." Magnar said. "I do know that Burgard McCaig did this to them."

Eason kicked over a stool. Of course, McCaig's son would be the one to do this to a helpless adolescent boy. McCaig, himself, probably hadn't left a tavern since he was twelve-years-old. He drank in the night and slept at the corner stool during the day. How he'd even managed to produce children was beyond Eason's capability to understand.

"Where is McCaig's son now?" Eason asked. Magnar shrugged, wrapping a blanket around a shivering Rose. The girl's eyes were nearly popping clean out of her head. She'd come around soon, Magnar thought, and then they wouldn't hear the end of how she got the best of the giant, Burgard McCaig.

"They were in a pretty good fight," Magnar explained. "McCaig almost won. But Rose saw what he did to Caiden and struck him with the hilt of a sword in the make."

Eason drew his brows together. This was a mere preview of all the backlash the clan would exhibit for allowing Rose to train with the men. He hadn't yet decided to let her. The repercussions would surely outweigh the benefits. But Rose, of course, being of his blood, would be too relentless to see the consequences. He knew exactly what the children must have been doing in the smithy, although it was likely Caiden's idea. He knew this would not be the last time they tried something like that behind his back.

Magnar dabbed the blood off of Rose's face as Cinnie began tending to her ribs. He could feel his breath quickening but dared not look in Cinnie's direction.

"This is your cousin?" She asked, eyeing Magnar with her sky blue eyes.

"Yeah, I'm his cousin," Rose replied, annoyed Cinnie hadn't asked her directly.

Magnar sighed.

"Aye, this is my cousin, Rose," he stated.

Cinnie continued holding cold raw meat to Rose's ribs to numb them, ignoring Rose's arrogant reply.

"And she has been under your uncle's care for how long?" she asked.

"About six years," Rose interrupted.

"About six years," Magnar confirmed.

Cinnie pursed her lips and nodded. "When does she leave?"

Rose attempted to cross her arms, but scowled at the jolt of pain that shot up her ribs.

"I dunno. When do you leave?" Rose asked.

"I don't think she will; she loves it here," Magnar smiled.

"You will stay too, right? You are of age; you can leave if you want to. But you will be Chief, so why leave?"

"I'll stay if you want me to," Magnar winked.

Rose began gagging, and Magnar shoved a basin under her as she vomited into it.

Magnar looked to Mabuz.

"How is my brother?" He asked, realizing that he had forgotten all about Caiden. Caiden had regained consciousness, but was lying spread-eagle on the couch, his eyes half-open.

"He only had a big whack in the head. He will need long hours of rest. I'd say for both of them, they shouldn't leave the house for two weeks at least."

"Oh! I left the venison cooking at home!" Cinnie declared, jolting up and grabbing her satchel.

"I'll walk you," Magnar insisted, standing with her, "your da isn't done yet."

Cinnie nodded and joined Magnar outside the house. Magnar placed his hands in the folds of his kilt after rolling his linen sleeves up to allow some heat to escape. As casually as he could, he walked beside her, aware of every step he took. Was he tilting too much to one side? Was he leaning too away from her or too much toward her? He took a deep breath and nervously picked at the stubble beginning to form on his chin.

"So McCaig beat them up?" Cinnie asked.

"Well, they beat him up, it seems." Magnar smiled, holding his head high.

"They seem pretty beat up, themselves," Cinnie replied, her face unreadable.

"Aye. I-I suppose so," Magnar replied.

Cinnie's house was but a block uptown, unfortunately for Magnar, who wanted to make every step with her count. However, every time he thought of something to say, the words were difficult to get out of his mouth. So Cinnie did most of the talking, and he just watched how her beautiful golden hair bounced with every step she took. He noticed how rosy her lips were, how they stood out upon her pale, round face.

"What are you going to do when you are Chief?" she asked him. Her voice was soft and quiet.

"Um...that's a long time from now," Magnar replied nervously. No matter how many times the people asked him this question, he never could determine exactly what to say.

"How do you know that? What if—the spirits protect him—our beloved Chief dies tomorrow? You would take his place."

They were at her door now, but she did not go in. She just stared up at him, an innocent look fixed upon her rosy cheeks.

“Maybe I’d make you my queen.” Magnar smirked, although his insides squirmed at his own remark.

Cinnie blushed, yet smiled, revealing the straight white teeth. Such teeth were rarities within the clan.

They stood like that for a little bit: dazed and silent. Finally, Cinnie rolled her eyes.

“Will you not kiss me, Òganach?”

And they kissed.

***

Eason paced inside, not quite knowing what to do, but positive that Christine would kill him if she were alive. In a straight, rigid stance, Gilbert stood at the doorway, ready to follow any order he was given. Only the slight tremble of his palms revealed the true nature of his emotions. Eason placed a hand on the man's back.

"Go get MacRay and then return to me. I know just what my nephew was doing."

Gilbert nodded and scrambled out the door.

Mabuz soon left as well, informing Eason that Caiden and Rose would be fine if they rested. Eason nodded, gave a sigh of relief, and thanked him with twenty gold beads.

Magnar returned home and lowered his head, rubbing his temples with exasperation. The poor boy had dark circles under his eyes and looked somewhat pale. Eason approached him and clasped his hands on the boy's shoulders.

"You did well," Eason praised him quietly, looking into his green eyes. Magnar sort of smiled and nodded his head. "I'm proud of you, lad."

Magnar's ears turned a bright shade of red or perhaps they had been that color the whole time. Eason did not know, nor did he have time to dwell on it.

In an hour, Gilbert returned with MacRay. Eason called the men to his office-bedroom. He paced back and forth behind the desk, while the two men stood in front of the door.

"What do you think of Rose, Gilbert?" Eason asked, still pacing.

Gilbert shrugged. "Pretty girl. Tough. I havena heard a greet of pain from her yet! She hasna even shed a tear!"

Eason let out a small smile. "Aye, she is. And Magnar tells me she put up a pretty good fight against McCaig's eldest son."

The two men were silent.

"I have orders for the both of you. I don't want arguments or opinions. Only your best work." Eason paused, retired from pacing, and looked them both in the eyes.

"Gilbert, I want you to make the girl the finest sword you've ever made. It must be sharp...and respectable." Gilbert nodded, allowing a small smile to shed light on his face. Eason leaned toward him and lowered his voice. "And if there is a shred of flowers or anything lady-like upon this sword, I guarantee you, you will be the first she wounds with it."

Gilbert's eyes twinkled and he gave a single, slight bow.

"MacRay, Rose needs a new bow; she has outgrown hers. I want you to make her the most impressive bow you've ever made. Make it a beautiful, detailed, light, sturdy and well-aimed bow. Then I want you to make her two hundred arrows."

MacRay bowed his head.

"You are dismissed."

Both men placed their hands on their hearts and left.

Eason lingered in the room for a bit, debating whether to call the men back and tell them he changed his mind. But at last, he gave a quiet grunt and returned to the kitchen-living room to make dinner.

the mold of life

Caiden had never been glummer. He had been in fights before, but not with anyone as ferocious as McCaig. He had to give himself credit, though, he had fought like a warrior. Not just any warrior, the kind that the Spirit Guide told in his stories and legends. Did he get knocked around a little bit? Maybe. But he still gave McCaig a run for his money. And he had done it all with Rose! Warrior twins? The clans would be telling stories about them until Ben Nevis shrank into a little pebble on the ground.

All this aside, the reason he was so glum was that he had to stay inside for two weeks in the summer! He had done nothing wrong, except try to defend his cousin's honor. Now here they were, sitting on the couch, missing out on sailing, fishing, horse-racing, tug o' war, stoolball, throwing stones and so much more. The possibilities had been so endless, and all the sudden they were next to nothing.

Every now and then, Gilbert would check in on them, making sure they were recovering alright. At one point the man brought draughts, Niddy Noddy, and knucklebones over, but these games entertained the Twins for no more than an hour. The Twins were not known for their patience.

Magnar did his best to provide entertainment for the children, but often he would take Valar out to hunt and train. This left the kids alone, with Eason off at meetings and working in his office. Once Caiden tried to teach Rose to whittle, but she accidentally cut herself a few times, then she carved the horse's head to come out between its hind legs. Needless to say, the two gave up on the hobby. So Rose took much of the time to tell Caiden about the things she remembered of the culture from The Outside.

"See they have this thing called a president in the United States. He kind of is a Chief, but kind of isn't. Scotland is right above the Province of Northern Europe. Hundreds of years ago, it was a bunch of countries like Germany and...France...aaaand Poland. And other countries. But then a big war started and the countries united against the United Kingdom, which is where we are right now. They destroyed everything here, and then realizing that they had killed all of these people, and thinking they had destroyed this land, the world began an international law that bans all use of nuclear weapons and bombs aaaaand guns. Yeah, I think that's it. So anybody who uses the weapons gets bombed. Which is ironic, if you think about it."

"Whoaaa." Caiden marvelled at this idea. "So if all of the people were killed, then how are we here?"

"Our people were few then, Caiden."

Both kids jumped in their chairs and turned to see Eason had walked through the door. Eason smiled. "They did not know we existed," he continued. "We lived in small numbers under the mountains, and because they did not know we were there, they did not bomb us. It was the protection of the spirits that allowed us to be ignored all of those years. Even before then, when we wanted to be left alone by the British, we could hide in the mountain's shadow. And then when the United Kingdom was evacuated, the five clans thrived without the weight of the industrialized people."

Without another word, Eason was out the door, leaving the Twins to their imaginations.

"How did Uncle become Chief?" Rose asked Caiden.

"Uncle ran away from my maw and your maw's family," Caiden said matter-of-factly. "He ran into the hills of Scotland, and his maw helped him. She told him that she had a brother in the mountains. Her brother was the Chief of the village, and if he went there, he could become chief and have a place to stay. So he did. Apparently, Grandma loved a man from the Outside, so she had to leave Scotland when she was Magnar's age. Then Eason's uncle took Eason in and trained him here. Then he died and now Eason's Chief."

"Oh." Rose replied. She had been expecting a great war story, but instead Eason had just been another man in line to become king.

Some days, Evander would come see the children, giving them complimentary pastries from his parents. They would sit and gamble nuts and berries, while Eason would play bittersweet songs on the violin by the fire. Evander tried his best to remedy their boredom, but there barely was anything he could do with them besides sit and play cards. They even tried gambling for gold beads once, but Eason barged in and yelled at them.

Even Gwen and Jean, the farmer's daughters, would come and bring the Twins vegetables when they found time. Rose had become friends with the girls after the tournament. In fact, they were the only girls that Rose could seem to stand in the city. The rest tended to scoff at her rants of adventure. But Gwen and Jean marveled at them.

"Perhaps we can go on an adventure," Gwen suggested one day over a game of niddy noddy. "We can explore the clans. I've always wanted to cross the sea and go to Mara."

Jean rolled her eyes. "Da would skelp us before we were out the door. Who would do the chores 'round the farm then?"

In fact, because of the chores on the farm, Gwen and Jean's visits were very infrequent, for their father often had them wake up before sunup and do their chores until sundown. Come sundown, the girls seemed drained of all energy, but occasionally, they dragged their feet to see Caiden and Rose, excited to break away from their normal routines.

When the two weeks were up (they had been counting), Caiden and Rose both asked Eason if they could go outside. Eason thought it would be better if they waited another week, for he didn't believe that they had fully healed. The children grumbled and threw themselves back upon their couch in despair. But the minute that Eason had returned to his bedroom-office, they began plotting.

"What are we doing?" Rose grumbled, rising from the couch.

Caiden shrugged.

"Sitting here, being bored, I guess." Caiden mumbled back.

"Well let's sneak out!" Rose suggested, her voice suddenly became enthusiastic.

Caiden straightened up in his chair, intrigued.

"Come on! You already told me you feel great, and my ribs are fine! Why do we still have to stay here?" She went on, shaking Caiden a little. "Come on, let's go have fun!"

Caiden sat still for a moment, his smile growing wider and wider. "Well, I supposed Uncle's wrath is better than sitting on the couch, getting bit by midgies[16]… Alright. Let's go."

They tiptoed out the door, inching it shut behind them, just soft enough so it would barely make a sound.

There was a chill in the air, and the Twins were grateful to have brought their cloaks along. It was a bit breezy; the wind was whipping their cloaks about, forcing them to grip the folds as they ran. Caiden grinned as the wind tossed Rose's hair every which way and she struggled to keep it out of her face. Ever since she was eight, it had grown into a wild, frizzy mass that blew in and out of her face.

"Let me braid it," Caiden insisted.

Rose nodded.

Caiden and Magnar had known how to braid for as long as they could remember. It was the easiest way to keep hair out of your face when you fought or played. But Rose had never cared to learn.

Caiden split the hair into three pieces and quickly braided it with practiced fingers.

"One of these days, you're gonna let me teach you to braid, and you will be the second-best braider in the clan. I'll be the first, of course."

---

[16] Flies

Rose smiled. Truth be told, she had avoided learning thus far because Caiden, as sweet and charming as he could be, was a horrible teacher. The boy was impatient and had no attention span for any matter that lasted more than ten seconds. If he wasn't the one doing it, he didn't have time for it. (She had learned this the hard way when Caiden had first taught her how to fish. He saw something interesting in the water, and before Rose knew what was happening, she was alone in the boat drifting out of Cheryic waters, while he swam after some kind of eel. It was hours before she was found again and brought back to Eason.)

"Thought ya couldna leave the house for another week?"

Caiden and Rose whirled around and saw Evander standing in the muck with a basket of biscuits.

Rose held a finger to her lips urgently.

"Drop the basket, and let's go!" She whispered.

Evander reluctantly set the basket on the ground.

"Go where exactly?" He whispered back.

Caiden shrugged. "Mountain?"

The other two nodded and began to pace away when Caiden stopped dead in his tracks.

"Wait!" he squealed, whirled around, and in one swooping motion, he took Evander's basket of biscuits.

Evander smirked, but Rose stood impatiently with her hands on her hips, tapping her foot dramatically.

"What?" Caiden asked sheepishly, his nose reddening, "for the road."

The three friends hiked to the mountain base, snacking on biscuits as they did. Rose noticed they weren't as fresh as usual, a little more stale and less sweet, but she was still grateful.

"Och!" Evander grunted, and he threw a dry biscuit on the ground. "I canna make biscuits."

"You made these?" both the Twins marvelled.

"Aye," Evander replied. "Well, my maw has been sick. That's why I haven't been around so much. Been tryna help out and whatnot. But, I canna bake. I'm no meant to be a baker. I mean, my da says I am. But, naw."

"Perhaps," Caiden grinned, "you should be a warrior with us?"

Evander snorted. "Us?"

"Me and Rose!"

Evander stopped in his tracks, taking Rose in as if assessing her capabilities, her strengths and weaknesses. "The Chief's letting you then?"

Rose shrugged.

"That's just a slight obstacle," Caiden waved his hand nonchalantly, "we can remedy it."

Evander smiled; the boy had some of the largest dimples either of The Twins had ever seen, and they grew profoundly deep when he showed his teeth.

Caiden smacked his back, "Sooner or later," he said, "you'll be a warrior too, Evander, it's just one of those things I know. I can see the future."

Rose rolled her eyes. "Oh wheesht Caiden, you couldn't see the future if it was written in big, bold letters in front of your face."

Caiden waved both his hands, disregarding her. "Eh that's just because I can't read. The letters get all jumbled in my head."

Evander nodded. "You've never once been right about the weather, in all the years I've known you."

"It's not my fault the weather's always changin'. Listen you two, this is fate. I can see Evander fightin' countless battles with us. Those Craotics will never think to attack Cheryic land again. You'll see."

The North Road was a rocky one, and the children had to look at their feet to assure they wouldn't trip. The number of buildings was beginning to wane as they closed in on the stretch toward the mountain. Now it was mainly homes of miners and guards, with maybe a tavern in between—a stall for horses here and there.

"I've been thinking," Rose said as she bounded over to where the stone of the mountain met the tall grass of the base. "Where's the door?"

"Door?" Evander asked.

"The door. There has to be one. The door they used to hide from the Outside all those years."

"The miners use it," Caiden replied, "Uncle took me once. It's huge. But it's round the other side of the ben.[17]"

Rose shook her head. "That's not it then."

"Why not?"

They were face to face with the stone now. Rose traced her fingers around the jagged edges and began to climb.

"Ever read *The Hobbit*?"

***

Eason paced around the room, back and forth, forth and back. His fists were clenched tightly at his side.

Where could they have gone? They could be anywhere!

The only thing he could do was sit and wait. There was no doubt in his mind that The Twins had run off themselves. He should have foreseen the idea brewing in their eejit heads!

---

[17] Mountain

He should...he should...he should get them a bodyguard. Perhaps then he could actually get some work done without constantly looking over his shoulder to see if they were getting into trouble.

McCaig's eldest finally would be punished in the morning for assaulting royalty. Burgard would be thrown into the woods for two months to think on his actions. The problem was when Eason had come out to deliver the news, the victims were gone.

Magnar lay on the sofa whittling a wooden block into the shape of a woman. Valar sat perched on the sofa's arm, intently watching him work.

"Where could they have gone?" Eason grumbled. "Caiden's idea to leave, no doubt. Or maybe Rose's. The two are so unpredictable. What have I done to deserve this? Have I not been decent? Have I not given you everything? Taught you all I know? How could they be so stupid?!"

Valar screeched.

"Och wheesht!" Eason yelled at the bird. It flew to the corner, tagging Eason's shoulder as it did. "Damned thing's a menace."

Magnar smirked and continued to whittle the woman.

"What?" Eason asked, annoyed.

Magnar just shook his head.

Eason stood in front of him and crossed his arms stubbornly.

"You worry too much, Uncle," Magnar reasoned. "Caiden's been out of the house loads of times. He said himself, this morning, he feels fine, and Rose's ribs are no longer hurting her. What's the worst that can happen? Relax, they're fine."

Eason narrowed his eyes. "Laid back, relaxed? Hardly the qualities of a future Chief."

Magnar rolled his eyes. “You *know* I’m not laid back *or* relaxed. I just-”

“You just don’t care about your siblings, your subjects. I don’t know of any good Chiefs who were careless with their people.”

Magnar smashed the woman down on the side table and stood up abruptly, face to face with Eason. “Uncle-"

The door opened.

Both Magnar and Eason's heads turned toward the door, hoping to see The Twins. Instead, Gilbert and MacRay walked inside with many packages. They were laughing ecstatically about something, but this was quickly terminated when they took in the tension of the room. Seeing the beat red faces of both Magnar and Eason, as they stood no more than a foot apart with their fists clenched, the men set the packages on the counter and scurried out of the room.

Magnar sighed and plopped back down to the couch, but did not pick his creation back up. "Late birthday presents, Uncle? For who?" he asked Eason, who was heading back to his pacing area.

"Rose." Eason replied, the floor booming with every step he made.

Magnar nodded.

"I can’t believe they are so old." Magnar stated.

Eason shook his head. “Amazing. You all were so little when you first came to me; now you are so grown.”

He looked down sadly at the packages on the counter, feeling their wrapping in his fingers. For a moment, Magnar wondered what he could be thinking. Streaks of white were beginning to run through his black locks and the lines on his face were growing deeper. Magnar wondered if he had been the cause of the aging man's worries. What would he look like if the two babies had not been dumped on his doorstep?

Magnar returned to his whittling. Both he and Eason had trouble with sentimental moments. So they chose to ignore them. Caiden was always the one gifted with the sentimental quality. Who knows how that happened?

There was a pounding on the door. Eason grimaced. The door's wood was so old and rotten, he half expected the hand in question to go right through it. Dust clouds filled the air with each pound.

Eason sighed.

"Are you expecting someone?" Magnar asked, his thick brows drawn together.

Eason said nothing but trudged toward the door and swung it open.

A man, with a deep red face and hair whiter than Ben Nevis's snow, stood in the doorway with an entourage of Outside men in suits behind him.

"Hello father," seethed Eason.

***

The children bounded home from the mountain with a skip in their steps, especially Caiden, his eyes widened and bewildered from a successful day's adventure. The first in what had seemed like years. He had been babbling to Evander incessantly since they had begun the hike home and Evander had replied quietly with "ok" and "Sure" or "you don't say?". But this was the nature of their relationship.

Rose hiked ahead of them. She had heard nothing but Caiden's babbling for two weeks straight, and she was happy to have someone else be his ear for the day. She strode ahead. But as the house came into sight, she stopped dead in her tracks and yanked both boys by their tunics into an alleyway.

"WHAT?" Caiden yelled.

"Wait, you numptie."[18] Rose whispered in a shouting voice.

She gestured her thumb over the corner, and both boys peered beyond.

Three men in the strangest, tightest, black uniforms Caiden had yet seen, stood carrying wide knives. Black glasses covered their eyes.

"Can we get closer?" Caiden asked, "It's not like they can see us with those things on their face."

Rose shook her head. "They're Outsiders. Those things help them see better. What are they doing here?"

Both boys shrugged and scrambled to peer out and get a better look.

Evander glanced over at Rose. "You...you dinna think they're after you...do ya?"

Rose's eyes widened and Evander grabbed her wrist before she could run.

"Lemme see what's happening. I willna tell where you are, and they willna think I'm with ya," Evander added.

Rose nodded and backed further into the alley.

The Twins ran through town square and began taking a shortcut through an alleyway to Evander's, but they were stopped midway by a few menacing boys smashing clubs to their hands. Caiden and Rose held their hands up in peace, eyes fixed on the clubs.

---

[18] Idiot

"I heard ye challenged my brother?" A voice snarled from behind.

Caiden and Rose turned.

Within the dim light of the alleyway stood a boy their age with a giant club in his hand. He, like McCaig, had a permanent scowl etched on his face. The boy's dirty orange hair fell past his shoulders.

"But ye ken what else I heard?" The boy spat, slowly making his way toward them with a menacing look in his eyes. "I heard that even the prince is too cowardly to fight one on one. He has to have his sister save him."

"Get away Fergus," Caiden warned, fixing his eyes on the flaming haired boy. He was fully aware of the boys behind him and sensitive to even the slightest sound they made.

Fergus put his hands up innocently. "I mean no harm. I'm no jessie. I just want a fight one on one with one of ya. Particularly you, prince. I'm no in the mood to beat up a lassie."

Rose laughed. "I can take you any day."

"Not without the help of your brother to save the day."

"Caiden, stand back and don't help me. Count to sixty. If he's not down within a minute, I owe you six beads," said Rose.

Caiden smiled quietly but said nothing. He stood with his back against the wall, praying she would win. He assessed Fergus calmly. The boy was skinny and pale, so she likely could take him. The one problem was that he had never seen her actually win a fight. Sure she did with McCaig, but well, she kind of cheated, as she had every right to. The point was, he had his doubts.

The boys stepped back against the alley walls as well, leaving space for Rose and Fergus to examine each other with cautious eyes.

"Start counting now Caiden." Rose ordered, not breaking her stare from Fergus.

"1 2 3…" Rose did nothing.

"28, 29, 30." She just stared at him.

"36, 37, 38." Nothing. Fergus squirmed impatiently, his fists in front of his face.

"48, 49, 50."

Fergus threw his hands in the air.

"WELL COME AT-"

BAM. Rose's kick met Fergus's jaw, knocking him to the ground. She didn't hesitate. She gave Fergus a final blow to the nose, assuring that he would be out long enough for the Twins to leave.

"60."

"Let's go." Rose ordered Caiden.

"Wait." Caiden stopped. "Does this mean I have to pay you six beads?"

Rose sighed. "We'll talk about it later. This is supposed to be our dramatic exit now."

And they left.

***

Magnar lay on the couch with his hands rubbing his temples. Eason had returned from his meeting with his father and was now pacing the room frantically. "If they're gone any longer," Eason fumed, "I'll call for the city to find them. And by the spirits, they won't be able to sit on their bums for weeks."

"How could you let this happen?" Magnar groaned, "you're destroying everything!"

Eason knew he wasn't talking about the Twins. He ignored Magnar as he paced more rapidly.

"They can't do what they're told. God forbid! Magnar, by the spirits, you better have children. If the Twins are left in charge, it'll all be in flames."

"It may as well all be in flames now," Magnar grumbled.

"What did you say to me, lad?!" Eason's voice rang out to maximum volume, and likely could be heard across town square. "I didna have a choice. It was the five clans who voted. I can't stand up to America unless I have the support of the clans, you daft boy!"

Eason stormed out of the room, slamming the door behind him. But he was soon back, clutching a map in his hand. He opened it in such a rushed manner, he ripped the edges. "Do you see this little strip of land up here? That's Scotland! Do you see this little tiny fraction of that land? That's our land! Do you see this giant mass of country on this side? That's America! Do you understand now why I'm trying to avoid a genocide?"

Magnar's face had turned a deep shade of purple, but he just pursed his lips together in protest.

"They will be here, among us." Magnar said, "They will be watching us. They will learn our ways. Now they can learn how to destroy us, from the inside."

Eason crumbled up the map and threw it to the fire. "The clans will come round in time...it will just take some convincing."

The door slammed open, Rose and Caiden bounded inside.

"Magnar!" Caiden ran to his brother's side. "You should have seen Rose! She took just ten seconds to beat up Fergus! Well actually it was a minute, but fifty seconds of that minute was just her standing in front of him doing nothing, so really it was ten seconds!"

(By this time, Caiden had managed to turn his shock into awe.)

Eason whirled around to Rose. "You what?!"

Both of the Twins' ears turned pink.

"Well…um…she did it…carefully..." Caiden defended.

"Hair's bonnie, Rose," Magnar nodded to her.

"Um…thanks," she replied.

Eason turned his nose up at the boy. Every remark he made anymore was enough to make him seethe.

"You could have gotten hurt." Eason growled.

Rose bit her lip.

"But I didn't?" She replied, twiddling her thumbs next to Caiden, whose head was drooping guiltily.

Eason's teeth clenched.

"Caiden, why did you leave with Rose? You know you can't do that!" Eason yelled.

"It was my idea," Rose confessed. The room grew quiet. Eason turned back to Rose, face red.

"What?" He asked, his voice dangerously low.

"I'm sorry, Uncle," she said with her eyes meeting his defiantly. "I grew bored. But, both Caiden and I felt fine. It was pointless to keep us locked up in here."

Eason boiled over. He pointed to his niece. It was all he could do to say, "Go to your room."

Rose obeyed.

Caiden still stood petrified next to Magnar, but after about a minute of awkwardly standing, he voluntarily went to his room.

Magnar smirked again.

"Oh, what now?" Eason groaned.

"When the girl arrived at your house, did you expect a princess or a soldier?" He made a tsk noise with his tongue. "Because in all of my history books, I've not read about a princess like her."

"You think this is a joke, lad?!" Eason growled, and he peered out the windows. Men in camouflage uniforms were standing idly throughout the city: leaning on buildings, sitting on stones and holding their machetes in their hands. He whirled around to Magnar and drew close to him, speaking in a low voice. "You must listen to me now. No matter what the other clans say, these men are dangerous. You do not eat anything they give you. You do not even look them in the eyes. If they talk to you, come directly to me. You are the heir to the Cheryic Chieftain. You are their secondary target."

Magnar gulped. He had cut himself with his whittle knife and now clenched his bleeding hand with his tunic.

"Your generation, your reign," Eason sighed, "has been handed one of the most difficult situations this clan has ever faced."

hands to break

It took a few days for Eason to soften, but as soon as he did, he gave Rose the most beautiful sword and bow she had ever seen. The silver metal glistened as she removed it from the scabbard; her hand fit around the hilt perfectly. Cheryic patterns wove along it, and she held the blade to her face, admiring the way she could clearly see her reflection in it. The bow also had Cheryic patterns, and something written in Gaelic that Rose was too giddy to ask about.

"Go on. Practice." Eason smirked. "I want you to be able to shoot anyone who gets in your way when you start school."

***

"It's the first day of school! Wake up!" Rose was jolted awake by the shaking of her entire bed as Caiden bounced upon it.

CRACK.

The mattress fell right through the bed frame, bringing Caiden and Rose with it. Caiden rolled off of Rose, holding his stomach as he laughed uncontrollably.

“Caiden!” Rose shouted, “Wheesht!”

She closed her eyes in an attempt to fall back asleep.

When he regained his composure, Caiden leaned over Rose and allowed a long line of drool to descend from his mouth. Rose opened her eyes as she felt something unpleasantly wet on her cheek.

"Ugh!" She impulsively pushed him off the mattress, and he tripped over the bed frame and landing on his butt.

"Ow." Caiden said in a monotonous voice. Rose jerked up.

"You deserved it," she replied, now wide-awake. She wiped her cheek with her sleeve. "That's so disgusting."

Caiden laughed. He scrambled back upon the floored mattress, which Rose began pushing herself out of.

"Where's Magnar?" She asked.

"Not up yet."

She nodded and turned to the window. Thousands of stars lit up the sky, creating an electric blue hue. At first, she marvelled at them. But then she slowly turned her head toward Caiden.

"What time is it?" Rose asked.

“I dunno.” Caiden replied, his face beginning to turn a shade of pink from straining to hide a laugh.

“What time is it?” Rose asked impatiently.

"Well...by the candle...which sometimes lies...3ish." Caiden replied sheepishly.

Rose gritted her teeth.

"And what time is school, Caiden Rankin?" she asked, beginning to walk toward Caiden. She picked up a piece of wood that had broken off of the bed frame and smacked it to her palm menacingly.

"What time is school?" She asked again in a harsher tone.

"Maybe it's 900; maybe it's not." Caiden placed his arms behind his head and relaxed on her mattress. Rose smacked the wood again.

"Why'd you wake me up so early, Caiden?" Her tone was soft and dangerous. Caiden suddenly jerked his head toward her. His closed smile, which abbreviated his high cheekbones, suddenly disappeared, and his eyes grew wide.

"Why'd you wake me up, Caiden?!" Rose yelled, diving for the bed. Caiden scrambled out of the way just in time and leaped toward the door. Rose chased him around the couch and into his room. Magnar lay sprawled out on the bed, legs dangling over each side, snoring softly.

Magnar's peaceful sleep was soon interrupted by Caiden pouncing on his bed and shaking him violently. "Magnar! Help! Help me! She's gonna kill me!"

Magnar's pale eyes fluttered open when he saw his brother and he glanced around wildly, trying to make out what was happening.

"What in the name of the Owen himself are ya doin'?" Magnar half-shouted sleepily. Caiden pulled at the front braids of Magnar's hair. Magnar's jaw tightened. He threw Caiden off the bed onto his butt.

"Really?" Caiden asked annoyedly, his smile faded.

Magnar wrapped on a kilt from the floor and tucked his tunic into it.

"Aye, really." He nodded. His smile widened as he dressed silently, doing a belt to hold the kilt tight. As soon as he glanced outside, however, his smile faded. "What the hell are you all up for?"

“Caiden woke me up,” Rose replied. She had been lurking in the corner of the room, waiting on the opportune moment to strike Caiden.

Magnar pounced onto Caiden, putting him in a headlock.

“Really, little brother? It’s your first day of school, and you want to be known as the boy who woke up in the middle of the night just so you can get ready early?”

Magnar gestured for Rose to come over and she began drooling on Caiden in the same fashion as he had done to her. Caiden struggled in Magnar’s grip, his veins bulging nearly out of his forehead. He tried to get up, but Magnar held his long brown hair to the ground. Magnar reached his hand above his head, threatening to punch, but brought it down on the side of the boy’s head instead.

"What are you doing?" Eason thundered. They all grimaced. His green eyes were flashing with fury. Magnar immediately dropped Caiden, who landed on the floor like a wounded animal. Rose stood up, wiping the drool from her chin. Eason looked toward her.

"Rose, what were you doing?"

She took a sudden interest in the dirt floor, so neatly compacted.

"Tackling Caiden," she murmured.

Eason's lips grew thin.

Magnar stood up.

"Uncle, we were only fooling arou-"

"You, I am most disappointed in,” Eason growled. “This is no behavior for a future Chief.”

Magnar hung his head.

“And at this hour?!” Eason continued, “If you want to make a racket, go outside! Some of us have a clan to run in the morning."

He turned and left the room.

“Why is Rose’s bed broken?!” Eason’s voice could be heard shouting in the hallway.

The Twins exchanged glances while Magnar just shook his head at the two of them. Eason stormed back into the boys’ room.

"The three of you go hunting, now. This is a punishment and there's no getting out of it."

“Even me?!” Rose asked excitedly, while the other two grumbled.

“Aye, Miss I-want-to-do-what-the-boys-do. Now go!”

And they were off.

The children ran out the door of the house, nodding to some Outside guards courteously, yet cautiously. Magnar had released Valar from its cage, and the bird flew ahead of them. When they arrived in the forest with their bows slung over their backs, all chaos from home quickly faded away. Not even a natural sound could be heard in the morning compared to the night, when masses of bugs and wolves cried out into the air.

The children chose not to oppose the forest’s noiselessness. Slowly, they crept through the woods, Magnar with much more practice than the other two.

Valar landed upon Magnar’s shoulder. He winked at the Twins as if to say, “watch this.”

“Sealg.” Magnar whispered to the bird, and it flew away, flapping its great wings in the air. “She’ll be back soon.”

Caiden had gone hunting a few times with Eason and Magnar, but had never shot anything. Rose had never hunted before. It was considered blasphemy to make a woman go hunting, for it was useless. A woman could not possibly kill a living animal. Rose had already decided that she would change the clan's point of view that day.

For about an hour they waited behind bushes for a deer or perhaps something similar. It was a stag that roamed through the forest with a great, proud chest. It seemed to have found food pleasing enough to bring his march to a pause.

Magnar nodded to Rose, who took out an arrow for her bow, which was already resting in her hands. Slowly and silently, she placed the arrow onto her bow and pulled it back. It took her a minute to be sure that she had found her target. But as soon as she did, she released. The stag fell instantly; there was no suffering. Magnar, Caiden, and Rose ran toward their kill, Magnar beaming at his little cousin.

"Congratulations!" He praised, placing a hand on Rose's back as they examined their kill. Rose's first kill. "You are already quite the archer, Rose."

"I practiced." Rose bragged, tossing her hair to the side.

Magnar pulled the arrow out of the stag's head. It had landed deeply right beside the eye of the great animal.

"Maybe, but why didn't you hit the stag in the eye, Rose? Ya missed!" Caiden teased.

Rose punched his arm.

Magnar took a rope from his bag and gave it to Rose. "Here's a first kill tradition. You get to carry your kill home." He smiled sarcastically, his lower lip curling slightly.

Rose rolled her eyes and began attempting to lift the stag onto her shoulders.

"Fine."

Suddenly a dead rabbit falling from the sky hit Rose on the head. Valar landed on Magnar's shoulders and screeched proudly.

***

As soon as they entered the house, the chaos returned.

"Caiden, for God's sake, lad! Brush your hair!" Eason scolded.

Caiden scrambled inside his room and grabbed a brush. Magnar made sure his braids were ok, which they were, as always.

"Rose, you do something with your hair too and change out of those rags, all of you! This is school we're talking about, not a trip to the river!" Eason ordered.

"But we have to run in school!" Caiden's voice whined from his room.

Eason sighed.

"Just wear something appropriate....but actually Rose...perhaps you should change into something of Caiden's to make running easier."

Rose ran to the now-crowded mirror and began braiding her hair the way Caiden recently had taught her. Caiden quickly changed into a blue tunic, then put a festively patterned jacket over that, along with fingerless gloves. Over this, he threw on a cloak.

Rose borrowed a white linen tunic from Caiden and slipped it over her corset. She also less willingly acquired a pair of brown trousers. Over these, she slipped on a dark blue herigaut and pushed the hood over her corset.

It was early September, yet they already needed various layers to go outside, the air was so bitter.

"Magnar, where's my sword?" Caiden asked, panicked from his position sprawled out below the couch. He searched beneath the cushions. He slipped his daggers into his boots and up his sleeves.

Rose's boots were on her feet before she knew it, and her cloak was fastened comfortably around her. She reached for her scabbard to find another sitting right next to it.

"Caiden it's in here!" She called from her room and attached her scabbard to her belt. She placed her bow and arrows behind her back and fastened her fingerless gloves on her palms. Caiden's hand could be seen reaching around, snatching his scabbard.

When Rose ran outside of her room, she found Magnar with his sword strapped to his belt, clasped in place with a leaf-patterned morse. She knew for sure he had two knives hidden behind his back—time for school.

The Twins' first "class" was Intense Training. The whole school had this, except for the rest of the girls. So the trainer, Andrew MacRay, (more commonly known for his work as a bowyer) put Rose with a group of ten beginner boys, including Caiden.

MacRay's light brown hair only just reached his shoulders, and he stood with his bowl chest out and his head held high. But his features were kind, despite being somewhat worn and scarred from battle. He had no beard except for a slight stubble, unlike most men in the clan, whose beards fell to their chests or lower.

He stood in the field, awaiting the start of class, talking casually with two Outside guards. They were here, according to one chunky boy, to protect the children from any harm from drunks, rogue soldiers, and wolves.

Rose lined up next to the other boys, who stared at her in a way that she hadn't experienced since she had first arrived in the clan. They looked at her like she was an Outsider. A few of them snickered.

"That's the chief's niece," she heard one of them say. She kept her distance from them and stayed next to Caiden, whose face was as red as a tomato. She felt fury build up within her and struggled to contain it. A boy with long orange hair and a menacing scowl pushed through the crowd.

"Ye lost, Miss?" He asked in a malicious tone. Fergus. The boy still had a purple bruise on his forehead from their last encounter. "Here, ye dinna need that." He reached to take Rose's sword from her scabbard, but she was too quick. She removed it and it was next to his neck before he knew it. Fergus froze. "Ye dinna have the balls."

The rest of the boys giggled at this play on words.

Rose probably would have stabbed him, but a hand gently nudged her sword down. Evander looked at her with gentle eyes and a facial expression that seemed to say *I got this*. He turned toward Fergus, his features hardening.

"Ya friends with this traitor lass too, Evander?" Fergus asked, beginning to back away.

"Is there a problem with that?" Evander spat.

Fergus smirked. "How's yer maw?"

Evander laughed, "How's yer brother?"

Fergus narrowed his eyes at the boy, who stood nearly a foot taller than him.

Evander placed his forefinger on his temple, the area that had been turned blue by Rose's kick a few days before. "Where'd this come from?"

Fergus simply responded with a spit to the ground.

Evander turned back toward Rose.

"Alright Evander," Fergus seethed, "but I wouldna count on her. She'd be no different than shaggin' a man."

Evander punched Fergus's mousey little face so hard that he was on the ground. Fergus clutched his bloody nose with one hand and propped himself up with the other, but said nothing. He gave Evander one last nasty look, then returned to his group of friends. Evander turned back to Caiden and Rose. His face had become a color that reminded Rose of bricks from the Outside.

He grinned slowly. "Welcome to school."

"Alright, class! Alright!" MacRay shouted, "First years, I'm MacRay. I am your Intense Training tutor. In this class, you will test your bodies to the limits, as you are sure to do if you become a warrior. If you canna complete this class, you may join the women in learning to become housewives." A few kids murmured Rose's name, others snickered, and the rest just looked disgusted. MacRay ignored them and continued. "Today we will start with a game."

This received several groans from a few boys in the back. MacRay continued to ignore them and led the group out back to the woods, where they came across a pit about a kilometer long, twenty meters wide and fifty meters deep.

The Pit was a phenomenon in the clans which had become victim to many Old Wives' Tales. Theories ranged about how it came into existence: The more religious clanspeople believed that the spirits casted all the demons of evil down into the pit, while those who deemed themselves wise believed that a star had fallen from the sky and plunged into the ground. Most clanspeople, however, believed that the earth had swallowed the Outsiders and this was what remained. It was a secret tradition for young men of the clan to climb to the bottom, a test of their bravery.

"Alright," MacRay began, after giving the children a moment to take in their surroundings. "Initiation begins now. Whoever makes it to the other side, without going around, wins. Go."

What happened next occurred in a series of phases. Phase 1: Everyone stood flabbergasted, their eyes fixed on the other side of The Pit, refusing to believe the impossible. Phase 2: Everyone casually looked around, still in disbelief, but hoping to find something to prove their theories wrong.

Caiden entered Phase 3 first: start actually attempting to solve the problem. In his own fashion.

"I know what to do." He whispered to Evander and Rose. "We're gonna win this."

Rose crossed her arms. "Okay Caiden, number one, I don't think this is a team activity and number two, please, oh please, don't say flying."

"It's a team activity if I say it is." Caiden scoffed, "and I wasn't going to say flying, that's ridiculous. But we can jump!"

Evander smacked Caiden's head, turning to Rose. "We could climb down, and climb up, but that may take too long."

Rose nodded. She could see out of the corner of her eyes that this was the approach Fergus was attempting to take. She didn't want to do what Fergus was doing. She wanted to do the complete opposite of anything he ever did.

She looked up. The trees towered above her, shedding light between their vast branches. "The trees."

Evander shook his head. "That's just as dumb as Caiden's thing. If you fall, you die."

In an instant, Rose grabbed Caiden's tartan and slashed a sturdy piece of cloth from it. She handed Caiden her sword in return for the cloth and began climbing hastily up a nearby tree. She could hear boys below murmuring notes of disapproval. One even said, "well, she lasted one day."

After clambering up a mountain at age eight, climbing a tree felt small and insignificant. She easily made it to the highest branch which could hold her. As it happened, Cheryic students were required to keep rope on them, just in case they were to go on an impromptu mountain climb. She tied one end of this rope to the branch and the other to her arrow. Ziplining, apparently, had been unheard of amongst the clans until this point, for the boys below gaped at her. She shot the arrow into a tree across The Pit, held the cloth in her hands and began to slide down the rope. It seemed it would be successful, until the arrow in the tree snapped. Rose desperately dropped Caiden's cloth, and caught the rope in her hands, which was swinging back toward the tree. She looked behind her, and with all her might, kicked off against the tree trunk, swinging herself over the pit, and to the other side. She landed with a thud, and rolled until she finally regained herself, and saw the distant figures Caiden and Evander cheering.

MacRay blew his whistle. "Alright class, good good good, now go to your next period. If ye have archery, meet me back at the field."

Rose, Evander and four other boys returned to the field with MacRay, who began setting up targets. Rose removed her bow from her sheath, and shifted towards Evander, away from the other boys, who were still intent on laughing at the girl.

"Have ye been practicing?" Evander asked, watching MacRay struggle to lift one of the targets.

"Yes, mom." Rose teased.

Evander broke his gaze from MacRay to look back at her and chuckle, his cheeks rounding out like small apples as his grin reached from ear to ear.

"Hey, I taught ya, remember?"

"I think I can beat you now," Rose assured him, lifting her bow and inserting an arrow.

"Oh yeah?" Evander asked, lifting his own bow.

"Ready, set, shoot." Rose commanded.

One hit the bull's eye.

Evander's hit just outside.

"Told ya," Rose scoffed. All the boys gaped at the arrow, their mouths dropping like idiots.

***

Magnar beat Rose home for lunch. In fact, when Rose arrived at the doormat, she heard raised voices. She paused, holding her ear against the door.

"I'm telling you Magnar! It's no right!" Cinnie's high-pitched voice stood out like wildfire. Rose thought about glancing into the window, but decided against it for fear of being caught. She did not want the intriguing conversation ceasing on her account.

"Listen to me; it's none of your business what she does!" Magnar's voice had already become deep as it did when he was angry, much like Eason's did.

"Aye, but it's your business! Imagine the reputation you've gotten, allowing your younger cousin to act the way she does!"

"How is the way my cousin acts wrong?"

"Women have no business on the battlefield! We canna even wield a sword! The whole clan kens that well, and they see her and they see you. They willna[19] allow you to be Chief, Magnar, if they see such nonsense. Not only that but...well, she doesna[20] respect our ways. She doesna deserve to be here. Many believe the Outside men wouldna be here if it weren't for her, Magnar. She's one of them."

Cinnie's voice was low now. Too low for Rose to understand, but she crouched intently on the ground, yearning to hear even a scrap of what Cinnie was saying.

CRASH! What must have been a piece of furniture getting slammed to the ground made Rose jump.

“You dare talk about my cousin in this way?! You dare talk about one of the heirs to the throne of Owen Cheryic himself?" Magnar's voice had taken Eason's dangerously soft tone. "Someday, she may be your Chief."

"You are first in line. You can easily rid the clan of her." Cinnie replied defiantly.

"Get away from here."

Cinnie snorted. "And she's put you under her spell, has she? She's a witch too?"

"Get out."

Caiden snuck up behind Rose, his hands casually in the folds of his kilt.

"Hey Rose, Whatcha-" Rose put her hand to Caiden's lips and shushed him, gesturing toward the open window.

"Oh come on, Magnar. What is it with you and her? She's not even your real sister. She's only your cousin." Cinnie's

[19] Will not

[20] Does not

voice had become a few octaves higher in her failing attempt to placate Magnar.

Caiden's eyes widened. "Is she talking about-?" He asked, pointing at Rose.

She nodded.

"That little-"

Rose shushed him again.

"No, Cinnie. What would you understand? You're a mere child who knows little about love, even the love between a brother and sister. I am responsible for them. Both of them. That is my job as Chief and as a brother." Magnar's voice had become quieter now.

At this point, two Outside guards were walking toward the house, one with a shiny white bald head, the other dark and smiley, both eyeing Rose and Caiden suspiciously for their obvious eavesdropping. "It's my house," Rose mouthed. They nodded and crouched down beside her to listen also.

"Oh Magnar, you're not even Chief yet, and for the last time, she's not even your sister. She's your cousin."

"Only by blood. Do cousins sleep under your roof every night? Were you there to see your cousin shoot her first deer? And do you forget that my uncle has been a father to me for as long as I can remember? She is my sister, and you should mind your place Cinnie Reid. She is a princess of this land. In the olden days, a prince would have had a woman hanged for speaking so harshly about the princess."

"In the olden days, the princess would no act as if she was a prince."

"And look at us now. Get out."

The Outside guards at this point, realized also that the two were talking about Rose. Baldy, as Rose called him in her head, was now tsking and listening intently. Smiley nudged Rose. “Not exactly the most accepting bunch, are they?” he whispered.

Rose shrugged. She was beginning to grow used to the Outsiders integrating with the clan. Some were quite friendly.

"Aye, and maybe when I get home,” Cinnie continued, “I'll convince my father to dress in a gown and sew by the fireside."

Rose felt her face grow hot.

"Get out of my house and never, ever, come back," Magnar said.

Rose could hear Cinnie's footsteps getting closer. Caiden moved to the far wall so its shadow would help keep him unseen. Rose did not try to hide. The wooden door creaked open and she pounced. Cinnie let out a squeal of shock.

Rose grabbed the girl by the hair and just started punching. She could see in her peripheral vision Magnar's blond head running toward her. She already felt Caiden grabbing her from behind, attempting to pry her off of Cinnie. All of this happened while Cinnie lay sprawled out beneath her, wailing like a newborn. The Outside guards jumped and sprinted toward the fight, but did not get there before Rose was yanked off by Magnar.

Nose bloodied and face red, Cinnie scrambled from the ground. "You little witch! How dare you?!" Cinnie snarled, and she began to march away, but then thought again and turned to tackle Rose to the ground. Rose began thrashing and kicking for Cinnie to get off, when suddenly Cinnie stopped. Her eyes widened and a line of blood dripped down the corner of her mouth. She fell onto Rose. Rose scrambled out from under her, getting tangled in the silky dress when she saw it: a machete had been plunged into Cinnie's backside.

Baldy yanked it out of her back, giving Rose a courteous nod. Smiley's eyes widened as he backed slowly away from the scene.

Magnar grabbed Cinnie as she coughed up blood. She choked and sputtered, her blood splashing onto Magnar's yellow stubble. People from the square were beginning to run over and shake their heads, whispering among each other. Two children ran for the doctor.

Cinnie sputtered once again in Magnar's shaking arms, but then her bloodshot eyes looked toward the mountain and she grew still.

Caiden began shaking and fell to the ground.

Rose looked to the Outsiders, screaming, "What have you done?!"

Smiley said nothing, but spun around to vomit by the house. Baldy shrugged. When Rose growled and nearly lunged at him, he grabbed her and whispered into her ear.

"You are lucky," he hissed. "Perhaps *you* are next."

Rose shuddered and bolted to find Eason.

When the school year ended, Eason called all three of the children to his office. The children all whispered brief prayers to themselves as they followed behind him, hoping that they hadn't flunked any of their classes.

"Children, I am going to a meeting with the five clans." Eason said, standing with his hands pressed against his desk. An I-mean-business look stood out on his face, but Magnar did not heed its danger.

"You dare speak with the Craotics, our enemy clan, on a day that's not a peace day? Uncle! Do you not realize the danger this could put you, all of us in?" Magnar asked, ears reddening.

"There are greater dangers than the Craotics now, lad. We must all come together to defeat them." Eason replied. "We cannot do it alone."

"Defeat who?" Caiden asked. He had remained silently in a chair the whole time, pleased that the conversation had not been about his grades.

Eason shook his head. "Too many ears linger around here. But the Americans are dangerous. Be careful. Someday, I will give you the full story." Eason dismissed them from his room.

In the living room, Caiden plopped on the couch, grabbing a whittling knife and a block of wood. Magnar just rubbed his temples as he lay on the carpet, defeated. "I can't believe he's doing this. Why is he doing this? Why won't he tell us or even me? He could at least tell me! No offense." Magnar babbled.

"None taken." The Twins simultaneously answered from the couch.

"Listen Magnar," Caiden began, chipping away at the wood with his knife, "if you're really concerned about Uncle, follow him."

Magnar rolled his eyes and sat up from the ground.

Caiden smirked.

"Oh come on, Magnar. You want information? Don't rely on other people for it. Find out for yourself." Caiden said, his puppy-dog eyes were beginning to light up, the way they did when an idea was coming to his head.

"It's too risky. I mean, we don't even know where Uncle is going." Magnar protested, but he knew that arguing wouldn't get him anywhere in this conversation. When Caiden set his mind on something, there was no stopping him. Magnar realized this with a sinking heart as Caiden's smile grew wider. Nope. He'd bolt the door and all the windows if he had to. These twins were *not* leaving the house on his watch.

Rose leaned forward in her position, whispering to the boys in a low voice.

"For a future Chief, you're not very observant, are you?" She said, "You didn't see the map on Uncle's desk?"

The boys shook their heads.

Rose sighed.

"He's going to Belfast to meet," Rose said a-matter-of-factly. "It's neutral territory."

Magnar grunted.

"That's in Ireland! We can't go all the way over there!" Magnar shook his head, suddenly looking much older than his mere sixteen years.

"Aye, but it's also a two week journey by horse, not even." Caiden gave Magnar his pleading puppy dog eyes.

"Oh, just two weeks in which we have to walk, worry about food, worry about the expense, and not to mention the fact that we have to cross the sea."

"We're royalty, Magnar. We can say we've come to hear complaints; they'll give us free food. Rose has already proved that she can hunt, and what do we have to pack? A cloak, a few snacks, maybe a few beads for the ferry? What else could we possibly need?"

"My bow if we want to hunt…" Rose added.

"Okay, that's true. But we'll be fine. We've gone camping many times before."

Rose crossed her arms. She tried to contain the excitement which made her arms shake and shiver: *We may be going on an adventure in a short time*, she thought.

"I dunno, Caiden. I'll think about it," Magnar complied.

Caiden seemed satisfied by this and went outside for knife practice.

Eason left around dinnertime after force feeding Caiden his dreaded haggis recipe. Rose concluded that she would go to bed and see what the boys would decide in the morning.

There wasn't much that she despised more than that one hour between going to bed and falling asleep. It was that daunting period when she was left alone with her thoughts that she envied the boys for being able to share a room. Sometimes, she dwelled on her mother. She wondered if she'd thought of her before she died. If she died quickly in that car or if it took a while. She wondered if the man who hit her and ran ever saw justice for his crime elsewhere...if he ever thought about her. She knew this: she was grateful she would never have to ride in a car again. After an hour of contemplating, Rose finally was able to shut her eyes in peace.

***

"Wake up, Rose!"

She jerked up, shouting, "what in the name-?!" Bam! Her head slammed into Caiden's, who went flying off the bed and onto the ground.

"Oh jobbyyyyy!" Caiden moaned, holding his hand to his head.

Magnar ran inside Rose's room, knocking on the door as he did, as if it made a difference.

"What happened?" He asked hurriedly, assessing the situation. He must have decided nothing serious had happened, for he turned to Rose, ignoring Caiden. "We're leavin' in twenty minutes."

Rose nodded.

"Sorry, Caiden." She said. She ran to pack food, her sword, her bow, arrows, and a blanket.

Magnar opened Valar's cage and released it outside. "*Lean mise*" he ordered, and the bird flew out of sight.

***

Magnar wasn't sure if he should ask Farmer McHenry for horses or just borrow them. He figured he'd ask, and if the farmer said no, he'd borrow them from the next farmer. Though the hour was late, Magnar got the nerve to approach the farmer's doorstep and make up a story.

The farmer sleepily opened the door in his gown and cap.

"Young Òganach, what brings ya here in this late hour?" The farmer asked, doing his best to be polite through tired, half-shut eyes.

Magnar bowed his head.

"Forgive me, sir, for waking you at this late hour. Errr by order of my uncle we are to meet him in Aviemore for an urgent meeting with Outsiders. Would you be of such good grace as to allow us to borrow three of your horses for the trip? We will be back in no more than a month's time, and I assure you, the horses shall be in the very condition they were in when we left with them."

Rose winked whimsically at her twin and Magnar, who turned a blind eye to it.

The man nodded his head.

"Saddles are out back. Take whichever ones ya please. Goodnight Óganach." And the door shut in Magnar's face.

They took a torch from the farmer's front porch and lit it. It took them a few minutes to find the saddles in the dark. Magnar put two fingers to his teeth and whistled the way he had seen Farmer McHenry do to call the horses. Five came galloping up the hill. Two of these five included Righ and Anam. Rose and Magnar took these. Caiden chose a dark brown one that appeared black in the dim lighting of his torch.

They had one flaw in their plan: the spare map they had found in Eason's drawer was nearly impossible to read in the dark and they scarcely had the light of the moon. But the biggest flaw ended up being Magnar allowing Caiden to be in charge of navigation.

So, they started blindly into the forest path, hoping they were heading in the right direction.

They galloped down the path for a few hours, until they decided to give the horses a break and set up camp until daylight. Magnar took a few minutes to get a fire going using an old Cheryic tradition involving bark and dried leaves. When the fire was ready, Caiden held the map to it.

"Oops." Caiden said.

Rose and Magnar groaned. "What?"

"Well, we should be following the river around the mountain, west then north." Caiden explained. "We just went south, so at least we didn't go the complete opposite direction."

"You're joking!" Magnar whined.

Caiden smiled apologetically.

"I wish I was," he replied.

"Alright, from now on, I navigate. Let's move. We have to get there before the meeting begins."

With that, Magnar took the maps and they headed west early. After five hours of riding upstream and crossing a few bridges, they finally made it to a man-made dirt road. At this time, the sun finally started rising and beams of light shed through the trees and guided the siblings.

When they reached the place where two ancient roads of a strange cracked material intersected, they allowed their horses a rest and they unpacked some food. Rose had packed four rolls, a container of nuts, two containers of water, and three apples. She took an apple and bit into it. Both Caiden and Magnar marveled at the road they sat on. It had crumbled into various cracked black stones with weeds growing in between. They'd never seen any road in such terrible, yet strange condition. It would be impossible to ride the horses on it, for they would surely get pebbles and whatnot stuck in their hooves.

Rose began talking nonchalantly about the condition of Evander's mother and how Fergus talked out of his arse all the time at school. When she finally realized the boys weren't listening but were staring at the road, a realization popped into her head.

"You've never seen an Outside road before?" She asked through a mouth full of apple. Her green eyes lit up.

Magnar swallowed nervously.

"Of course I've seen a road. This is just different. Why did it need to be so hard? What's the purpose if it hurts a horse's feet?" Magnar asked.

Caiden continued to stuff his face with a roll, his eyes glued to the gleams of light which reflected off of the pavement. They looked like stars on a blank, black canvas.

"Cars," Rose replied. "The Outside uses them to get around. They never use horses. God, it seems like ages ago I was in one of those. I suppose I have spent almost half my life here, though."

She laid down with her hands beneath her head, her eyes far off in a daydream. Magnar did not want to disturb her as she reflected on her past, but they needed to leave. He stood up and reached out his hand out to her.

"Come on," he urged.

She smiled, took it, and he hoisted her up.

They continued on the road for hours and hours, walking and galloping in half-hour intervals. Sometimes, Valar would come into sight, soaring above them majestically. Once the bird even dropped a dead rat on them, which the Twins refused to eat. Most of the time, however, the bird was out of the sight, and the children were on their own.

They walked on the Outside road, through the woods, and over bridges. After a week, they still hadn't ridden through any villages.

When they set up camp, Caiden looked over the nibbles of food they had left. (They were not exactly sufficient packers.)

"I'm hungry," Caiden grumbled.

"Good observation, Caiden." Magnar replied sarcastically, trying his best to make a spark for a fire.

Rose giggled. The girl was too excited to be on an adventure to have her spirits dampened by a grumbling stomach.

"Come on, Magnar, at least let us hunt. Rose can go with me." Caiden pleaded, Rose stood up.

"Aye, I'll go." She agreed, grabbing her bow from her quiver.

"It's different here. You could get lost or hurt. We don't know this place like we do back home." Magnar argued. "We need to stay with the horses."

"But we'll starve." Caiden whined. "Please? We won't go far."

"It's dark!"

"No! That moon is almost as light as the sun!"

Magnar sighed, rolling his eyes. What could he do? Thanks to his irresponsible packing, they might starve if someone didn't hunt.

"You build the fire; we'll come back with a mighty beast." Rose insisted, already walking toward the woods, "Or a rabbit or something…"

Magnar sighed again and nodded.

"Fine," he said, "but don't disturb the forest."

***

Caiden's stomach felt as if knives were stabbing him from the inside.

Ok. Maybe that was a bit of an exaggeration, but he still felt hungry. The people had a saying...what was it? "If ye bairn's[21] wee famished, best feed him before he kills the cow himself." Basically, you better feed your teenagers before they become cranky and take all the food for themselves. (The children of the Cheryic Clan were typically well fed year-round.)

Caiden was relieved that Rose had volunteered to go with him. He was not the best at shooting in general. Sure, he was skilled with a knife or dagger, but that had to be pretty close range. Rose hit the bullseye every time with her bow. In hunting, it was all a matter of finding the animal. After that, it didn't stand a chance against Rose.

They continued wandering through the forest until Rose stopped abruptly.

"What is it?" Caiden asked.

She put a finger to her lips, shushing him.

"I heard something. A rustle or branch or something." She explained.

---

[21] Child

"Maybe it's the wind." Caiden replied.

His comment was repaid with a classic you're an idiot look from Rose. The air all week had been eerily still, so quiet you could hear a pin drop. Perhaps not the best cover for the children, but they could've heard anyone approaching from a mile away. Perfect for travelling.

The Twins stood there for another two minutes, listening intently for some animal they could shoot. Caiden was about to suggest continuing on when CRACK! Another stick broke, not far from where we were standing. A low drawling snarl came from the position where the stick had broken, not ten feet from the Twins.

They whirled around.

A deer could be seen grazing in a small opening of the forest. Rose inserted an arrow to her bow, pulling back for aim.

"Rose." Caiden whispered.

She shushed him.

"Rose."

She released the arrow and watched as it landed deep in the deer's eye.

No later than when the deer hit the floor, a wolf leaped above the deers' corpse and lunged at Rose. She dove backward, sword in hand as the wolf sprung right on top of the blade. It snarled and bit at the air, though impaled.

Three other pairs of eyes were looming in the dark, circling them. The twins stood back to back. Rose raised her sword toward two of the wolves, which drooled through snarling teeth. They were bone-thin, their rib cages protruding through thinned fur.

"You see that sword in your sheath Caiden?" Rose whispered, "It's actually pretty useful when you're getting attacked."

"Yeah, yeah." He mumbled, and slowly removed his sword from his sheathe, waving it around as the wolves' eyes followed it back and forth hypnotically. He giggled to himself, despite his predicament.

"I'm failing to find the humor in the situation," Rose said from behind him.

Caiden laughed a little more, and waved his sword again, this time with sound effects. He began by swooshing. *SSSSHHHHHWAAAAASHSHOOOOOSH.* Getting bored with this, he barked and growled. He could feel Rose tensing up behind him.

"Wow, you really are going to die a child," she said.

That's it. Caiden thought. *I'm done playing games. They were the prey, not him.*

He lunged after the front wolf with his sword in hand.

I'll name him claws, he thought. Claws pounced on him, but Caiden was ready. He deflected his pounce with a slash of his sword. The blow wounded the wolf in its chest. Claws backed up, trying to buy time to recover. Caiden took that moment to stab Claws all the way through. The wolf made no sound; it fell in silence.

Caiden turned around to find Rose fighting the last wolf. She had already killed her first culprit, who was bleeding out on the ground. Now she was in an eye to eye war with the second. Caiden did not intrude. He only looked to see if his help was necessary. It wasn't. Her efforts were truly paying off. Beast (that's what Caiden had named the other one) was missing a leg, yet still fighting valiantly.

Eventually, Beast was slain, beheaded by the great warrior, Rose. They bid him farewell and took his two friends back to camp to roast over the fire. (There was nothing quite so delicious as eating a wolf that tried to kill you for dinner.)

Caiden barely acknowledged how slowly Rose was walking behind him. He assumed it was only because the wolf she carried was heavier. He didn't even notice her limp.

***

Caiden and Rose returned with a wolf on each of their backs. Now, Magnar had expected them to catch either nothing, a rabbit, or if they were lucky, a deer. But wolves were not on his list of expectations. So he sat holding his hands to the warmth of the fire, unable to verbalize the millions of questions shooting through his brain. Eventually, he took a professional approach and cleared his throat, readying himself for the interrogation.

"How did you get those?" Magnar asked, maintaining his calm the best he could as he poked the fire.

Caiden and Rose gave each other a weary look and shrugged.

"We just saw them in the distance," Caiden began, hastily skinning the thing on his lap. "They were chomping at this deer, so we decided wolves for supper was better than nothing."

Rose nodded, somewhat pained in her expression, "Yeah, I've never had a wolf before, so this'll be interesting, to say the least."

Magnar had known his brother for nearly fifteen years now. It had taken him two to master Caiden's tells when he was lying. Thirteen years later, Caiden still lived under the illusion that he could pull the wool over his brother's eyes.

On the other hand, Rose had skills when it came to lying. She could easily add a quick convincing detail between Caiden's babbling rants, which almost made Magnar doubt himself. She did have one fatal tell: When she appeared to be telling the truth, she was hiding something. If she looked to be a liar, she was telling the truth.

At this moment, Rose could have had a halo over her head, the way she was innocently batting her lashes. This left Caiden to hold the Devil's Blivet.

"What happened?" Magnar asked again patiently, kicking himself for allowing the Twins to go out on their own, but also wondering how they could manage to screw up one simple hunt.

"We just saw these wolves in the woods. Are wolves edible?" Caiden asked, widening his brown eyes at Magnar, knowing full well that he looked like a harmless puppy-dog as he did so.

Rose rolled her eyes. "Of course they're edible, Caiden, they're meat."

Magnar pursed his lips. "That's all very well, Caiden, but did you know that wolves taste absolutely terrible? Why would you kill an animal you don't know is edible?!"

None of the Twins spoke, but both squirmed uncomfortably.

"I'm just famished." Caiden replied, cutting the meaty bits out and flinging them into the pot over the fire. They all groaned as a putrid aroma filled the air. There wasn't much meat on either of the wolves; they must have had a difficult week, which is why they turned on the Twins in the first place.

"Did we bring a medicine bag?" Rose interrupted.

Caiden turned toward her, drawing his brows together.

"Don't change the subject." Magnar ordered, believing she was playing on his gullibility. His wall of suspicion was impenetrable.

Caiden turned back toward him, now raising his brows.

"No, seriously, did we bring a medicine bag? She needs it." Caiden asked him.

Magnar thought about it. *Did I pack a medicine bag? Yes, I remember, I packed a few bandages, alcohol, and a needle and thread. Wait, stop...they're still distracting you.*

"If you tell me what happened, I'll give you whatever you need," Magnar bargained.

Rose scowled, unwilling to give in to his mind games.

"We were attacked by three wolves," Caiden informed him. "We beat them, though. Obviously. We're alive. I almost died, but Rose saved me. Thanks for that, by the way."

Rose shrugged like it was no big deal.

Magnar just sat stunned for a second. Then he remembered the medicine bag.

"What do you need?" he asked Rose.

Caiden turned to her questioningly.

"Yeah, what do you need?" Caiden asked, and Magnar realized that Caiden had been as uneducated as himself on Rose's wound.

"I'm fine, really. One of the wolves I was fighting bit me, and it had a pretty good grip."

"Jobby! It bit you? Where?" Caiden asked, receiving a scowl of disapproval from Magnar at the word "Jobby."

"Just my leg." She gestured toward her blood-soaked leg, which they realized she had been covering with her arms as she sat.

Panic swelled through Magnar's veins and his head jerked toward Caiden.

"Was it rabid?" Magnar asked.

Caiden shook his head.

"I don't think so, Magnar. They weren't foaming at the mouth or anything. Plus, all four of them attacked us, not one. I think they were just starving."

Magnar let out a sigh of relief. He jumped again, remembering Rose's leg. He pulled out a medicine bag from one of the horse's saddlebags. Out came bandages, alcohol and a cloth. Magnar lifted Rose's skirt slightly, revealing a complete bloody mess. He could almost see the bone beneath her shin.

"Next time you are bleeding to death, can you let us know?" Magnar asked, scowling at the messy wound.

"I did let you know," Rose reasoned.

"Not soon enough," Magnar spat. He poured the alcohol on the cloth and dabbed it on Rose's leg. She tensed a bit and said nothing. Magnar couldn't help but laugh out loud.

"What?" She asked, annoyed with his good humor.

"Whenever Uncle dabs alcohol on Caiden's cuts, he goes: 'AAAAH. Jobbyyyy, you're killing meee!'" Magnar laughed, using his best whiny Caiden impression. "Most times with even more profanities."

Caiden smacked the back of Magnar's head.

"That was a long time ago!" He objected.

"Aye Caiden, a month is a very long time span for a youth such as yourself," Magnar laughed.

Under his cloth, Rose's leg shook.

"You ok?" Magnar asked her.

Her smile was clear as day, even revealing her large pearly teeth.

"Aye, sorry, I was just laughing," she remarked.

Caiden grunted.

"Cook the wolves, Caiden," Magnar ordered. "We might as well get something out of this experience, even if it will taste like rotten meat."

Caiden trudged back to the pot over the fire. It was hard, chewy, and slightly burnt due to Caiden's skills, but they ate until they were satisfied. When they were finished, they took out their blankets and wrapped themselves, shielding their bodies from the chill in the early spring air.

They rode swiftly for days after that, Rose grimacing the whole way, but never complaining. Magnar watched her pale face carefully and constantly insisted that they took breaks so he could search the wound for any sign of infection. When they reached the river, they mounted a ship to Ireland, and the journey over sea only took a day. It was a relief for Rose not to have to ride a horse. She could lay on the floor of the lower deck, finally resting her wound.

They arrived at Belfast right on time. In fact, within an hour of their arrival, the meeting between the five clans would begin. In a valley, there was a campsite filled with the representatives, scribes, guards and other servants of the Chiefs. The children were relieved to see the bustle, for they could cloak their faces and move easily through the crowds. They walked throughout the camp, keeping two eyes out for Eason. They were afraid to even think about what Eason would do if he caught them.

Without warning, a horn sounded and a man in colorful clothing read from a long parchment.

"The host of this event, Chief Akir Triact of the Triact Clan, has called the meeting to the great tent at this moment. All gather now."

The Twins turned to Magnar. He could barely recognize them by their chins. It was hopeless trying to distinguish their lips as well, for they were exactly alike, Magnar realized.

"Where to?" Caiden asked in a hushed voice.

Magnar looked around. One tent stood taller than the others by several meters, and all of the men at the camp were swarming toward it.

"I have a feeling it's that one," he said. The Twins pulled their hoods down even more, paranoid of recognition, and started toward the tent.

They walked inside the tent and sat on the ground with the other common men. Three large thrones sat on a platform in the middle of the room. One of which, Eason sat in, hastily sifting through documents. He looked worn from his travel, dark circles forming beneath his green eyes. Another gray streak appeared to have grown in his dark locks. But he also looked regal, sitting tall with broad shoulders and thick boots to carry him. To the children's horror, his throne was practically facing them. They lowered their heads and began praying.

In another throne, sat a white-haired chief with an impressive braided beard. He looked about seventy, ready to keel over. Everything about him looked thin, grayed, and sickly—the Craotic Chief.

In the third throne, a man with slight stubble and black curly hair sat. Out of all the men in the room, this man scared Magnar the most. He was not a man; he was a boy. He looked barely four years Magnar's senior, yet he sat in the position of a Chief. How did he become Chief so young? Magnar shuddered when he realized that something must have happened to his father. What would he do when Eason passed on to the spirits? Would he live to see that day? Magnar prayed that he would not, but then, who would look after Caiden and Rose if Eason and Magnar had both passed on? Perhaps one day, they would learn to be careful and not as reckless as in their current nature. Perhaps.

The colorful announcer stood in the center of the tent and opened his faded scroll.

"Wheesht! Wheesht!" The announcer cleared his throat as ambassadors from the clans and men in tight black suits and machetes gathered to the spaces surrounding the circular formation of thrones. Tight black suits. Magnar realized the Outsiders were here. This was not a meeting about them; it was one with them. "We gather here today because on the day October 1st, the guests of our clans, The United States, have violated our peaceful ways by stabbing an unarmed girl in the back with a machete."

Peaceful ways. Magnar had to restrain himself from snorting, *Go to any tavern or schoolyard. You may want to use a different word.* It was at this moment that Magnar noticed an old man...tall for his years, with eyes that resembled a cat's. They were so bright, Magnar swore that if the tent were pitch black, they would still be seen. His hair could have been a mountain of snow piled thickly on top of the man's head. He was red in the face, a sagging face, unmoving and unreadable, and he gazed around the room. He wore a tight black suit as well.

Magnar's gaze focused on the middle-aged woman behind him though, with curly dark hair and wide lips, nodding as she quickly jotted notes down. He was startled as she caught his gaze. At first, she smiled as if it were her birthday, then returned to her jotting. But suddenly, as if realizing something, she looked back at Magnar, her eyes sick with an expression he had never seen before. Was it fear? Looking back at the Outside man, she returned to her notes. All in a split second.

Magnar shook his head.

"We shouldn't have come here."

Caiden looked in the direction of the woman also, and his eyes widened. "Maw!"

Magnar grimaced. "No Caiden, come on; let's go."

"Wait!" Rose whispered.

"The United States of America apologizes on behalf of this guard, who was put in Scotland to protect the people of the clans." The Outside man began, his voice was low, slow and melodic. "We would like to ensure the great union of the clans that this man has been removed and sent back to the states where he will be put on trial and sentenced to due punishment."

Murmurs chorused through the people surrounding the thrones—some of wariness, others of approval. Patiently, the Outside man waited for the murmurs to cease.

"To seek forgiveness, we will provide you with all resources Scotland requires. Food, medicine, or any other supplies Scotland will be in need of."

"We need nothing," boomed a voice from the opposite side of the room.

Eason had risen from his seat and was squeezing the hilt of his sword nervously.

"The Cheryic Clan, while it does not speak for all, wants the United States to leave our clan once and for all," Eason boomed.

The Outside man stepped back for a second, assessing Eason carefully.

"My son," he said. "We have wronged you. But with other nations seeking your land, this is no time-"

"It is not other nations seeking our land. It is you," Eason spat.

The Outside man nodded slowly and rubbed his lower chin.

"Very well," he said. "we will pull our men out of Cheryic land."

The room erupted with murmurs, shouts, and cries of approval and disapproval alike. Eason looked as if he had just run into a wall. His lips had parted, and his eyes did something of a somersault in shock.

"Wheesht!" The announcer yelled, making a downward gesture with his left hand.

"We will pull our men out of Cheryic land." The Outside man said again, "and any clan that wants out of this agreement. I am willing to let the Chiefs decide. It is your land, after all."

The room had taken on a life of its own, with men whispering amongst each other like little birds.

Eason nodded slowly, his eyes wandering from Chief to Chief.

"I would advise you all," he began, "to follow my lead, for the clans should stand united in such matters. *I* will not be responsible for the ultimate demise of the Great Clans of

Scotland. So I will not allow American troops to touch Cheryic soil again."

The Triact Chief rose to his feet suddenly, pausing for a moment as he took in the crowds and then looked to Eason. He looked to the Outside man, fear masking his dark young eyes. He froze for such a period that the room began shifting uncomfortably.

The Triact Chief nodded at the Outside man.

The Outside man nodded back.

"I demand that the American troops leave my land as well," the Triact Chief added. "All of them have until tomorrow morning to evacuate."

The Fisher Chief rose as well, if a bit slower and shakier. "The damned troops aren't on my land at the moment, but ye can bet their bloody arses that if I find one wanderin' about my land, he'll have an axe plunged into his back."

This was rewarded by a serious of ungentlemanlike roars from what must have been the Fisher people's ambassadors.

Next came the Farmer Chief, but he stood up more hesitantly, looking back and forth from the Outside man to Eason.

"In truth," he began, "I dinna ken what to do here. My people have suffered greatly from attacks in the south. And they have stopped since the Americans have protected us."

He glanced nervously at the Outside man, who watched him without a single blink.

"But I ken," he said, "it is the Americans who have facilitated these attacks, and to let them in our walls would be idiotic indeed. I say the troops must leave all land of Clan Duchannon."

All eyes turned to the Craotic Chief, who slounched in his throne, fingers tapping his hilt. He raised a brow at the Outside man and slowly leaned on his sword to push him up to his feet.

"I do not have the lands, the resources, and the Outside knowledge to support my people as Chief Rankin does," The Craotic Chief said. "I have the opportunity now to do what I scarcely could before, to be the Chief who protects his people from the dangers of the world. If Chief Rankin believes that I will turn down this opportunity, he is gravely mistaken. I put the safety of my people before the pride of a young lad who ran away from home."

He glanced toward Eason at the last sentence, and the room stiffened. Every eye in the room was glued to Eason, anticipating his next move. Eason's face turned a shade of crimson so dark, Rose worried he had stopped breathing. Through gritted teeth, he could only squeeze out the words, "You will regret this decision," and he stormed out of the tent, followed by an uproar of murmurs and laughter.

As Eason stormed out of the room, the children yanked their hoods further over their faces, praying the shadows would hide them.

They did not.

Immediately after Eason fled the tent, they heard him call back, "Children, we're going home!" And they hung their heads and trudged out the door.

"Eason!" The children heard as they were leaving, and both they and Eason whirled around. The Farmer Chief was following close behind them and raised his hands to Eason as a sign of respect.

"I want to apologize."

Eason raised his brows. "Why? You have done nothing wrong."

The Farmer Chief lowered his eyes, an action not commonly seen among the royalty of the clans. "Not yet."

Eason waited patiently.

"I must move my people. I hear there is land here in Ireland, which we will sail to. Ye must understand, I dinna want to leave ya exposed, but you have the protection of the mountains and the forest. We have no such thing but open plains. If what ye say is true and the Outsiders want Scotland, then my people are too weak to fight."

Eason stood very still for a minute, allowing the information to sink in. He opened his lips, as if to protest but then sighed.

"You are right," he said. "I have no right to ask your people to be our shield from the storm."

The Farmer Chief took Eason's clenched fist to his heart, thanking him and returned to the tent. Before he entered, however, he whirled back around.

"I am certain ye ken this," the Farmer Chief said, "but I most warn ya anyway to get it off my conscience. I'm afeart that even if my people werena leaving, ye'd still have the Craotics to the south. They're right below ya…as ye ken, and with the Outsiders…well they're up to something. That man's been after yer land for years."

Eason nodded. "Thank you. I am glad I am not the only one suspicious of the Craotic Chief's motives."

The Farmer Chief nodded once and disappeared inside the tent.

Eason said nothing for what felt like years to the children. They remained frozen, hoping the encounter with the Farmer

Chief had made him forget about their existence. But after a moment, Eason grunted and said, "Let's go."

"Wait," Caiden grimaced.

Eason glared back at the boy, his eyes narrowed.

"Might I take a leak first…?" Caiden added with a boyish grin.

Eason rolled his eyes and stomped toward his horse.

"Hurry," he said without looking back.

Caiden ran into the trees. He went deeper than usual, searching for the perfect bush to dig a hole behind. (He may have lied to his uncle about only needing to take a leak.) When he found it, the camp was no longer in his sight range. He was beginning to dig when he noticed something under the bush...it was white and black...his vision focused...an eye. Caiden took a step back and realized that surrounding the eye was an entire mangled body. When his eyes focused even more, he realized he recognized the stubbly cleft chin, the dirty blond hair, the narrow eyes, the thick stone neck.

Burgard McCaig was dead beneath the bush that Caiden was about to do his business in.

Lilias the bold

The mysterious demise of Burgard McCaig never was resolved. The boy was brought back to his family, mainly his brother Fergus. Fergus stopped bothering Rose after this, and seemed to disappear from school altogether. Perhaps he'd become a drunkard, like his father.

It was two weeks after the children had arrived at home that winter set in. The snow formed a permanent sheet on the ground, and Rose knew she would see no trace of grass again until April, maybe May. This set the Twins into a prolonged seasonal depression, for Eason would never permiss them to venture too far into the snow. School was put on hold during this time of year, fearing for good reason that if any of the farmer's children ventured up in the snow, they would catch cold and die. So The Twins were stuck inside yet again, only allowed to go as far as the square. This is why when Eason awoke one day, put on his best kilt and cloak, carefully wrapped a fresh package of salmon, turned to the children, and said "We're going to the O'Connors," the Twins hesitated, thinking it to be a trick of some sort.

Magnar immediately stood, threw on a black wool cloak and said, "So it's time then?"

Eason nodded grimly.

"Time for what?" the Twins asked together.

Eason did not reply but squeezed his foot into a thick black boot.

"Evander's maw," Magnar said to him. "She is dying."

"How is she *dying*?" Caiden asked. They were halfway down the hill, nearly the only people on the road in this dark hour. He clutched his cloak near to him.

"Perhaps Rose will know," Eason replied, his face carefully concealing all emotions. "Have you heard of cancer, Rose?"

"A long time ago. Aye."

"Here, we call it Broden's Illness. It's how Broden Cheryic, the second Cheryic Chief passed on. We don't know how to treat it. From my understanding, the Outside does not either."

"No." Rose said, blinking bits of snow off her eyelids, "but I thought-"

She hesitated.

"Yes?" Eason asked.

"Well, this will sound ridiculous. But isn't the reason that Outsiders never came back here because of...well Broden's disease- or illness? I always thought...I guess that Highlanders were immune."

Eason shrugged. "Perhaps some are. The people believe that it is the spirits who protect them from such diseases until it is their time. Others believe that the cause for disease never was here in the way the Outside detected."

"Well what do you believe?" Rose asked.

Eason smiled slightly, "There are some things, Rose, that cannot be explained."

They were outside of the little bakery now. Snow had piled in front of the shop, and Magnar was forced to push it out of the way so the door could be pried open. The four of them stood awkwardly in the very room in which Rose had first met Lilias O'Connor. *She was kneading something,* Rose thought, *just behind that counter.* It had been bustling with heat, Lilias's singing, Evander's thrashing around upstairs, and Andrew O'Connor always out and about. Now it was eerily silent.

"Right," Eason mumbled, "let's get this over with."

The O'Connor bakery was dark, but they let themselves upstairs anyway. Rose had never been upstairs, and she realized quickly that it was one single room with two beds. Evander sat at the larger bedside, holding a candle in one hand and his mother's hand in the other.

"It's damned cold in here," Eason grumbled. "I'll start a fire in a moment. Evander, here's some salmon to cook for dinner. Lilias, how are you feeling?"

There was an awkward silence until Evander managed to say, "She's not talking anymore...I dinna think she can."

"Right," Eason said stiffly. "I'll start a fire then. Children, keep Evander company. Evander, where is your father?"

Evander shook his head. "I dinna ken."

Eason approached the bed for a moment, beholding Lilias's hollowed, frail face. For a moment, he thought she was already dead. But he thought better of checking and started to go off to look for wood.

"Wait." Evander said and he reached for the bedside stand. "She asked me to give you this."

He handed Eason a sealed letter, which Eason anxiously fumbled to open. It was one line. It read: ***Watch over my bairn***.

Eason nodded once and quickly went off to find firewood. Andrew O'Connor did not return to see his wife's death. But Eason was there, although he had sent the children home. He assured Evander that he would not have to witness it alone, and when she passed, he lifted her blanket over her face and allowed Evander a rare hug.

Lilias was burned on the mountain top to join the spirits, as is tradition in the clans. When Andrew did not turn up for that either, Eason took the boy in to live on his couch, at least until he was back on his feet, claiming, "I'm already running a damned orphanage so what's one more?" Eventually, Andrew O'Connor turned up in a nearby tavern and claimed his son again. This father and son relationship lasted a few months, until Andrew kicked him out of the house, claiming, "If ye willna be a baker like yer da, what's the point of ye?" This time, Evander found his own place and continued to train to be a warrior with the Twins.

Three Years Later

let go of the moment

For the next few years, the Twins seemed to forget the information they'd learned about the clan's danger from the Outside. But for Magnar, the Outside haunted his every action. He became distant from his usual friends at home, avoiding their camping trips and hikes. He never left his siblings' sides, constantly trailing behind them wherever they went. The only time he left the Twins' sides was when he and Valar practiced an attack by setting up dummies in the forest.

It wasn't until the summer of the Twins' eighteenth year, just before their final year of school, that life seemed to collapse on itself. On a beautiful spring morning, Magnar, Caiden, Evander, Gwen and Rose all went scavenging for crayfish in a small brook in the woods. The Twins playfully would poke each other with the crayfish, attempting to pinch each other with the little claws. Magnar and Gwen went downstream to look for some more there, claiming that the "six-year-olds" were scaring away the crayfish. After a while,

Caiden, who had taken a liking to Gwen, left "to chase Magnar" with the little pinchers as well.

This left Evander and Rose in the middle of the brook, overturning rocks and flinging the creatures into the buckets, fantasizing about buttered crayfish for dinner. They were motivated to continue searching despite the chilly spring air.

At once, however, Rose felt a cold sensation on her back. She whirled around to Evander's splash. His wavy blond hair was soaked with water. He was one of the few clan members who took the time every day to shave his face neatly. The once scraggly teen was now two heads taller than Rose. His face had tanned from the many days training in the sun.

He was a man now, just like Caiden and Magnar, a new anomaly that Rose wasn't sure she could get used to. The boys were growing up and she wasn't exactly getting any younger herself.

Rose sighed. Much like Caiden, Evander's actions had not matured with his looks. But neither had Rose's. She splashed him right back, soaking his shirt. Evander laughed but did not reciprocate.

He nodded toward the crayfish in his bucket. "You can have mine; if ye want."

Rose drew her brows together.

"Are you sure? There's plenty for all." She lied.

Evander pushed her playfully. "There are about two for each of us and ye ken it. Take them. I'm right scunnered[22] and want to head back. Want to come?" He asked, his brows scrunched, and the corners of his lips tilted up.

"Sure." Rose shrugged. Her bare feet tingled at the feeling of the soft spring grass as they made their way into the fields

---

[22] Bored

and mounted their horses. When they were about a quarter of a kilometer from the gate, Evander stopped suddenly. Rose's horse nearly tripped over its own feet as she tried to halt it as abruptly as he did.

Evander grinned and grabbed her arm, helping her regain her balance. She thanked him as she held herself steady, cursing her clumsiness.

"I talked to your brothers today," he said, blue eyes meeting green. His eyes were so focused, Rose felt herself shifting back and forth uneasily.

"I talk to them every day," she replied, trying to shrug off her discomfort. "I'm pretty sure you do, too."

Evander let out a small nervous chuckle and nudged her arm. This comforted Rose a bit, but she still wrapped a messy lock of hair around her finger awkwardly.

"It's what I talked to them about that concerns you." he replied. "I wanted permission."

Rose probably shouldn't have laughed, but the situation was too strange. "You asked my brothers for permission. Why? To do what?"

He shrugged and smiled, his lips drawing into a thin line. "Caiden has been my friend for my entire life. And Magnar, Magnar is a different story. He is so protective. Of course, it's a good thing he is, he loves ya a lot."

Rose grinned, her eyes flashing to Evander's feet and then back to his face. His eyes had little specks of green throughout them, just like his mother's used to. She could see so much of her gentle smile in his.

"RUN!"

Both turned abruptly to see Magnar and Caiden galloping full speed toward them yelling.

"Where's Gw-?!" Rose began to ask, but Magnar smacked the butt of her horse, jerked it to a sprint so fast that Rose's neck strained and she let out a cry of pain.

"Just run!" Magnar shouted at Rose.

Rose looked behind her to see what must have been a thousand people emerging from the forest, wearing the Craotic red and gray kilt. Shock numbed her as she ran blindly with Magnar and Evander's guidance. (Caiden was being dragged on the other side of Magnar.) The guards were sounding the alarm as they allowed the children to sneak inside the village gate hastily.

BONG! BONG! The bells rang, and panic commenced. Soldiers filed out of their quarters, their weapons at the ready. Magnar, Caiden, Evander and Rose all galloped back home, doing their best to avoid hitting people in the ensuing chaos. The streets had suddenly become crowded as everyone ran home to their loved ones, screaming out names. The children only knew to go where Eason would be waiting for them.

Gwen was dead. Magnar had watched in horror as she had been shot down with an arrow from a distance. She had travelled too far down the river. He couldn't do anything about it. Caiden and he hadn't even had time to watch as her body floated downstream, never to be seen again. Magnar had been forced to drag a shocked Caiden and Rose into the city, with the help of Evander, who somehow had developed a knack for keeping a cool head.

Eason waited for them on the front step, dressed for battle, his longsword in hand.

Caiden immediately snapped out of his trance and his anger took over. He darted up the steps, but Eason grabbed his arm. Caiden struggled, trying to free himself from Eason's grip in a raging frenzy.

"Get off of me!" He shouted, more vehemently than Magnar had ever heard him. "I'm getting my sword!"

Eason held Caiden firmly, but Caiden was a young man now and bore the strength of one. He was nearly a head taller than Eason and looked down upon the graying man, which is why Eason became grateful when Magnar ran to his aid.

"Listen to me, Caiden," Eason ordered. "Listen to me!" He took Caiden by the ear and brought him inside. Evander, Magnar, and a petrified Rose followed them.

Eason threw Caiden on the couch. The boy flailed around, eyes wild. Suddenly, tears poured from them. He quickly covered his eyes with his hands in embarrassment. Magnar ran to comfort his brother; he placed a hand on his shoulder as he lowered himself to the couch next to him. Eason looked from Rose to Magnar to Evander. He saw that Evander was the only one neither petrified nor occupied.

"The Craotics are attacking, yes? This is not unexpected...what happened?" Eason asked the young man.

"They're different, Gliocas...stronger, greater numbers." Evander replied, his voice shaking.

Eason swallowed, his Adam's apple moving steadily beneath his black beard. "Did you bring Gwen home? She went with you, did she not?"

The children looked around at each other, searching for the person with the strength to tell the truth. Caiden's head lifted from his hands.

"They shot at us, as we were running from them," Caiden choked out. "They…they…she's…"

Eason nodded slowly.

"Stay inside. Do not leave this house until I come back with word of what to do."

Evander stood up.

"What about my father?" He asked, face pale.

Eason put his hands on Evander's shoulders.

"I will see to it that he is safe."

Evander nodded.

"Where are you going?" Rose shuddered, waking from her daze.

Eason sheathed his sword and opened the door, holding it with his boot.

"Where I belong, to help protect my home," He replied, eyes sterner than ever. He turned to Magnar. "Take care of them."

Magnar nodded, wishing he had more to say, but he could not think of the words.

Caiden darted up from his seat and grabbed Eason's arm. "Let me fight too."

Eason shook his head.

"You have not completed your training yet. I need my heirs safe and sound. Remember, a clan is not lost, until it is leaderless."

Caiden clenched his jaw.

"I'm not a child anymore. I'm eighteen-years-old now, I became of age two years ago! I can fight for my people," Caiden said, his finger jabbing his own chest.

Eason just shook his head sadly and left.

As soon as Eason's figure had disappeared behind the door, Caiden stomped to his room, like a pouty, grounded teenager. Rose ran to hers in the same fashion. Magnar sat down on the couch and put his head between his hands.

Evander stood awkwardly in the corner near the door and drew his lips into a thin line. "So, the village is being attacked, huh?"

Magnar allowed a small smile.

"Mhm. Now what news about my sister?" he asked, hoping to distract himself from reality.

Evander raised his eyebrows.

"Your sister?" He asked, a small smirk creeping across his lips.

Magnar chuckled. "Aye."

Evander grunted. "Heehaw[23], really, I was just asking her and didna get an answer before, ye ken..." He looked down at the ground in embarrassment. "I canna believe this happened."

"Go comfort her." The words left Magnar's mouth before he'd even thought them through.

Evander looked back at him in surprise.

"It'll be alright," Magnar assured him.

Evander walked slowly and awkwardly toward the girl's room. He knocked on the door. "Rose? You okay?" He asked loudly, glancing back at Magnar.

No reply.

"Rose?" Evander asked. Magnar gestured for Evander to peek inside the room. He did. Then he opened it all the way and walked inside. Magnar stood up, angling his body to get a glimpse of what was happening.

"She's not here!" Evander shouted, jogging back to the living room.

No. Panic arose within Magnar as he realized what was happening. He ran inside Caiden's room and found that both

---

[23] Nothing

he and his weapons were missing. The window was propped open. He ran to Rose's room and found the same.

Magnar cursed himself for being such a fool.

***

Rose had known the whole time what Caiden was actually going to do when he ran into his room. He had never been one to hide in his room from his problems. Rose had known this, and Magnar should have known this, but his head had been so clouded with past events, he didn't have a clue. Rose followed Caiden's example and stormed into her room as well. As soon the door was shut, she grabbed her weapons, and escaped from the window to find Caiden waiting for her outside.

"How did you know I'd follow you?" Rose asked, suspiciously raising an eyebrow.

Caiden shrugged.

"You're cannier than Magnar, more predictable, and pretty reckless," he answered nonchalantly.

Rose smirked.

They ran around the side of the house, and Rose glanced warily through the living room window. Evander's curly dirty blond locks ambled toward Rose's bedroom. Magnar watched from behind, his thin, short frame anxiously shifting his boot.

"Run." Rose ordered Caiden. She knew that as soon as they found the Twins gone, Magnar and Evander would come after them. The Twins darted down past town square, which had now been cleared out as people took shelter in their homes. They ran down the hill and through the remainder of fields, which stood between the gates and the city. They were still uphill enough to see what lay below the city gates, when they saw the Craotics, driven up against the city wall, in numbers which outdid their men a hundred to one.

"Caiden, I don't think we're going to win this one," Rose said under her breath.

Caiden shrugged, "well maybe...maybe if we went out there...well that's an extra two...and that could make a difference, right?"

"Caiden, we need to evacuate the city." Rose replied, realizing only as she said it, it was true.

Caiden hesitated, but soon nodded grimly. "But how...the only way out is the way they're attacking. I'm sure they've surrounded the side entrances too."

The twins' eyes widened as the revelation came to both of them at once. "The Mountain! " They shouted.

"Round up the villagers in the square." Rose ordered, "we must go quickly and quietly."

Though the Twins had found the passage years ago, they kept it secret. They enjoyed having the power to save an entire village in only their hands. So over the years, they had taken trips only to explore, always confirming they were not being followed before they did.

Caiden nodded. "We'll move faster if we split up."

Rose gave one quick salute and turned to go east.

"Wait!" Caiden called, and Rose felt herself being enveloped into a massive, warm hug. She felt the bristles of his stubble on her head as he kissed it. "Be careful. I need you to live for me."

Rose nodded.

"Don't do anything stupid," she joked, then darted east, knowing that she would not be able to stop her tears from flowing if she looked back.

***

The Twins didn't have a chance running from Magnar. As Valar flew overhead, Magnar easily found and followed their tracks. He knew the curve and crest of the Twins' boot prints like the back of his hand. Also, he could guess that the Twins would be drawn to the battle. He and Evander followed their tracks through an empty town square, down the hill, until they reached the southern gate.

Magnar cursed.

The Craotics were gaining more and more ground, taking Cheryic soldiers' lives as they did. It pained Magnar to think of who the motionless dots on the horizon could be, and if they were wounded, or worse, on the ground. He knew he would recognize many of them. He also had never seen the Craotics gain so much ground on their walls. They had attacked in Magnar's lifetime. But they had been brief ambushes, meant to take cattle or food for the winter. This was different. He didn't even know that the Craotics had such great numbers nor did he know what would motivate them to lose so much to obtain Cheryic land? Magnar rigidly sucked a breath in as he realized the Cheryic soldiers would soon retreat. But where to? There was nowhere to go.

They need me, Magnar thought, *but so do my siblings.*

"Do ye think they're down there?" Evander asked worriedly, waking Magnar from his thoughts.

Magnar examined the tracks even further and cursed some more.

"They split up," he said.

Evander wiped his brow.

"Why would they do that?" He asked, his face flushed. Magnar gazed down at the armies of Craotics in the distance. *What would Rose do?*

Then, it hit him. The Craotics were making progress. The Twins would want to get the civilians out of the city before real problems began.

"They're trying to get people somewhere safe...but where?" Magnar stated, his voice barely audible under his breath.

Evander's eyes widened and he examined the track further. "The ben."

"What?"

"Years ago," Evander said, his eyes distant in a memory, "when we were fourteen or fifteen or so, we found this passage to the mountain. It was secret, covered. I think only the three of us know of it. It didna mean much to us then, just a secret hideout. But...I think you can use it to get out the other side."

Magnar rolled his eyes. Just another thing that the Twins had managed to hide from him. He wanted to question Evander more, but there was no time.

"We should split up too," Evander told Magnar.

Magnar nodded slowly.

"You go after my sister; I'll go after Caiden," Magnar told him. He placed two fingers in his mouth and whistled loudly.

Valar swooped down, landing gracefully upon his left shoulder.

"*Lorg Ròs,*" he commanded, and the bird was in the air again. He turned back to Evander. "Follow Valar, she will lead you to Rose."

Evander nodded and broke into a sprint toward the great bird.

Magnar ran off, thinking about how strange it was that his brother's best friend was in love with his cousin.

Caiden was not difficult to find. His feet had always been quite large and rather clunky. His boot prints were the same as Magnar's: both had round crests in the soles which were in the form of eagles, the symbol only given to the princes of the Cheryic Clan. After about ten minutes, Magnar didn't even need to look for Caiden's prints anymore. He could hear him, loud and clear.

"Attention! By order of Chief Eason Rankin, the village must gather around the square!"

Magnar searched through terrified crowds of people rushing toward the square. A tall boy, no, a man, with a large nose, round brown eyes, and stubbles of a brown beard stood not ten meters away from Magnar, shouting at the crowds. Caiden.

Magnar pushed through a herd of hurrying women clutching their children to their chests. As soon as he caught up to Caiden, he did what any caring brother would do: he punched that eejit[24] in the face.

Caiden went down in shock. He shot up a helpless look to his older brother, his eyes wide as he rubbed his cheek with his left hand.

"What was that for?" He asked, removing the hand from his cheek and staring at it as if checking for blood.

Magnar rolled his eyes.

"For scaring me half to death, you eejit! I was worried you went to fight and got killed!" Magnar felt his face grow hot.

---

[24] Idiot

His little brother was not so little anymore. In fact, he was a few inches taller than Magnar was. However, in Magnar's eyes, he would always be the over-excited boy who jumped up and down on the couch when Eason would bring home the fall cider. Magnar's puppy-dog eyed, baby brother with a huge smile always imprinted in his face. His stupid, reckless, little twerp brother who never looked before he leaped.

"Geez…I'm sorry." Caiden mumbled, rolling his eyes in return.

Magnar bared his teeth.

"And to be even more stupid, you split up with Rose!" Magnar yelled, spit escaping through his lips and onto Caiden's face. Magnar didn't care. Caiden deserved it just as much as he had deserved that punch.

Caiden pushed himself hastily from the ground. He turned his giant eyes to Magnar.

"So…are you gonna help, or…" he asked, his foot brushing sheepishly over a few loose pebbles on the ground.

Magnar groaned.

"Ugh, Caiden! I'll help you because I must, but don't think Uncle won't hear about this," he lectured.

Caiden nodded acceptingly. They ran farther west, looking for more clueless villagers, shouting orders of evacuation.

***

A crying child stood in the middle of the pathway of scurrying villagers. His older sister looked about eight and held his hand, eyes wandering aimlessly through the crowds.

Rose hurried toward them.

"Where are your parents?" she asked. The girl's pale hair was knotty and caked with mud; tear stains removed a line of dirt from her face.

"My da's fightin'," she replied, a small pout pursing her lips together.

"What about your maw?" Rose asked her, crouching down to her level.

"Dinna have one," she answered, her eyes drifting down to the dirt road and ears turning crimson.

"Well, that's alright. Neither do I."

Rose took the children by their tiny hands and began walking north with them. The little boy stopped crying, distracted by keeping up with them.

"Well then, miss…what's your name, dearie?" Rose asked, attempting to sound jubilant.

"I'm Eara and this is Wallace," She replied, gesturing to the four-year-old boy with his full fist in his mouth.

"Well, Lady Eara, allow me to escort you and Wallace to a tunnel full of adventures."

"What kinds of adventures?" she asked with a wide smile that reminded Rose of Caiden.

Rose laughed.

"Well, it wouldn't be an adventure if we knew exactly what was going to happen? Would it?" Rose asked.

Eara frowned, pondering over all the possible adventures that could be awaiting them. Wallace began wailing again, his face turning beet red. Rose swooped around Eara, picked Wallace up by his underarms, and rested him upon her shoulders. She continued holding Eara's little hand as the new friends walked north.

Wallace laughed at his new point of view of the world. The boy was surprisingly light upon Rose's broad shoulders. She could feel his tiny hands resting on her head, and every once in awhile, he would squirm on her shoulders, pulling at her long hair as he did.

Suddenly, Rose felt a sharp grip on her back and then a release. She looked up and saw Valar gliding away. Wallace laughed playfully, reaching for the bird.

"ROSE!"

She whirled around. A tall figure with wavy blonde hair and a neatly shaved face was running toward her.

"Evander?" She asked, although she already knew the answer. A sinking feeling overtook her. Magnar and Eason would both kill her and Caiden for running away. But Rose wasn't so sure how Evander would react. He paused in front of her, acknowledging the children.

"Who are they?" He asked quietly.

Rose twisted the corner of her lip.

"This is Eara and this little guy is Wallace," she replied. "Their da is fighting and they don't have anyone to take them north."

She avoided talking about the mother, hoping to avert an awkward situation. Evander fell to one knee and took Eara by the hand.

"Pleased to meet you, Lady Eara." He cast the girl a ridiculously charming smile; she giggled. "Would you also like a ride north?"

She nodded, her ears turning crimson once more.

Evander boosted her up on his shoulders with ease. With that, they began walking to the square all over again.

"Are you mad at me?" Rose asked after they had walked for a few minutes toward the mountain.

Evander glanced at Rose.

"I was never mad at you. Just afeart.[25] So many have died already. I wasna 'bout to let you die too," he said, looking at the path ahead. He smiled. "Magnar, on the other hand…"

Rose nodded as much as she could with a little boy on her shoulders. She hadn't forgotten about the talk that they'd had just a few hours ago. Had it only been a few hours ago? It felt like years ago. Still, she knew the question he had wanted to ask, but she still hadn't thought of the answer.

When they arrived at the square, most of the women and children within the city were waiting, some holding knapsacks with supplies, unsure of what would happen next. Evander took Rose's hand and squeezed it before she mounted a stone and raised her palms towards the people. One by one, the chattering and murmurs ceased and they held their hands out to Rose as a sign of respect.

"People of the Cheryic Clan. You know by now that the Craotics are attacking. Now, this is only a precaution, but we must leave the city to ensure the safety and survival of our people."

Whispers erupted amongst the crowds, most of them the high-pitched voices of women.

"And how exactly are we supposed to do that?" One voice called above the others.

"Aye...well that's the thing...there is a passage."

Another murmur of voices erupted.

"All of the passages are closed off!" someone shouted.

"Not this one." Rose replied, "it's through the mountain. You must follow us."

"We canna leave our homes."

---

[25] Afraid

Rose took a breath. “I’m sorry. I know better than most of you how hard it is to leave your homes. But what matters is that we leave together. And I hold my life in the spirits’ hands when I make this vow before all of you: We will return.”

***

The Craotics refused to retreat. There were too many of them against Eason’s timid army. How were there so many of them? He had sent a messenger to call on other villages for help, but by the time those would be reached, it would be too late. Eason cursed himself for his stupidity. He should have evacuated the villagers immediately when hearing about the Craotics’ attack. But they never dealt with numbers so large before.

Eason watched from a hilltop as the men he knew and had grown to love, were being crushed by weapons superior to their own. He shuddered upon feeling a pat in the back and looked to his side to find an old man, with warm crinkles around his eyes, smiling beneath his armor.

“Do not try to stop me Gliocas,” Farmer McHenry grinned. “For I ken that in the land you come from, old men do not fight for their children. But this is the honorable way for a Cheryic to die.”

Eason stood, frozen, unable to speak to his old friend. The man hobbled to the battle, but before he quite reached the fighting, he looked back at Eason and said, “Do not weep for me, Gliocas.”

In the blink of an eye, Farmer McHenry was lost in the crowds.

A soldier he recognized arrived where he stood: Just on the outskirts of battle. Eason realized that he would have no choice but to reveal the secret of the mountain passage.

The man stood with his palms at his sides, awaiting orders. Eason turned to him patiently, "There is a passage in the mountain. One only the Cheryic Chiefs of the past have known of. The symbol of the great Chiefs of that past is upon a flat stone and above it is a great tree. Find the passage and take it," Eason commanded him.

The man stood there, hesitant and unsure.

"Well, what are you waiting for?"

"The city is evacuating, sir. I thought you told your niece and nephews to alert the city," the soldier replied.

A million thoughts swarmed through Eason's brain. Whose idea had that been? Perhaps it was Magnar's, although Magnar was not one to disobey his uncle. Did they realize how much trouble they would get in for leaving home? How did they know about the passage? Rose and Caiden would have left home without hesitation, but not Magnar. Did Magnar realize that they left, if they had left?

Eason's thoughts were interrupted as he realized the soldier still stood before him, awaiting his orders.

"William, right?" Eason asked, ignoring the voice within him which warned that this was not the time for curiosity. But the soldier must have been in his mid-thirties, still quite young. "You have two bairns waiting for you back home."

The soldier nodded.

"Aye sir. A bonnie eight-year-old girl and a strappin' four-year-old boy. Eara and Wallace."

Eason nodded. He watched the soldiers fall in front of him, their eyes full of terror.

"Go to them. No doubt they are on their way to the mountain by now." The young man hesitated, but thanked Eason, bowing his head and sprinting for the gate. "Wait!"

The man turned, his face showing a complex mix of emotions. Eason could have guessed that he was horrified he would be called to stay after given the hope of being with his family, but willing to do what he could to protect his children. A true Cheryic soldier.

Eason fumbled with something in his pocket. A booklet. "Give this to my children. Tell them they will need it when the time is right."

The man nodded, snatched it away and ran toward the city, not turning back.

Despite their rebellion, Eason couldn't help but feel pride for his children. He knew that he should have been angry with them, but they had surprised him today. Perhaps the city would not burn down on the day of their reign.

He unsheathed his sword and ran where the fighting was heaviest. The nasty line, which first split the Craotics and Cheryics apart, was now blurred as the clans intermixed with each other.

Eason stabbed the first Craotic he could find, thrusting his sword into a yellow-toothed Craotic's chest. In the corner of his eyes, he saw an axe make its way toward his head. He ducked and found his sword automatically cutting the axe-bearers leg off. The next Craotic that he saw managed to block his blow to the head, but before long, the man was spread-eagle on the ground in a bloody mess.

More were coming; Eason didn't know how long he could continue to keep this up. He was beginning to feel old and...tired. He felt stretched in every direction, like a hectic morning of getting his young children out the door to do a day's work. But they were not young anymore, and he scarcely remembered how he had mustered the energy to get them out the door in the first place.

After about an hour, he breathed in and realized that his men would need to begin retreating to the mountain also. But what could they do? They could not outrun all of the Craotic men! They would only end up leading the Craotics to the clan. No. It was best to kill as many as they possibly could here and buy the clan time to run away.

He looked to the man on the ground. He had just slit his throat a few seconds ago and now he wondered, *does he have children of his own waiting?*

"Gliocas!"

Eason took a swift look beside himself to find the captain of the guard fighting next to him. He had a terrible bloody gash in the side of his head and his face and beard were caked with dirt.

"We must retreat!" The captain gasped. "We canna hold them for much longer. All the men who remain here will die."

Eason pursed his lips. His decision, he knew, would decide the fate of his army, his clan, and his children.

"Let all who choose to, leave. But we must protect our clan. We must buy them all the time we can."

At that moment, Eason knew for sure that he would never survive this battle. However, the people would. His children would. That was all that mattered to Eason.

The captain nodded his head and began to shout the orders.

With that, Eason took his sword and with all his might, beheaded a tall Craotic with a thick, sectioned beard. For the next hour, he slashed, beheaded, and stabbed Craotics while simultaneously ducking and dodging their axes, swords, and knives. But before long, they were swarming him, and it took all of his wits to stay alive.

Where did they get these weapons? He found himself wondering. They were beyond the technology of any clans he had seen around him. The swords were razor sharp. The blades were strong enough to withstand any axe. He'd even seen some spears fly through the air at such velocity that he'd taken a half-second to marvel at them.

He glanced at the ground and to his horror, the lifeless body of Farmer McHenry lay sprawled in a broken mass.

"Ah!" The cry escaped him before he even realized it. His vision blurred; his head throbbed and his back felt as if someone had set it on fire.

Burning…burning…why wouldn't it stop burning? He wondered. He heard a cry in the distance. Was it his own? Was it someone else's? He couldn't feel anything now. His vision blurred into a soft, dream-like state.

"Uncle! Uncle!"

Eason whirled around. "Magnar! Get back in the bath!"

The boy stood there, no taller than Eason's knee, his knuckle in his mouth. A brown mushy substance caked his golden locks.

"What...what's that on your head, lad? Mud?"

The boy shook his head.

"Unky! Unky!"

A tiny boy toddled over, his pants fully gone.

"Little laddie, did you go poop all by yourself? Lemme wipe you!"

Eason grabbed the boy under his arms and carried him over to the makeshift kiddie toilet he had made for him. He looked inside. Nothing was there.

"...where did you poop Caiden?"

Caiden said nothing, but pointed to Magnar, standing in the doorway, his head caked in brown crap.

Eason sighed.

"What does this song mean to you, Rose?"

Eason and Rose sat cross-legged in front of the fire, while a man playing a harp sang a melancholy tune in Gaelic. Eason knew he had tutored her enough in Gaelic to recognize the words, which in English, roughly translated to:

"Goodbye, my love, I am sorry I could not see winter's end.

Farewell Father, although you thought you would be the first to go.

Goodnight, daughter, remember forever I love you so."

Rose shrugged.

"You have no idea what this song means?"

Rose shook her head.

"Come now, Rose; you are nine years old, old enough to know what's what. What do you think it's about?"

Rose refused to make eye contact with Eason, although he could see that she was glassy-eyed. At least he knew that she understood the song. He decided to spare her from trying to explain the meaning herself.

"The man is dying. He is saying farewell to his loved ones."

Rose nodded slowly.

Eason smiled and patted her on the head. "Go on and play with your cousins, lass."

"Ready position, Rose. You can't look as if you're falling asleep in the field of battle; you must be on your guard."

Rose raised her sword just above eye level determinedly.

"Bend your knees."

She did so.

"Good. Now strike!"

She hesitated.

Eason sighed.

"It's alright, Rose. I'll block it; I promise."

She shook her head.

Eason scowled.

"Just do it, Rose."

She raised her sword, and with the blunt part, tried to strike Eason in the shoulder. He blocked it easily. She struck at his legs. He blocked it again. She tried to the other shoulder. Once again, Eason blocked it.

"Will I ever get good, Uncle?" She asked, her big eyelashes making her look terribly innocent.

Eason nodded.

"Does it comfort you to know that you are better than all the women in the Cheryic clan?"

She shook her head.

Eason sighed and smirked. Perhaps the girl would make a soldier after all.

"You are good, Rose. I am just better for now."

Rose laughed. "Nothing can kill you, can it, Uncle?

Eason's smile grew wider. "Let's just say I will be there for you for a very long time."

"Eason, please." Helen begged him through desperate eyes. "You must save them. He can't find out."

The hour was late. She wore a cloak that covered herself from any recognition she could receive from the clans. It didn't matter. Nobody was awake anyhow. Except for Eason now.

"Have you once visited me since I arrived here? Have you even sent me so much as a letter?"

"How am I supposed to send you a letter in the Highlands?"

"Nevermind," Eason grumbled. "What's she done this time?"

"She's reportin' him. Domestic abuse, violence...she's gone crazy. Eason please, you gotta take them, he's gonna kill us all, I swear. He's tryna run for president soon...oh Eason please." Her voice was coming out only in incoherent sobs now, and the boys both wailed with her, too young to comprehend anything that was happening.

"Eason, you know him. You know he'll do whatever it takes. If he finds out about my him...he'll kill him. And Magnar...I can't. You know I can't. He can't know. He can never know. He's too...he's too damn religious. That's his whole base, see them religious folk. They won't take kindly to this at all. No please, take them. Christi's gotta start a whole mess. Oh God, Caiden, sh, sh, ssssh."

She clutched the boy to her chest as he wailed, sniffling in the cold.

"Stay with me." Eason said, "you can live here with your boys. Free."

She shook her head quickly. "That's what daddy needs—another scandal. Daughter gone missing. No. I have to stay. Everything's gotta go back to normal. He doesn't know about them, Eason. He can't. They're all I got."

All in a second, she shoved the boy in Eason's arms and threw the other inside. Then she was gone, without even a look back.

***

Eason awoke from the memories feeling extremely tired. The sky was moving, but he wasn't sure how. He heard distant shouts, someone was calling:

"Gliocas, Gliocas, Gliocas..."

He found himself repeating names to himself, silently.

"Rose, Magnar,

Caiden,mmmRosemmmmMagnarrrrrCaiddd..."

His vision faded and he soon found himself staring right into the eyes of his favorite sister.

***

The Cheryic Clan had reached the Great Tree. Rose and Evander marveled at the flat rock beneath with an ancient Cheryic symbol etched upon it. They both lifted it.

"How did you know where this was?" someone asked, gaping at the newly revealed tunnel. Stone stairs led down a dark and narrow path, wide enough only for two people. Rose realized that there was no time to lose. A woman handed Rose a torch, and she started down the stairs. Wallace still sat upon her shoulders, now laughing playfully. Rose could not help but feel jealous of his naïveté.

"I saw something like this in a movie once," Rose explained.

"A movie?"

Rose nodded, "Aye, it's a…" she turned to see the clueless expression on Evander's face. "Nevermind."

The tunnel was dark, with the exception of the eerie glow of the torches some civilians carried. The walls were layered with stones, likely taken out of the mountain itself. They were black with glints of sparkles in them. They reflected the torch as Rose and Evander passed them. The ground's dirt was compacted beneath her feet, yet it was damp. It seemed that the air had taken on a dense, cool feeling beneath the mountain, as if they had taken a wet rag and cooled their face from the heat of the sun.

Suddenly, the tunnel opened to a gaping room with pillars that must have been a mile high. The room was the biggest any in the clan had ever seen, and all who entered paused to gape at it for a moment. Rose felt goosebumps trail down her arms as she strained her neck to get a glimpse of the ceiling. She could not see it: it was just a black abyss.

It was a city. Rose had heard the stories over and over. After Culloden, the clan had taken refuge in the mountains and built this great place. It was hidden from all British eyes as the clan built a life of its own, carving out room by room. They all were connect by this great hall.

She remembered the situation and cursed herself for wasting a moment. They had explored these tunnels a few times as children. She knew the way. They had to leave this room. It would be a slaughterhouse if the Craotics caught them in here. Rose started across a bridge wider than the tunnel had been, but still one that could only hold three or four people across the width.

"Àille!" A man called out to Rose from behind. She turned to find a man in his mid-thirties with curly, pale hair running toward them.

Wallace saw the man first. "DA!" He yelled, his high pitched squeal exuding so much joy that Rose felt tiny tears well behind her eyes. Eara turned to see her father as well. How her face lit up! It seemed that someone had switched on a light behind her eyes.

Wallace squirmed to be let down, and Rose complied as the boy scrambled to his father. Evander did the same for Eara. They ran into their father's arms, and he responded with a warm smile and teary eyes. When they finished embracing, the father approached Evander and Rose, who kept walking. They could not hold up the crowd, which was steadily forming in this room.

"Àille."

Rose smiled politely, awkwardly turning her head so that she could see him while she walked.

"Thank you for getting my children to safety. I am forever in your debt."

Rose shook her head. "It was a pleasure escorting your children to the mountains. They are fine people." (Eason had finally taught her how to speak politely to strangers.)

"Aye. They are. Well, I thank you."

"You came from the battle; did you not?" Rose asked.

He nodded; his eyebrows drawn. In the torchlight, she could see specks of blood dabbled on his face. His shirt was another story, and had streaks lining it vertically…someone else's, no doubt. The man himself had a few gashes here and there, but did not look otherwise hurt.

"Is my uncle alive?" she asked.

"When I left, he was."

"Are they still fighting?"

"Aye. But your uncle was kind enough to let me leave so that I may father my bairns."

"Did you see my brothers on the way back?"

As if on cue, a cry was heard from behind them, at the beginning of the tunnel.

"Make way!"

Four soldiers carried a stretcher with a body on it.

"The Chief is dead!" One of them called, carrying the stretcher high above their heads.

There were a number of wails from the crowd. Rose froze.

The Chief is dead. If only I knew who the Chief was…

"May I see him?" Rose asked, swallowing down a lump in her throat, wondering why she felt dread. She could not think straight. *Chief? What Chief?*

They lowered the stretcher.

I know no Chief. I know no Chief.

She fell to her knees, holding back her tears.

I cannot cry, she thought, *not in front of them, not in front of my people.*

"Make way! Make way for the princes!"

Two boys shoved their way through the crowd, their faces stained with tears as they made their way toward the stretcher. The dark-haired one fell atop of the dead man; the fair one stood where he was, gaping at the dead man in disbelief.

A girl was in Rose's face: Eara. Her bright blue eyes looked into Rose's. The small girl lowered herself onto Rose's lap and wrapped her arms around her.

"Eara," her father called in a tone that warned her to stay away from Rose.

The girl did not seem to hear it. She rested on Rose's lap, not wavering.

"Was he your da?" She asked Rose, who winced at the way the girl had used past tense when she referred to her uncle.

"No he was…" Rose paused and thought about the question. "Aye, he was my da."

"Was he nice?" Eara asked her, playing with Rose's hands. Rose bit her lip.

"Very."

"What will you do now?" she asked innocently.

Rose thought about this question, trying to stay out of the clouds that her mind kept falling into. What would Eason want Rose to do? She looked to his body as if he might sit up and give her answers

"A clan is not lost until it is leaderless," she could hear him say in his usual calm voice. Had he known then that he would die? She ruffled Eara's hair playfully.

"I will protect all of you."

Rose stood up somewhat shakily when Eara pranced from her lap.

"Oh," Eara's father began, "My name is William. The Chief…well…he had asked me to give ya this before I left."

William handed Rose the booklet. She vowed to read it later, but there was no time now. Magnar and Caiden were staring at Rose through teary eyes.

"We've gotta avenge him, Rose," Caiden said shakily.

"Not yet." Rose replied. She bit her cheek, praying to Eason that she was doing the right thing. She was. She knew she was. She turned to Magnar.

"You understand you're in charge now, right?"

Magnar shook his head through teary eyes, his lips wet with tears.

"No…I can't."

Rose nodded slowly. "Start by taking us to the Baile Beatha. We can't go back to the city. We have to keep moving. If we have reinforcements, and we are attacked again, we can defend the clan. But we have to get there. Now go. Run ahead with Evander. I'll stay in the back with Caiden."

Magnar nodded and did as Rose told him. She felt sorry for Magnar. She had always known of his fear of leading before his time. She had seen the way he had looked at the young Triact Chief with frightened eyes all those years ago. But he had no choice now. She also knew that Evander wanted to be with her. But Caiden and Magnar weren't necessarily stable at the moment, so she thought it was only right for at least one sane person to be in each group.

Rose hoped she was sane.

"Keep moving, people!" She shouted. "Let's go!"

The crowd continued to move, carrying the fallen Chief high on a stretcher. The Chief's niece held her head up high, erasing all feelings from her mind.

***

"Welcome Eason." I smiled; my light brown hair flowing past my waist. My palms fell to the side of my silky dress, which swayed slightly in a light cooling breeze.

I could see in his face an expression of recognition, then he looked relieved. I knew he thought I was my daughter, and I gave him a moment for him to realize I was not. His expression changed again to something of bewilderment.

"Christine!" He gasped.

Eason looked around him. We were in the middle of a beautiful plain with tall grass that wavered in a slight breeze that Eason could not feel. The sun was high in the sky, yet he could not feel its heat. Beside him, a clear, small pond sat in the ground. I sat patiently in front of it, watching. I could see that he wanted so badly to touch the pool, but decided against it.

"Where am I?" Eason asked, afraid of the answer.

I smiled. I knew him, though he did not know me anymore.

"The lower section of the afterlife." I replied, and Eason returned his gaze to me, studying me. I knew I looked different than the girl he had once known. I was older, perhaps, more dead.

"I never imagined hell to be so beautiful," Eason replied.

I laughed.

"No brother, this is the lower section of what those on Earth call 'heaven'."

Eason stood, stunned, beholding beauty surrounding him. He stared at the pond, still fighting the urge to touch it.

"That is the Pool of Apperception." I told him.

"What is it?" he asked. "Why is it there?"

"You have a choice, Eason." I said, my smile fading. "You can either be reborn again into another life; there's no telling what life that could be. You can walk up these stairs to the higher section of heaven."

Golden stairs appeared beside me that seemed to go up forever and ever.

"Once you go up those stairs, you can never go back down. Or you can sit here by the pool and wait."

This puzzled him.

"What do I wait for?" he asked.

"Is it not obvious? Your children and mine. I've been waiting for my little girl whom you so graciously have watched for ten years. I'll wait for a hundred if I must."

So many questions overwhelmed him; he needed to pause to sort out the most important ones.

"And I wait with you?" he asked.

I nodded.

"As long as it takes."

the Twins hold

Eason was dead. Gwen was dead. Caiden also wanted to die.

He desperately wanted to go back to the battlefield and fight in Eason's name. But as much as he hated to admit it, Rose was right. Eason had always put the needs of his people even before the needs of his own family. He thought of Magnar's eyes, sunken with fear and misery, and his chest tightened. Magnar would never do the same, Caiden realized, and he prayed he would never have to.

They finally reached the end of the vast room and found a narrow path, so small it almost seemed ridiculous to have it connect to such a place. Magnar and Evander, having led the line of people, had managed to pry open the door that enclosed the tunnel. The Twins allowed the people to go ahead of them, hoping to be as far away from their uncle's lifeless body as possible. They continued to trudge at the people's heels, willing them with their minds to move faster. They weren't sure if there would be enough time to escape before the Craotics found the tunnel.

There wasn't. The length of the tunnel must have been a few miles. The people made it safely to the opposite side of the mountain and out the door, but just as Caiden and Rose were emerging outside, they heard a vicious roar coming from the other end of the tunnel. The people froze for a moment, taking in the chaotic scrambling noises from the inside of the tunnel. Then one girl screamed, and as if on command, all of the people took off, running into the trees. A few soldiers stayed behind, willing to defend the royals' lives. Caiden was about to follow the people and run when Rose grabbed his arm.

"We can take them!" She told him, gesturing to the dark hole in the side of the mountain. Caiden shook his head.

"What, are you off yer head? You just said we had to stay with the people! Not even our whole army could defeat them!"

She rolled her eyes. "Caiden, the tunnel's only wide enough for two people! They probably have run out of arrows by now. They obviously didn't take the time to get more weapons and our army narrowed them down!"

"Yeah, it narrowed them down to the best fighters."

Rose groaned. "That's ridiculous. These are Craotic trained soldiers. We are Cheryic trained. We can beat them."

He thought about her words. "Tell that to the dead Cheryic soldiers."

Rose rolled her eyes again.

"Just do as I say," she told him. She took out her bow and placed a few arrows in it skillfully. Caiden removed his sword from his sheath. He could hear the swords being removed from the sheaths of the soldiers that had stayed with them. "Leave the torches outside." Rose ordered the soldiers.

They did so, and Rose led them back into the dark, so far in, that the light was just a speck in the distance. Without the light from a torch, they could not see their own hands when they held them in front of their eyes.

We can do this. Caiden thought, trying his best to stay positive. It wasn't working. They kept their backs to the walls, carefully listening to the tunnel. Caiden swore that he heard a hum coming from the soul of the tunnel. It grew louder and louder until it turned into a growl. Two torches, at first merely orange dots in the distance, grew closer and closer. Caiden grew fully aware of his breathing, and attempted to quiet it, but found that it was only becoming louder as he became conscious of it.

As soon they could see the whites of the leading Craotic's eyes, Rose shot an arrow in the bridge of his nose. The men's storm of fury ceased suddenly, as they observed the fate of their leader, and Rose seized the opportunity to shoot another in the heart. This enraged the rest and they charged, searching aimlessly for the source of the arrow. Rose shot them, one by one, until a pile was forming, making it difficult to maneuver in the tunnel. She had finally used her last arrow when Caiden turned to her.

"Let me have some, okay Rose?" Caiden asked, afraid she would kill all of the enemy within their first battle. He *did* want at least one war story to pass on to his children.

She smirked.

"Fine, let's go."

They ran ahead of the soldiers, keeping to the sides of the wall to avoid the torchlight, and they emerged like demons, slicing their enemies from the abyss. The element of surprise was still on their side as the Craotic men jumped where they stood and backed away, flailing their torches here and there. Rose beheaded one. Caiden slit one's throat with his sword. The Cheryic soldiers behind them scarcely were able to kill any at all. Caiden took his knife and threw it at an approaching Craotic's head, and it sank deep into his eye. He stabbed one in the gut, beheaded one, cut one's arm off, then beheaded him again. It was the twins' first kills, but they did not think about it. With every Craotic man who approached them, they became obsessed with the idea that this could be the man who killed their uncle. They insisted upon taking revenge. Soon, the tunnel was swarming with bloody Craotic bodies.

***

Magnar walked ahead of his people, scared stiff and unable to breathe. The daylight had faded and he was left guiding his people to Baile Beatha in the dark. It occurred to him that they had no food, no water and the people were slowing down. He would have told them all to set up camp, but it worried him that the Craotics might be nearing them. So he simply allowed his clan to take a brief rest and soon they would be back on the road.

"Gliocas!"

He automatically turned to look for Uncle, but soon he remembered the unfortunate events of the day and turned to the speaker.

"Yes?" Magnar asked politely. An out-of-breath boy of about sixteen years appeared before him.

"I have a message from the prince and princess."

His breath caught in his chest as a million scenarios raced through his mind.

"Give it to me then," Magnar ordered, deepening his voice. The boy handed him the faded, muddy, parchment with handwriting so messy, it had to be Rose's.

Defending tunnel. Keep leading.

~Twins

Magnar read the paper over and over again. He checked the back: nothing.

He cursed under his breath. Fools! They would be killed for sure! Two against hundreds? Sure, they had been narrowed down, but still! He panicked, trying to figure out how to save his siblings.

What would Eason do?

He took a deep breath. What would Uncle do? Eason would have stayed and led his people to safety, then attended to the Twins. But Eason was different. Magnar worried too much about them to ever do such a thing. Could the Twins defend the tunnel?

He looked to the sky. *Where is that dammed falcon?* He thought, *of course now is the time it goes off for a hunt.*

Magnar sighed.

"Evander." He turned to the blond soldier beside him, who awaited his orders patiently. "Lead them to Baile Beatha. I need to find my siblings."

Evander shook his head. "Magnar, no. The people need you-"

"The Twins need me too." Magnar snapped. Before Evander could say another word, Magnar was running back to the mountain.

A trail of murmurs followed him away, as the people felt the stab of rejection with their new Chief abandoning them.

Evander sighed. Caiden and Rose were old enough to make their own choices now. If this was theirs, then he was grateful for the spare time. The sun had finally set after a long, stressful day and Evander looked to the stars.

"Please keep them safe, Eason."

***

To Caiden and Rose's surprise, the Craotics ceased to continue to come through the tunnel after only a few hours of fighting. To say the least, they were grateful. One of them had whacked the back of Rose's head with the hilt of their weapon. She had an annoyingly bloody gash and was beginning to see stars. Caiden seemed to have a few cuts and bruises here and there, but nothing serious.

When all of the Craotics seemed to stop coming, the twins took a minute to regain their breaths.

"Are you alright?" Caiden asked Rose warily as she leaned on the wall.

She nodded. "Been better. You?"

"Been better." Caiden offered her a grim smile. She stared down the tunnel, expecting more of the Craotics to come.

She listened carefully for the soft hum of their growl. She gazed back at the exit of the tunnel, which they were finally approaching.

"We should barricade the tunnel." She told Caiden.

He looked toward her wide-eyed.

"What if the army is still on its way?" He asked.

Rose's heart melted with sympathy toward her hopeful kin. However high the hope was, she needed to cast it down to reality.

"They aren't coming, Caiden." She told him.

He looked to his feet and began to speak.

"Hawl!" They held up their swords in readiness for whoever or whatever made that noise.

Someone held a torch up to them. A familiar face showed through the orange glow of the torch: A boy their age with a permanent scowl etched into his pale face.

"Fergus?!" the Twins yelled.

The boy smiled sadly. One side of his face was caked in blood, but otherwise, he seemed unharmed. "I ken about the Chief. I have to say, I never was in love with his politics. But he was a good man. I'm sorry."

Rose stepped back, caught off guard by his politeness.

"How did you escape?" Caiden asked, his face filled with hope.

"We held them back until they got to the tunnel entrance, when we were sort of fightin' on the side ya see. And about twenty men still lived and I did too obviously, so we were fightin' and fightin' and tryin' to get to the tunnel, but couldna until all the Craotics that were still fighting were in the tunnel. We chased them and killed them, but by the time we got here, well I was the only one who got here alive…did you kill all those Craotics?" He looked around at the stacks and stacks of bodies on the ground.

"Aye." They told him, restraining themselves from bragging too much.

He stared at them, wide-eyed.

"How…?"

The Twins posed with their weapons, standing back to back as they showed off their form.

"Ah." Fergus said awkwardly.

There was a long silence.

"We're going to barricade the exit so that they can't get through." Rose informed him, getting back down to business. "Are there still Craotics in the city?"

"Aye, many swarming throughout houses and burning them." Fergus's voice cracked, and he looked to the ground, embarrassed. "How are you going to barricade it?"

They began walking toward the exit, glancing behind them every few seconds out of paranoia. They searched around for any means of blocking the gaping hole. Rose looked at the top of the tunnel, where loose rocks and dirt had been blocked by a giant boulder embedded in the ground.

"If we can find a way to get that rock loose, that debris would block the doorway."

Fergus shook his head.

"That debris would come crashing down on us."

Rose smirked.

"Then move." She removed a branch from a dead tree by the exit and began climbing up the mountain with it.

"I wouldna do that if I were you," Fergus warned her cautiously. She ignored her old rival.

When she had climbed to the top of the doorway, she stuck the stick beneath the boulders. It was about her height the whole way around. She kept as much distance as she could from the boulder as she added pressure to it as if it were a lever. Seeing that she was making no progress, Caiden climbed up on the other side of the boulder with a branch. He also wedged his branch beneath the boulder.

"Ready…push!" He ordered, and slowly the boulder came loose. When it started to roll forward, Caiden and Rose dove out of the way. The debris came crashing to the bottom of the mountain, which happened to be the entrance to the door, in a small landslide.

Caiden glanced back at Rose and shrugged.

"That works."

"What in the name of Owen Cheryic himself is happening here?" A voice boomed behind them. Magnar stood with his arms crossed behind the group, his face as red as a cherry. His blond locks were now matted in sweat and dirt.

"Magnar, you should've seen Rose." Caiden began, "She saved everyone! She saved the entire clan. And I mean, I don't want to brag but...I did some saving myself."

Magnar did not look impressed.

"What are you doing here?" Rose asked him, her tone hostile. "You are the Chief; you cannot leave your people! Not now!"

Magnar rolled his eyes. "Well, you can't just leave and throw your life in the hands of the Craotics and not expect me to follow!"

Rose slapped him in the face. "I will throw my life away for the sake of my people, because they are my people! Just like Eason! You should be proud to have such siblings!"

"Proud?" Magnar spat. "Proud?!"

He could no longer muster words. He attempted to think of something, anything that could embody how he felt. But he could not.

"We are leaving!"

to measure the meaning

When Magnar, Caiden, Rose, Fergus, and the remaining soldiers did return, the clan moved swiftly and silently, with only the sound of Magnar's commands and a few people crying quietly. They had refused to leave without their Chief, but had lost a day in doing so. They murmured to one another silently about his lack of devotion to the clan. If Magnar was being honest, he couldn't help but feel a trace of jealousy when he learned about the Twins' success in holding off the Craotics. Magnar also wanted to avenge his uncle, and what kind of Chief has not killed any more than a stag?

He withdrew to his thoughts for the remainder of the trip. Would they ever take back their homeland?

The questions raced through his mind like poison, possessing his thoughts no matter what he did to evade them.

He stopped walking and looked around. The sun was setting again. The worn travellers would soon be exposed to wolves and bears alike. They were sheltered by high trees and nearby he heard the sound of running water. They would be in Triact territory soon.

"We set up camp here," Magnar ordered.

The people went about setting up camps silently. There were still a few men left: the elderly, non-soldiers who had families, soldiers who had been sent back and those who had not quite completed their training. They set about chopping firewood. Most of the young men were gone. It was a trait of the Cheryic youth to marvel at the idea of dying in a blaze of glory on the battlefield. But now, it was a waste. They could have used those young men's strength.

A few fires were quickly built, and what was left of the Cheryic Clan huddled around them. Magnar sat in front of one fire, surrounded by Evander; Chelinda Reid; her husband Old Man Maccus Reid; Gilbert Stowe; Spinster Gricelda Blackwood; Cinnie's father (Maccus's brother) Mabuz Reid; the fat drunk (Fergus's father) McCaig; and the Spirit Guide, Stewart Wallace. All of these people sat awkwardly around the fire, roasting a skinned rabbit. Nobody said a word until it was nearly ready, when Gricelda Blackwood cleared her throat.

"Well, I think it's obvious what's happened," Gricelda said.

"Ooo aye and what is that Gricelda?" McCaig slurred. (The man had managed to snag a bottle of ale before they left.)

"Them." Gricelda spat on the ground and nodded at Magnar.

"I beg your pardon?" Magnar said, his ears turning pink.

"Face it," she said, "the line's been corrupt ever since yer uncle came into the mix from the Outside. Yer not one of us. Ye'll never be one of us."

"Wheesht!" Evander shouted, "Gricelda y'ol spinster, ye ken as well as I do that Magnar has known nothing but the clan his whole life. He was raised as one of us, and he is one of us. It is in his blood. He will forever be a Cheryic Chief."

"Aye," Gilbert added, "the lad's right. Magnar's uncle was a good Chief, and I am sure the lad will be a good one as well."

"Yer off yer head!" Mabuz Reid stood up. "Mind that it was his uncle that allowed in our walls the Outsiders who killed my daughter. It was his uncle that allowed our clan to be invaded by an enemy with much lesser resources than ourselves. Eason was a terrible Chief and so will his kin be!"

Magnar could feel all eyes on him, even those from the adjacent fires.

"Well, what do the spirits say?" Gricelda looked to Stewart, who stared sheepishly into the flames. "Because it seems to me that ever since these Outsiders have come into our lands, the spirits have brought bad omens upon us all."

Stewart sighed, "The spirits use their voices in ways too complex-"

"Yes, yes," Gricelda interrupted. "The spirits are mysterious and all-powerful, but sometimes the spirits skelp ye in the face to let ye know what you're doing is wrong, and it seems to me that they're doing so right now. So we must please them and cast these Outsiders out of our clan!"

"No!" Evander shot up, "Eason was a good, kind Chief. Under him, we scarcely had poor. He listened to our needs and supported them. He brought in his kin as acts of mercy! It was the Craotics who betrayed him, and he could have done nothing about that without starting a war. How can we cast out his kin as an act of cruelty?"

"It is not cruelty if it is listening to the spirits, lad," Maccus Reid chimed in.

"Oh, finally, Maccus Reid, good of you to join us!" Evander shouted sarcastically, "it's nice that ye show some care for the clan now. Tell me, where have you been for the past sixty years?"

"Be careful, lad!" Chelinda pointed a heavily ringed finger at him.

"We have strayed too far from the descendants of Owen Cheryic!" Maccus Reid claimed, "we must find who is next in line that is not an Outsider. Who would that be Stewart?"

Stewart rubbed his temples. "I believe it would be Rory Silver."

A young man, one fire away, stood up, his hair reminded Magnar of the cold morning in Ben Nevis, with the ground completely covered in a pale white frost. "I am Rory Silver," the man said. His voice was so soft, it was nearly carried off with the wind.

Across the fire, a young woman with pale hair that reached her waist stood up, her face glimmering with tear stains.

"Stop!" Jean said, "Yer all haverin[26] and it gives me the boke![27] Magnar is the rightful Chief by blood *and* virtue. How can ye deny that?"

It was madness, left and right people were arguing as if Magnar was not even present. He grimaced whenever he heard his uncle's name and thanked the spirits that the Twins

---

[26] Talking nonsense
[27] Makes me sick

had gone out to hunt. All he could hear were the dull throbs of clans people arguing against him. Perhaps three people spoke in his favor. It continued, in agonizing torture, for nearly an hour, until it seemed as though all of the clan had joined in the argument. Most were against him.

Finally, he stood and raised his hands to the people. They immediately fell silent as they looked to him.

"It is my understanding," Magnar said softly, "that my reign is being challenged before I have even come into it." He paused and looked around at the people's trembling faces. "You all are afraid. I understand. So this is my first gift to you, as your soon-to-be-chief—a choice. If you truly believe Rory Silver to be your true chief, you will cast your vote to Stewart on his parchment. If you believe me to be the chief, you will cast mine."

"Magnar, no, this is ridic-" Jean began, as she raced toward his side.

But Magnar's decision was already made. He nodded toward Stewart and walked alone in the darkness.

He returned around midnight. Stewart had only just finished counting the votes and gave Magnar a pitiful look. Magnar gave one small nod and Rory Silver strode from the fire, his hands in the folds of his kilt.

"All pay your respects to Rory Silver," Stewart ordered. "King and Chief of the Cheryic Clan."

Rory nodded, but did not waste time on taking the people's respect. He looked to the trees and said, "My first order as chief is that we leave for the Triact Clan tonight to seek shelter." He paused and looked to Magnar, his eyes cold and unapologetic, "and no Rankin shall ever set foot in the Cheryic Clan again."

Magnar sank to the ground and put his fist to his chest as the clan began to pack their things and put out fires. Gilbert approached him.

"In my youth lad, I would have stayed with ya." He smiled, showing his crooked yellow teeth, "but I fear I would be more of a burden to ye now than a help. So I will go with the clan and do all I can to convince them to send for ya, when the smoke has cleared away."

Magnar nodded. "Thank you, Gilbert."

Gilbert's face grew much more rigid suddenly, as he looked upon the body that lay on the stretcher, away from the fires.

"But he would want to stay with ya," Gilbert said, "send him to the spirits, even if it is not upon the mountaintop where the past chiefs have been sent. They will find him and he will find them. He is strong, ye ken."

Magnar nodded and took Gilbert's fist to his heart. "I will remember you, Gilbert Stowe," Magnar said.

Gilbert gave a slight nod and hurried to pack his things, but then quickly returned to Magnar.

"I nearly forgot," he said softly and handed Magnar a large gray sack. "I managed to grab some things from your house that I knew your uncle would want. But also, make sure you keep his sword. You ken he would want you to have it."

Magnar nodded, and Gilbert disappeared again.

"Evander." Andrew O'Connor stood in the firelight. He still wore his apron from the bakery.

Evander stood with his arms crossed. "So yer alive then, are ya. There was no hurry to find yer son, was there?" he said.

Andrew ignored this. "I ken what yer thinkin. Ye belong with the clan. Come with us son, dinna stay here where there is no future."

"I belong with my family," Evander said, stepping behind Magnar.

Andrew looked sadly to the ground, but said nothing. Then he was gone.

Before long, everyone was ready to go. A few, mostly women that Magnar had known in some way, held their arms out spread-eagle to Magnar to show their pride for him. But then he was left alone by the fire.

Well, alone except for Jean and Evander, who would not budge.

"Go." Magnar commanded them. "Your life is not here."

"Why did ya do that?" Jean asked. Magnar could see how beet red her face had become, even without the red hue of the fire.

"The people have been through so much…" Magnar said. "Their homes *and* their loved ones have been taken from them...I shall not take their dignity from them as well. They deserve something they can control at least, even if that something is me."

Jean smacked the back of Magnar's head, who shot a startled look at her.

"You're not royalty anymore," she said, "I'm allowed to do that."

Magnar snorted.

Evander did not look up; he stared off in the distance as he drew in a deep resounding breath. "When my maw passed, I desperately wanted someone to blame. I chose my father because he had spent most of his time in the taverns. He could not bear to see her go, so he just did not come home. I blamed him for her death. But, even after I wanted so badly to blame him, if he had fought for me, I would have lived with him. If he had shown he cared and wanted me, I would have taken care of him when he grew old. That's where yer wrong Magnar. The people tested ya to see if ye would accept the blame, and ye failed them."

Magnar hung his head between his hands.

Evander ignored him and nodded at Eason's body.

"We should send him to the spirits soon," he said.

Magnar shook his head. "We must wait for the Twins. We cannot send him off without them."

Jean shot Evander a worried look, but Evander did not seem concerned. Magnar wondered how he could be that way. Through all of the perils that Evander had seen the Twins get into, Magnar had never once seen him worry. That was the difference between the two of them: Evander had always focused on the Twins' uncanny ability to get out of trouble, whereas Magnar had only seen their ability to get in trouble.

"Hawl! Look what we killed!"

Everyone whirled around to see Rose, Caiden, and surprisingly, Fergus, galloping over on horses, grinning. But then they all sobered upon seeing Eason's body, dismounting slowly.

"Where have you been?" Magnar asked, unable to hide his annoyed tone.

"Hunting," Rose replied. "Are you lost? Where is everyone?"

Magnar grimaced slightly as he picked a blade of grass from the ground. "We are no longer part of the Cheryic Clan."

The Twins stood dumbfounded.

"Even me?" Fergus replied.

Magnar rolled his eyes. "No, not you, they just left. Hurry and run after them and you'll catch up."

Fergus stood awkwardly, looking from Rose to the trampled grass revealing the path the clan had taken.

"Go!" Magnar ordered.

Fergus dashed away.

Rose stared down the path that Fergus had taken, unamused. "Funny. I thought we were becoming friends."

Magnar shook his head. "Everyone is afraid. People turn on each other when they're afraid."

Caiden looked from Jean to Magnar to Rose to Evander back to Magnar back to Rose.

"IS EVERYONE IGNORING THE FACT THAT WE HAVE BEEN THROWN OUT OF THE CHERYIC CLAN?" Caiden shouted, his face beet red.

Magnar stood up and dusted off his kilt. "Aye, but before we acknowledge that, Uncle has been waiting long enough to go to the spirits."

Everyone grew quiet.

"Get wood," Magnar ordered.

"But..." Caiden said. "The mountain! He needs to be sent off with the Chiefs."

Magnar shook his head. "They will find him."

Rose, Jean, and Evander set about the forest looking for wood and branches and piling them up. Caiden just stood, dumbfounded, wells of tears forming in his gigantic eyes.

When the pyre was formed, Magnar turned to Caiden. "Help me lift him."

Caiden shook his head, "I can't."

"Do it."

Rose jumped and grabbed Eason's legs as Magnar heaved beneath his arms and Caiden hesitantly lifted the arch of his back. They gently placed him on the woodpile and stood silently for a moment.

"Soooo what now?" Rose asked.

"There's no spirit guide." Caiden added.

And Jean sang. And it was soft and beautiful and everything the children needed. Well, they were not children anymore.

It was an ancient song, often sung at funerals, so Caiden joined in, his voice cracking in inconvenient places. Magnar listened for a little while, appreciating the beauty in Jean's voice. Then he also joined in, his voice clear and rich. Evander followed, less majestically, and more quietly. Rose did not. She just stood, listening, taking in her uncle's face. She remembered when those lips had kissed the top of her hair before bed, countless times. Those eyes which now were closed once beamed a beautiful shade of bright green, just like hers. His long dark locks still were braided proudly down to his strong bowl chest. He was not a large man, but it took a fool not to say that he had been a proud one. And now he was gone.

When the song ended, Magnar dropped a torch on the pyre, and Jean took his hand as they said goodbye. Rose allowed a tear to be released when she realized she would never see this man's beautiful face again.

When the deed was done, Magnar sat and opened the sack Gilbert had left for them. He chuckled a bit, imagining Gilbert rummaging through everything to see what was important. He had certainly nailed it: There was a loaf of bread, a small bag of oats, a tiny sack of salt, three potatoes, an onion, an oatcake, a bag of nuts, a canteen for water, a painting a Cheryic woman had made of Eason and the children, Rose's extra supply of arrows, a "photo" of a woman, and a pair of Magnar's stockings.

Magnar picked up the photo. He had seen Rose stare at it before, taking in every detail. It was a woman with curly chestnut hair holding a little girl in her arms. Magnar had never understood the concept of a photo. Rose had tried to explain it multiple times, but Magnar could not seem to grasp how the artist got the likeness to be so…real."

He handed it to Rose, who held it to her chest in relief, taking in the details again. She put it in her pocket, taking out the booklet as she did.

"Eason's memoirs," she said, flipping through it hastily.

Magnar nodded. "For a later time."

Magnar took Eason's sword, and removed it from the scabbard: "*Chan eil tuil air nach tig traoghadh*," he said sadly.

"There isn't a flood that will not subside," Rose repeated starkly.

Magnar patted her on the back. "Uncle told me that when I broke my arm."

"It's yours, Magnar. He would have wanted his heir to have it."

Magnar shook his head and put the sword back in its sheath. "His heir no longer."

Rose realized the despair Magnar was feeling and she raised her brows. *He believes that we will wander through the world without purpose!* A part of her thought.

"Magnar, we will come back and lead our people," Rose said.

He gave her an *are-you-really-that-stupid* look.

"And what will we do in the meantime? Wait? Starve?" Magnar asked skeptically.

Rose took hold of Eason's sword, which Magnar still gripped with a gloved hand.

"We'll fight."

Magnar scoffed.

"And…we'll build an army. We will find people to be in our army!" Pride filled Rose's chest, for she was quite pleased with her spontaneous idea. She smiled and stared wide-eyed at Magnar in anticipation.

Magnar nodded slowly and looked down at the sword, which she let go of.

"How will we convince people to join a clanless army of four?" He asked.

"Five...Jean's here too, you eejit!" She replied. Magnar threw his hands in the air in a *sorry-but-hey-she's-not-a-soldier-so-I'm-right* way. Rose grunted. She couldn't think of how exactly they could convince people to join their army, but that could wait until later.

"Wheesht," Magnar said. He laid down and closed his eyes for some long-needed rest.

Suddenly a dead rabbit fell on his head.

Magnar snorted as Valar perched itself on the nearby wood pile. "Nice timing," he grumbled. The bird pecked his hand affectionately.

Rose was not yet tired, so she took the memoirs from the bag and began to read them eagerly. Her eyes remained glued to the papers for about ten pages and her imagination stirred as she was reminded of all that Eason had gone through. Eventually, her exhaustion got the best of her, so she laid her head down as well. Her mind, however, would not let go of the papers that she had read, even as she slept. Her memory raced through Eason's memoirs in the form of a dream.

"Come o'er here, boy!" A voice snarled.

Rose was in a dark narrow room, with clothes hanging down from the ceiling. The door opened, revealing a warm light from the outside.

A thin girl in a cropped tank top and a dark ponytail grabbed Rose's arm. "Mom?" She wanted to say, but no words came out of her mouth.

"Eason, you gotta get out of here!" The girl said, "Daddy's gonna kill you for real this time!"

She yanked Rose's arm so hard that Rose swore she would pull it off.

"Where is he?!" A deep voice yelled, and she heard a high-pitched woman arguing with the man downstairs until finally, she heard a loud crash and the woman was silenced.

"Mama told me to give you this and we collected enough money for you to go here. Go to Mama's brother's house. He'll be waitin," Rose's mom said, as she opened the window and ushered Rose to get moving. Rose clumsily climbed out the window.

The scene changed and Rose was standing at home now, facing a tall man with a long gray beard.

"Yer maw sent ye here?" The man asked.

Rose felt herself nodding.

The man grunted. "Serves my sister right for leaving the clan for love. I am Chief and King William Cheryic."

There was a long moment of silence and then a lanky, freckled boy walked out of Caiden and Magnar's room wearing nothing but a towel.

"This is my bairn, Hamley. I suppose he's yer brother now. Ye'll train together and learn the ways of our clan with him."

The scene changed and Rose was fighting Craotic men next to Hamley, who was now an older lanky boy, but still lanky nonetheless. She fought for what seemed like days until she looked to her right, and Hamley's head was rolling on the ground.

The scene changed again, and Rose was home, caked in blood, standing in front of Chief William.

"The Prince is dead." She told the Chief.

"No…" the Chief said, "no, he is not."

She reached to steady the Chief, but he collapsed anyway.

"Help!" She called. "The Chief has fallen! Help!"

A dozen hands ran in to grab the Chief and help him to his room and bed.

The scene changed once more, and Rose stood in front of Chief William, his face pale and motionless in his bed. The spirit guide stood before him, carefully watching Rose with pitying eyes.

"The Chief is dead. In his final words, he named you heir, Eason Rankin. Do you object to being our Chief and King?"

Rose looked around at the dozens of faces staring at her, assessing her, scrutinizing her. "No...I mean...I have no right...but...Hamley was heir…"

"Welcome, Chief Eason Rankin!"

***

"Rose, wake up!"

Rose was shaken awake to blue eyes as Evander nudged her shoulder gently. She moaned, wiping the sleep from her eyes.

"I-I dreamed of Uncle." She said, tears streaming down her face. "How he became Chief...it was so awful. His cousin was killed in battle and…and Chief William died of grief. He was never meant to be Chief."

"He was *always* meant to be Chief." Evander said, pulling her in for an embrace as he used to do in their youth. She wanted to stay there forever, surrounded by his warmth, but she shuddered to realize what a fool she was and broke away.

Rose looked around. She had no idea where they were, and she doubted anyone did. Magnar had given up, unwilling to care about where they were going and why. Caiden pretended he knew, but the boy couldn't tell his left hand from his right. They were approaching mountains, but everything was mountains in the highlands, so this gave no navigational aid.

"Rose." Evander called softly, waking her from her meditative state. She turned back to him, batting her eyelashes teasingly and laughing. "There's something we found you must know about."

"Yes?"

Evander stepped aside, revealing a small boy standing idly with his fist in his mouth. Caiden had found him wandering the forest when he was out searching for firewood. The poor boy was so famished, Caiden nearly gave him all of their food supplies.

"He told me his parents were kidnapped along with his village," Caiden explained when the group was all together again.

Rose kneeled to the boy's level. The boy was currently munching on an apple, paying no mind to the rest of the world.

"Where do you come from, little wolf?" She asked, smiling softly. He giggled nervously. His kilt was worn and tattered, and he had holes throughout his muddy tunic.

"Where are you from, lad?" Rose asked again.

"Oir Coelle." He answered shakily.

Magnar's eyes widened. "Caiden, the map!"

Caiden fumbled with a few things in his back and took out a crinkled, dirty map. Magnar spread it on the ground, straightening the folds with his palms.

He looked to the river on his right, and the mountains below them, then he closed his eyes. "If we're near Oir Coelle, then we must be here." He pointed to the map, just below the tiny dot that said Oir Coelle.

"But that would make us-" Jean began.

"In Triact land," Magnar finished. "When were you attacked?" he asked the boy.

"Uhhhh yesterday."

Rose glanced at her companions; Caiden's brows were drawn together in thought and his mouth hung slightly open. Magnar stood, lips pursed, rubbing his totem nervously with his thumb. Jean's eyes were fixed on the ground, cheeks still freshly stained from mourning over her sister. Evander looked to Rose, staring as if he wanted to send some sort of telepathic message.

"Who attacked your village?" Rose asked the boy.

The boy cried.

Rose nodded; she had known the answer all the along, but she had to be sure the boy had been attacked by Craotics.

"What's your name, little man?"

"Peter." The boy whimpered, hugging his scraped knees in the grass.

Evander spoke up, kneeling to Peter's level alongside Rose. "Peter, how many do you think there were?"

Peter's eyes widened as he looked up at them. "There was one really tall one. I heard maw say he snuck up on the police. And then there were ten others. They surrounded us and Da told me to count."

Caiden began to entertain the boy by showing his collection of wooden animals that he, for some reason, had insisted on carrying with him since he was two years old. Rose, Magnar, Evander, and Jean huddled by the fire.

The breeze blew Rose's hair across her face and brushed over the blades of grass, which waved peacefully. Rose held her hands to the fire, allowing the heat to radiate onto them. After a long while, Magnar drew in a breath, expanding his full chest, his eyes lost in the flames.

"If Caiden and you," Magnar gestured toward Rose, "have taught me anything, it's to not stand by and watch as our world goes down in flames."

Rose let out a laugh of relief, darting from her seated position to wrap her arms around Magnar. Before Magnar took her in, he held her shoulders.

"If anything should happen to either of you, I'd never forgive myself," he warned. "I will go after you if you are reckless."

Rose shrugged this off and tousled with his hair playfully.

"We can raid the village during nightfall," Magnar sighed.

"What about Peter?" Evander asked, gesturing toward the boy. "He canna come with us."

Magnar shook his head, tracing his thumb through the dirt beneath him. "No, but we need him close. We cannot split up too far apart. It's risky searching for each other in these lands."

Evander looked to Rose as if she could resolve their crisis, a small grin forming on his face.

"What?" she asked him. She was unsettled by the mischief brewing on his face, a phenomenon she had not seen since before Lilias's death. Evander let out a small, breathy laugh.

"You're an excellent archer," he grinned.

"Duh." Rose replied, batting her lashes.

"Plus, ye certainly aren't afraid of heights," he added.

"I used to be," Rose objected.

"Och yeah, right!" Caiden shouted, unable to hide that he'd been eavesdropping from his position with Peter. "You nearly gave me a heart attack when you swung across The Pit a few years ago!"

Rose rolled her eyes. She could feel Magnar tensing beside her, disliking where this conversation was going. She ignored him. He would have to let her go some time.

Evander chuckled. His hair had grown greasy in the past couple of days and matted on his head. It was shorter than the rest of the boys'. His mother had liked it that way, and Rose couldn't help but agree, despite it being a total mess at the moment.

"So ye can scale the roofs of the houses and be sure the areas are clear," he proposed.

"Aye, I suppose," Rose responded, cracking her knuckles slyly in an attempt to mask her excitement.

"I dunno Rose-" Magnar began.

"Magnar, wheesht." Rose said, "How will you ever manage not to explode if you always worry about Caiden and I, as well as the clan? Let us take care of ourselves."

Magnar jabbed his totem so hard with his thumb, it turned white. "Fine," he said, "but I go with you."

Rose nodded. She turned to Jean, who had been silent so far. "Will you take care of the boy while we go?"

"Aye," she said, but as Rose turned away, she spoke again. "I mean, no! I canna stand by while you avenge my sister for me! Naw, I must go too."

"Jean, you haven't been trained." Rose said quietly.

"I ken that," Jean began and sat quietly on the ground, contemplating. She pushed a strand of pale, nearly white hair behind her large, mouse-like ears. Her knees were clutched to her chest, yet her toes were pointed together, tapping incessantly as she thought. "I'll make a deal, Rose," she said, "If I die, it's no on any of ya, it was my own choice to be with my sister. But if I survive this fight, then ye train me, Rose, so I can fight in more. Ooooh Gwen would love that. Getting back at da by learnin' to fight like a man."

Rose looked to Magnar, who nodded sharply in return.

"Works for me," Rose replied, "but that still leaves Peter…"

"I'll take care of him," Caiden volunteered. "I'm still a bairn myself."

"It's settled then," Rose stated triumphantly and puffed her chest. "I am a genius."

Caiden chuckled softly, not turning away from the boy. "Well then," he said. "Would you want a ride on my shoulder's Peter?" Peter giggled and nodded his head. Caiden grabbed the kid from his armpits and hoisted him onto his shoulders.

"Off to Oir Coelle we go!" Caiden sighed, pointing in the direction of the woods.

no delay

The companions left their supplies in a nearby cave as they approached the town. They arrived at an array of empty wooden houses with roofs that Rose hoped would be sturdy enough to hold both her and Magnar. Magnar reluctantly agreed to allow her to run ahead and scout, seeing that she was the lightest and most graceful of the group. But he only accepted this with the condition that if she did not return in one hour, Magnar would come after her himself.

The group decided to move deeper into the town. The town was located on one of the rare plains of the highlands, and without the cover of trees, they were fully exposed. Here, they could find a place for Caiden and the boy to hide. Caiden went along ducking under roofs and marching over stacks of hay. Magnar instructed the crew to be silent, afraid that there could be spies within the buildings. The silence made Caiden weary of how loud his steps were as dry grass crunched beneath his boots. Every move they made could have been their last. Caiden began to imagine arrows shooting at them from the trees. What if it ended just like that? What would happen? He thought it unfair that lives could end so quickly, without warning. Perhaps that's why Gwen's death had shaken him so much.

"What's your name?" asked a small voice behind Caiden.

Caiden gasped, realizing he hadn't even told Peter his name yet. He smiled to himself. The boy reminded him of Cheryic children in the village, innocently laughing as they would weave through the forest trees for a game of manhunt.

Tears welled up in his eyes. He longed to be as innocent as this little boy again. After a few years of hunting and playing in the woods with Rose, Eason had given them work, sometimes at the smithy, other times fishing, farming and a few days of mining. Then most of the playing subsided. Eason always said that his heirs must know the people, so he gave them people's work.

"My name's Caiden." Caiden finally told him.

Peter laughed. "Caiden? That's my da's name!"

Caiden raised an eyebrow.

"Really?" Caiden asked, struggling to maintain an enthusiastic expression. He could not stop himself from scanning the trees for the glimmer of a weapon.

"Aye. My da always says that his name is the second-best in the whole world!"

Caiden laughed to himself, realizing where this was going. "He's right. Do you know what the first best name is?"

"Peter."

"You got it. Hush now, little lad. We'll see your da soon."

Peter smiled and reached up to grab Caiden's hand. He stared ahead at the path, absentmindedly putting his other hand in his mouth.

***

As they waited for Rose, the companions found Caiden and Peter an abandoned hut, far enough in the town that they could be reached, but surrounded by a fortress of buildings and hay to hide in. They needed only to wait a few minutes before-

BAM!

Rose landed on Caiden's back, his feet giving way beneath him. They tumbled to the ground with a thud. Caiden lay wide-eyed for a minute in shock. Then he looked up at the roof of the shed from which Rose had sneakily attacked him.

"Really?!" he asked, somewhat amused, but still shaken up from the fall.

She shrugged and held out a hand to Caiden, helping him off the ground.

"Everything's clear until you get to the center of town," she said to the crew. "Boys, can I talk to you alone?" She gestured toward the kid nervously, signaling young ears shouldn't hear.

Rose ushered her siblings away from Peter, leaving Evander and Jean to distract him.

"What's wrong?" Magnar asked in a hushed tone. "Are there more Craotics than the boy told us?"

Rose shook her head.

"They've kidnapped the townspeople. They are going to assassinate them...one at a time. I thought they just wanted our land but...it seems like they're trying to be the last clan standing so that they can take *everyone's* land. They want to see us suffer. What do they have to gain from this? First the Cheryics, then the Triacts?"

Rose returned her focus to Magnar.

"We need to get there as soon as possible. I can go in first with my bow. "

Magnar nodded, "I'll go with you now."

Caiden hoisted Peter up onto his waist and hid inside the shed.

***

Evander weaved in and out of huts, sword in hand, with Jean trailing close behind him. Magnar had allowed her to use his old sword, but it felt so heavy and awkward in her hands. The two of them glanced around. This village was so...poor. The houses were composed of old wood, with leaks and holes throughout. Inside the open huts were merely tiny straw beds. Sections of houses shared communal fireplaces outside. Evander had heard of the destitution within the Triacts, but he'd never imagined the people lived in horse stalls!

When the sheds, or he supposed shops, were close enough to jump to and fro, Jean turned to Evander.

"How did Rose get to the roof?" She asked, wide-eyed as she tried to imagine Rose jumping from one to the other noiselessly. Jean herself was known for many things in the clan, being the Farmer and wife-beater's daughter, being poor, being Gwen's older sister, and even being beautiful. But she was never *ever* known for her grace.

Evander examined the buildings, rubbing his gloved hands against the stubble that was beginning to protrude from his face. "You should have seen her in school," he grunted. "She was like a squirrel, climbing here, leaping there. Nobody ever understood how she did it." He eyed a target shed, backing away from it slowly. Then he darted back toward it, taking a giant leap and barely catching his hands on the roof's ledge. He grunted as he pulled himself atop of the roof.

Jean had not been through the training that Evander had, so this activity came harder to her. But being a farmer's daughter, she had the muscles to pull herself atop of the roof. Magnar's sword dangling awkwardly against her waist.

"You love her, don't ya?" Jean asked, smiling obnoxiously.

Evander shrugged, allowing a hint of mischief from his youth to reappear on his face. "No more than ye love Magnar."

Leaping from roof to roof, the unlikely pair made it to the town's center in no time. As they neared the square, Evander caught a glimpse of the hair on the tops of people's heads in a crowd. He quickly shoved Jean down, nearly pushing her off the roof in the process.

"Look down there," Evander mouthed. Jean stuck her head over the roof to find about a hundred people sitting on the ground below them. They all were hunched so tightly together, they had to sit criss-cross or hug their knees. Around them stood about twenty Craotics. Jean stared at them for a while, realizing she'd never seen the enemy so up close before. She'd grown so used to the Cheryic brown and pale blue kilt, that her eyes had to adjust to the new array of colors before her. The Craotic men wore red and navy kilts, faded and overworn. The men on the ground wore green and navy, the Triact colors.

A Craotic man interrupted Jean's thoughts, yelling: "Next!"

He scurried into the crowd and grabbed an old man, dragging him to the front of the crowd.

A chill went down Jean's spine as she noticed the pile of bloody bodies next to two of Craotics. They had come too late. One of the Craotics kicked the man and the rest laughed as if this was a Christmas present. The Craotic warriors grabbed the man and threw him on the ground; one of them raised its axe.

WHAM!

The axe fell to the ground with a dull thud as the Craotic warrior desperately grabbed at the arrow protruding from his throat, gushing blood. He fell with a gargling wail. Before the Craotic man next to him had figured out what was happening, an arrow impaled his scalp.

The old man sat dazed for a moment, but soon snapped back into reality as he ran for cover.

"Aaaargh!" A menacing noise came from one of the Craotics below Jean; a sound she guessed was a signal to attack Rose. She watched as Magnar pounced from the roof and landed with a thud upon the Craotic's back. He then realized the fault of his sudden outburst. He hadn't drawn his sword. He quickly placed a hand on the scalp of the man and another on the shoulder and jerked the neck sideways as hard as he could. And that was it. It was the first man Magnar had ever killed. The man fell lifelessly beneath him, and Magnar caught his balance before he fell with him.

Jean gasped as she realized Evander was jumping from the roof and attacking the nearest Craotic as well. Four down, sixteen to go. Jean took a breath and prayed silently to Gwen, yanking out her new sword and dangling awkwardly from the roof.

Jean took in her surroundings briefly. The people were watching with awe as four Craotics darted toward Evander and Magnar, ignoring Jean altogether. Magnar struggled as he tried to focus on the two Craotics he was fighting, but he was too slow. One raised his axe to Magnar's head, just in time for Jean to stab him in the back.

"Thanks!" Magnar said surprisingly.

It took all of Jean's strength not to stop and gloat.

The Craotic men whirled around in confusion, and Magnar and Evander seized the opportunity to strike at them.

Two others ran towards Rose. Big mistake. They were struck down with arrows before they could draw their axes and hammers.

Magnar slashed his sword at an incoming Craotic; he deflected it with a grunt. The Craotic man took the offense and aimed for Magnar's throat. Magnar jerked the man's sword up with his own and took the chance to stab him in the gut. The next one came at him with an axe, which Magnar ducked beneath, and stabbed him in the crotch. (Ugly, yes, but it was necessary.) Then Magnar bounced back up and beheaded the man. Jean, seeing she was no longer needed in the fight, shouted to get the crowd's attention, assuring them to stay calm and everything would be alright. They listened to her intently, for although she had never been graceful, Jean had always been gifted with charisma and eloquence. Suddenly, someone screamed. Everyone whirled around. A woman in her thirties with dirty blond hair clutched the towering Craotic's arm desperately as it held a knife held to her throat. The Craotic man didn't say a word; he just glared from Rose to Magnar to Evander to Jean.

"I dinna give a coo's lick[28] if ye kill me ye brute." The woman snarled, unafraid of the knife to her throat. The man growled. "Ye killed my husband! Ye took my son! Kill me and they will kill ya like ye deserve." She spat out each word.

---

[28] I don't care

Magnar looked to Rose's position, but she had disappeared. He searched the square desperately, wondering where she had gone when they needed her most. The Craotic man growled.

Magnar awaited Rose.

The Craotic man squeezed the woman tighter.

Magnar waited.

The man pressed the knife to the woman's skin.

Magnar prayed.

The man slit the woman's throat, roared and disappeared from the square.

The woman was dying. Rose was nowhere to be seen. Magnar ran to the woman's aid. She lay in a bloody, choking mess on the ground. She seemed to be trying to say something, but could not get the words out. Magnar realized the words she said were about her son. She wanted what Eason had wanted: for her son to live in peace.

"Your son will be safe," Magnar told her, gently caressing her hair. She nodded slightly, eyes fluttering, and her bright eyes stared off to the distance. Magnar closed them and whispered a small prayer to her spirit. "Be at peace." He finally told her, then stood to find his sister.

Evander found her first. She laid behind the roof that she had perched on, sprawled out on the ground. A bloody gash stood out on the right side of her forehead. The boys darted to her side.

"Is she breathing?" Magnar asked Evander.

He nodded.

Magnar turned to the crowd. "Are there any physicians here?"

"Aye." A man stood up and jogged toward Rose's body. "I'll help."

***

The shed was an old wooden one, much like the ones Caiden had seen back at home. The floor was damp dirt and the roof had many cracks, which gave way to tiny beams of moonlight. Caiden hated this. It gave him too much time to think as he crossed his arms, leaned against the wall and reflected. Was it two weeks ago that Eason was scolding them for placing their weapons on the table? And that quick kiss Gwen had stolen from him...was that all for nothing?

Now he sat in an old shed with a destitute six-year-old boy, wondering if the rest of his family was alive.

"Caiden?"

"Yes?"

"I have to tell you something."

Caiden glanced down at the small boy with his long white hair and wondered who on earth could have given him such strangely bright hair. It was nothing like what he had seen back in Cheryic City. His eyes were just as bright, practically a neon shade of blue.

"The Craotics were gonna take me away from my maw and da." The boy began, trying to pass the time, "I was afeart. They tried to tie me up, cause they said my da wasna behaving. They tied me up and locked me in a dark room. But they didna ken that my father was from the fisherpeople and he told me that if I place my hands a certain way when they try to tie me up, I can free my hands. So I freed my hands and untied them and ran far away. Then I found you."

It took Caiden a moment to let the information sink in. He remembered when *he* was six and he cried about losing a tooth. *This boy* had escaped a ruthless clan's siege and ran a day in the woods by himself.

"Peter, I'm so sorry," Caiden told him, rubbing his head, exasperated.

"I'm gonna be brave like you, Caiden," the boy said.

Caiden smiled sadly at the boy, for he seemed to know more about bravery than himself and even any of his friends, except for perhaps, Rose.

"You're already one of the bravest lads I know. You're even braver than adults," Caiden told him truthfully.

Peter laughed and shook his head.

"Naw. Some of the adults fighted. My da did."

Caiden considered this for a minute. "When my cousin Rose came to live with us, everyone thought she would be the clan's new Outside exotic princess, you know? She was the first princess the clan had seen in a long time, so they didn't know what to expect. Then she turned out to be a fighter. More than that, a hero. She's left behind everything she's known twice now."

"Wow," Peter gasped. "That *is* brave."

Caiden laughed, unsure of what his own point had been. "Aye, she is brave. Never known any soul braver."

Caiden began to pat Peter's head, but hesitated, for he heard a terrible growl outside the shed. Then there was a crackling sound.

"What was that?" whispered Peter.

Caiden put a finger to his lips. Slowly, Peter crawled onto his lap. Caiden put his arms around the boy's fragile figure protectively. He was so small…too small to have such pain in his life. Caiden would have taken it all away from the boy if he could have and brought it upon himself. But alas, he had nothing left to give the boy. The crackling sound continued, but the growling ceased. Peter looked up at him.

"Do ye smell something?" Peter asked.

Caiden sniffed the air…now that he mentioned it…Caiden did smell something. It was…it was…

Smoke.

Caiden pulled Peter up quickly and drew his sword. If there was a fire, it was spreading fast. The air already had a foggy hue to it, which Caiden had neglected to notice. Peter was beginning to cough.

"Let's go," Caiden commanded, picking Peter up in one arm and holding his sword in the other.

Caiden ran outside with the boy in his arm, gaping at the roof, which had caught fire. In fact, the buildings surrounding him were rapidly catching fire, lighting up the night sky. Caiden dropped Peter to the ground, attempting to keep their heads below the smoke.

Perhaps he was hallucinating, but Caiden swore he could see a pair of pale eyes through a window, and a rotting smile laughing at them. Then it disappeared, leaving only a trail of flames in his wake. Caiden searched desperately for any means of escape. He made Peter pull his shirt over his nose, and Caiden did the same thing with his cloak, though it didn't help much. They began coughing laboriously. Caiden decided they should try and make their way further into the village. Holding Peter in one arm, Caiden shakily stood and ran as fast as he could through the flames, hacking and coughing as he did. Hot…so hot... *Focus,* he told himself. He could feel his sweat immediately evaporating in the air as his body struggled in vain to cool him down. Caiden stopped and looked toward where he thought he was going. The ground…it was moving…up and down, round and round. Caiden had to lie down. He dropped Peter again and fell to the ground, which took him in like a pillow on a frosty evening.

"Caiden, get up," said a voice.

Caiden squinted his eyes, searching wildly for the source of the voice, when he saw it—a dirt road. He had no idea where it led, but he pushed himself up, still clutching Peter, who was now dangling unconsciously. With his final ounce of energy, Caiden sprinted through the street, clutching Peter. His vision remained groggy, but his destination was clear in his head.

He could make it.

Magnar stops thinking

Rose blinked her eyes open, but closed them almost immediately. The light was painful as beams made its way through the exposed hut she lay in. She blocked the sun with her hand and opened her eyes again. Evander's face hovered above her, startling her to the point of laughter. She poked his cheek.

He grinned, realizing how ridiculous he must look. He pulled away from Rose to give her space.

"What happened?" Rose asked groggily.

"We took the village back."

Rose reached toward her head and felt a rough cloth that had been tightly wrapped around it. She grimaced as the pain came flooding back to her, waking her out of her dazed state.

"Did Caiden and Peter come back yet?"

Evander shook his head. "Magnar's out looking for him."

Rose stared into Evander's blue eyes. One of Evander's talents had always been concealing his emotions, something neither Caiden nor Rose could ever do. There was something different in Evander's eyes today. Something he was hiding.

Rose began pushing herself up, grimacing at the wave of nausea that washed over her.

"Careful," Evander told her, his face guarded. He subconsciously traced his fingers over the mole on the top of his right cheekbone.

"What?" Rose asked him, annoyed at how casually he was acting when they literally had just saved an entire village from imminent death.

"What do ya mean?" Evander asked, drawing his brows together, forming deep lines that made him look much older than his mere eighteen years.

Rose crossed her arms as fast as her head allowed her to do so.

"Evander, I've known you for eleven years...what's wrong?"

Evander smiled. "I always ken in my heart that no matter what reckless, stupid, hell-bent act you're getting into...you'll come back. At least that's what I tell myself. But it just occurred to me today...what happens if I'm wrong?"

Rose shrugged. "Please," she laughed, "I am invincible."

Evander rolled his eyes and shoved her back into the hay. "Yer the worst person to be serious with, ye ken?"

Rose giggled. "I know."

***

Droplets of rain doused his hair as Magnar struggled to find his brother. He had seen the far end of the town go up in flames, but due to some miracle which he could only attribute to the spirits, the rain was beginning to fall. Hard. Magnar ran as fast as he could toward the flames, which slowly fizzled out, letting big clouds of steam rise up.

There they were. Caiden plodded toward Magnar, just outside the buildings of fire. Magnar watched in awe as Caiden set Peter down at Magnar's feet and then fell to his knees, gasping and heaving, grabbing his brother's hands for support. Then he fell unconscious. His mouth dangled open as his face pressed against the mud. Peter was conscious again, showing resilience to the smoke. Magnar told Peter to climb onto his back and he cradled his brother like a babe, carrying him back to the camp.

***

Caiden awoke to Magnar's loud whispers.

"Well, we can't tell him right away...the boy…the boy is fine-, no give it a few days, what can we do about it now? He looks…"

Suddenly a face hovered above Caiden, blond locks hanging down and brushing his nose. Caiden sneezed.

"He's awake!" Magnar said.

Two other faces hovered above Caiden.

"How are you, little brother?"

"Alright," Caiden lied. His head throbbed and his hands quivered, unable to grab a hold of anything without shaking profusely. Magnar returned the response with a pitiful frown, his lower lip curling. Caiden smiled and rolled his eyes.

"This is my fault," Magnar began. "We let a Craotic man escape. He must've tried to wreak havoc on the way, setting fire to the outer huts-"

"Where's Rose?" Caiden interjected.

Magnar grunted, "You and Rose can't seem to stay out of trouble."

Caiden began pushing himself up as well as he could manage, but coughed uncontrollably.

"Ah-ah-ah," Magnar said, nudging Caiden back down. "She's just got a bit of a gash on her head. Nothing to worry about. She'll be up and running in a week."

Caiden tried to remember what had happened. It came back in fragments: the flames, the shed, seeing the Craotic through the fire, Peter. *Peter.*

"Where's-"

"Peter's fine. He's…he's fine." Magnar interrupted.

A sinking feeling overtook Caiden. "What do you mean he's fine?"

"No Caiden, really, he's physically in better shape than you are. There's something else."

Caiden studied his brother; his hair was tousled and dirty. His clothes were covered in blood. He had a small cut below his eye, and his face needed some serious washing. His eyes were pink, swollen, and baggy. He had a piece of straw between his fingers and was breaking it into little bits subconsciously, his mind elsewhere.

"Tell me," Caiden ordered. Magnar glanced up at Caiden and then back down at the floor.

"We found out who his parents were."

"If you're gonna tell me that Peter's dad is dead, he already told me," Caiden interrupted.

Magnar hesitated, still avoiding eye contact with his little brother.

"When we attacked the Craotics, we...we missed one. But we killed all of the others." Magnar let out a breath, then quickened the talking pace. "I was such a fool to assume victory. There was a woman, a blond woman, who the tall Craotic man threatened with a knife. I had assumed Rose was on the roof aiming for him, so I never commanded anyone to lower their weapons. He slit her throat, Caiden; it killed her. Then when she was dying, she tried to tell me to find her son."

A tear ran down Caiden's cheek as he realized what Magnar was alluding to.

"Her son is Peter."

***

After a day, Rose moved to Caiden's hut so she could watch over him. She regretted it almost instantly. Magnar and Caiden fought endlessly over the next week. Caiden, being the dreamer he was, insisted upon adopting Peter. Magnar, being the logical mind, claimed that this was a stupid idea because they were, in fact, homeless. Rose just watched, unsure of her take on the matter. She supposed she agreed with Magnar; they were in no position to care for a child, but she admired Caiden's passion.

One day, however, Magnar growled hopelessly and stormed away, leaving Caiden with Rose, Evander, and Jean, who had come to dress his burns. Jean, of course, had overheard the whole thing and remained silent as she often did. Jean's silence often annoyed Rose in the past. She thought Jean was a horrible example for the women of the clan, often keeping her opinions to herself when arguments erupted. But lately, Rose had begun to appreciate it.

Jean was a wallflower. She stopped and observed the ongoings surrounding her, formulated her opinions with poise, and found ideal moments to utilize them. She was silent, but strategic. When Magnar stormed out of the hut, she took Caiden by the hand and used her gift.

"The Triacts have an orphanage that we can take the boy to," Jean said firmly, holding her hand up before he could interrupt. "They can care for the boy until we reclaim our home. Then Caiden, when the time is right, you can come back for him, and give him the home he deserves."

Caiden nodded, too weak to complain anymore. He drifted off to sleep in his mound of hay. Jean gave a small wink to Rose and Evander, then left to find Magnar.

Evander exhaled dramatically, leaning against the wall of the hut with his eyes closed.

"Caiden's depressed," he said blandly.

"He's had a long week," Rose added.

Evander nodded slowly, fiddling with a wooden necklace in his hand.

"What is it?" Rose asked.

Evander hesitated a moment, then realized she was referring to the necklace. "My maw's."

Rose scooted herself beside him, holding her hand out eagerly. Evander half-tossed her the necklace, which she examined. It was a simple design, yet beautiful. A wooden circle enclosed a tree, which spread its branches out to each of the sides. Rose smiled and tossed it back to Evander, who wrapped it into a bracelet.

"She was beautiful."

Evander glanced at Rose, shaking his head and grinning. "She always loved you, ye ken. She said you would be the one to set the women free."

Rose grunted.

"You ken Rose, I tried to tell ye this that day. That terrible day…when The Chief…"

He looked back down shyly, his fingers sifting through sawdust.

"He was like a father to me as well...which is why this is so awkward..."

Rose laughed, "spit it out, Evander, the entire clan has known what you're about to say for years now."

Evander blinked.

"You love me, no?" Rose batted her eyes innocently.

Evander's cheeks flushed. "Caiden canna keep a secret, can he?"

"Aye, you should be wiser before you spill your heart to people."

Evander laughed heartily. "Well, so should you. I heard that ye love me too, and even told a wee midgie that ye'd want to marry when the time is right, of course."

"Aye, perhaps." Rose grinned.

"Really?!" Evander let out a sigh of relief.

"You just said you heard that!"

"I was attempting to be smooth."

Rose rolled her eyes. "I'm a soldier now, but I've a heart still. Aye, I used to think it'd be great to die in a blaze of glory at the field of battle as Caiden always says. But I- I want more. And who better to teach me more than the man who taught me to shoot?"

Evander pulled Rose up off the ground, whirling her around to a silent tune.

"It's settled then," Evander cheered. "Perhaps in our old life, I would have requested permission to court from your uncle."

"And he would have said, *nope.*"

"Or aye...which is what he said."

"You asked?"

Evander shrugged, his eyes twinkling.

"Wait," Rose paused. "Does this mean I can't make fun of you anymore?"

Evander considered this. "I imagine it means you have much more time to make fun of me than you would've otherwise."

"Soooo…" Rose began, "this hair…"

She pounced toward his shaggy blond hair, tripping over Caiden in the process. The poor boy moaned. The two froze, looking down at the stirring sack on the ground. They had forgotten he was there.

A bell sounded in the distance.

Evander and Rose darted up, and Caiden batted his eyes open.

"Wait here." Both Evander and Rose said to Caiden, who drifted to sleep again.

The new lovers ran off to find Magnar, who stood conversing with Laird Gavin, the young freckled-faced laird of Oir Coelle.

"Was that a warning bell?" Rose asked. "Are Craotics coming back?"

Magnar shook his head. "Naw, it is the Triact Chief and some of his army."

Rose hesitated. "Army?"

"It appears our Chief knows not your intentions in lingering here." Laird Gavin replied, placing a hand upon Magnar's shoulder.

Magnar turned to Rose. "Do not make your presence known until I say it is safe to do so."

"Where are you going?" Rose asked.

Magnar brushed out his hair, attempting to make himself look presentable. He hastily dusted off his kilt and threw a vest on over his tunic.

"To talk to the Triact Chief."

***

The Triact Chief was a short and stocky young man, with black locks and eyes that reminded Magnar of a bottomless pit. These contrasted with his skin, which resembled the moon. This was a typical trait of the Triact people. Most lived north and beneath the trees of the forests. There was no sun exposure to add any color to the skin.

The Chief sat straight upon his horse, walking it through the village, paying no attention to the commoners bowing their heads beside him. Behind him, forty men marched in eight neat rows of five.

Magnar approached the Chief with Laird Gavin. Immediately upon sight, two of The Triact Chief's archers aimed their arrows at Magnar, awaiting an order to strike. Civilians screamed in fear, for they did not want their saviors to be shot.

Magnar raised his hands above his head. "I come in peace, Gliocas."

The Triact Chief looked down upon Magnar, narrowing his eyes.

"This town is mine," he said, "it has been Triact land since Aklen Triact claimed it with his own sword. Ye canna take it."

"I don't want your land, Gliocas," Magnar said, his hands still in the air. "There are far too many dangers in the world now for us to be haggling over soil."

The Triact Chief hesitated, then gestured for his archers to lower their bows. "You sound like your uncle," he said.

"Aye, he was wise."

The Triact Chief dismounted his horse and led Magnar to a hut away from the soldiers and townspeople. He poured Magnar some ale. Magnar took it and thanked him graciously.

"Why are ya here, then?" the Triact Chief asked.

Magnar shrugged. "The village needed saving from Craotic mercy, so my kin and I saved it."

The Chief laughed a deep, hearty laugh. "You and your four friends, ya mean."

Magnar bit his lip.

The Chief grinned and peered out the window. "Aye, I ken about your friends. Mind, your people are with me now. They came to us a week ago with their new Chief. But let me tell ya, rumors are spreading fast around the Triact clan. Legends of how the four of ya stopped an entire Craotic army spread like wildfire, see. They believe you will be the one to get Scotland out of the mess it's in. Jean the Eloquent, Evander the Cunning, Caiden the Dauntless, Rose the Fierce and Magnar the Honorable will reclaim their homeland."

Magnar rubbed his beard nervously, unsure of where this was going.

"Here's my offer," the Chief said, leaning in toward Magnar, "I love my land. I dinna want to see it go to ruin, for then there would be nothing left of me. But already, my name is going to dust due to...well…that is my own business."

The Chief took a deep breath. It was hot, for a Scottish day, yet he still wore a large coat of black fur.

"I want to give ya two thousand of my men so long as ye do the leading and fighting. But ye must clear my name."

Magnar froze. "Clear your name?"

"I am young, Magnar, and I was too young when I became Chief. I didna ken not what I did. My people admire you, Magnar. They'd rather see you as their Chief than myself. So I ask ya...include me in yer legend. Make it known that I was happy to support the defense of Scotland, that I was a key part in this great war."

Magnar nodded, too shocked to speak in more than a whisper.

"Gliocas," he said, "if what you say is true, and you are giving me two thousand men...then you are not only a key part of this war, but a hero of it."

The Triact Chief smiled contentedly, his eyes reddening with joy and relief. "I return to your people, Magnar," he said, standing up to leave again. "We ride home to Baile Beatha."

Before he left, he turned back to the young prince.

"Magnar."

"Aye?"

The Triact Chief seemed conflicted with what he was about to say, his eyes deeply pained. "Yer people are happy. I think it best that ye keep yer distance from them. Least for a while. Best not to overcomplicate their lives."

Magnar felt as if tiny knives were stabbing him inside out.

"Aye."

***

"You sent for me, Gliocas?"

Evander stood with a poised posture and hands held behind his back. They had remained in the Triact village for a few weeks to ensure both the Twins' recoveries. Evander was clearly becoming antsy from staying in the village for such a time.

Magnar laughed. "I am not Chief, my friend. And even if I did become Chief, I do not want you, of all people, to treat me with such formalities."

Evander relaxed his stance. "Magnar, it is my suggestion that in public, I treat ye with the proper respects, so ye may gain the respect of yer men as well."

Magnar nodded thoughtfully. "I am not Chief, Evander. I never will be."

Evander took a seat in the hay of the hut and waited patiently for Magnar to do the same.

"We have two thousand Triact men, Evander," Magnar began from his seat. "The Triact Chief is more than generous."

Evander widened his eyes. "We can win."

Magnar shook his head. "No...no this war is much more than that. Southern Scotland is swarming with more than just Craotics... The farmlands in the south, which the Farmpeople once possessed, have been destroyed in a fire. The Triact spies tell me this was a natural disaster, likely caused by dry lands."

Evander sat like a statue, unmoving, with his emotions heavily guarded. Magnar assessed him, trying to see if he had reached the same conclusion as he had, but Evander did nothing.

"We are not in a drought. There have been no reports of droughts. But if it was not a natural disaster, then who did it? The Farmspeople have always been neutral allies, with their land useful to feed the hungry of both Craotics and Cheryics."

Magnar studied Evander some more, until finally Evander let out a sigh and said what Magnar wanted to hear: "We are being attacked by the Outside."

Magnar nodded.

"But that violates so many laws of Scotland; they canna use the Outside against other clans."

"No," Magnar said. "They can. They just are not allowed to. I was there, Evander, when the Craotic Chief was the only one to not cast the Outside out of their lands. I am positive that the Outside is backing the Craotics. My uncle was afraid of the Outside, of their destruction. The Craotics are fools if they think that the Outside is doing this for their benefit. If the Outsiders win, Scotland, as we know it, will change forever."

Evander wrung his palms on his lap. It was enough of a demonstration for Magnar to know that he was just as alarmed as Magnar felt. They both knew Magnar's words rang true, but neither one wanted to fully accept this reality.

"But why?" Evander asked quietly.

Magnar shrugged. "Land."

"But they've plenty! What do they want with ours?"

Magnar shook his head. "I don't know.

"What happens when they've driven us to the northernmost tip of Scotland?"

Magnar shook his head.

Evander crossed his legs and propped his elbows upon his knees, leaning forward.

"And you think two thousand men is no enough?"

Magnar took a bite of an apple. "It may be enough to hold the border in an open field...but that won't help us for long. The Outside has numbers, even with the weapons ban."

Evander waited for Magnar to continue, but Magnar's eyes wandered into the clouds.

"What do ya propose?"

Magnar awoke from his little daydream and focused back on Evander.

"We unite the clans," Magnar smiled, awaiting the protests from Evander.

They came quickly.

"Are ye daft?" Evander gasped. "That hasna been done since Owen Cheryic himself ruled over Scotland."

"Aye," Magnar said, "And even then, these lands were separated into two countries. And our people hid in the mountains, separate from the Outside."

"So how?" Evander asked, crossing his arms skeptically.

Magnar shrugged. "When the Triact Chief spoke to me, he told me that rumors travelled and the people are holding us up on pedestals. They see us as legends, my friend. We can use this sort of immortality to charm the Chiefs of the two remaining clans in Scotland."

"The Duchannons and The Fisherpeople."

"Aye."

The door slammed open and a wriggling body was thrown on the floor by Laird Gavin. The boy quickly struggled onto his knees the best he could with his hands tied behind his back. His face was covered in flaming red hair.

"This boy claims to know ya. Been lurking about the village, calling for ya," Laird Gavin spat.

The boy blew his hair from his face.

Magnar and Evander gasped.

"Hiya lads," Fergus's voice cracked through bloody teeth.

"Well?" Laird Gavin asked.

"Aye," Magnar muttered under his breath."We know him."

Laird Gavin looked from Magnar to Evander awkwardly, then began backing toward the door.

"Well...I'll leave ya alone then." He mumbled as he left.

There was an uncomfortable tension in the room as the three boys stared for a while, until finally, Magnar said, "What in the name of Owen Cheryic himself are ya doin' here?"

Fergus laughed for a while. He looked about twenty pounds thinner, and his smile created hollow holes in his cheeks.

"Untie me, will ya?"

Evander looked to Magnar, who nodded his head at him. Evander took his knife and cut through Fergus's bonds. Fergus stretched and rubbed his wrists, leaning his back against the hut's wall.

"You're a fool, Gliocas," he muttered.

"How dare ya?!" Evander yelled, holding a knife to Fergus's face.

Magnar held a hand out to Evander, calling him back. Evander relaxed, but remained on his guard, not taking his eyes from Fergus's hands.

"Well, ye've been through a lot, have ya?" Fergus said, his head still comfortably resting against the wall. "Yer much quicker to violence now."

"What do you mean, 'I'm a fool', Fergus?" Magnar asked, kneeling to Fergus's level.

Fergus sighed. "Our people are suffering. The Triact Chief...he's taking us as slaves. Our men are forced to work in the fields and our women as servants. The Chief has already executed three men as demonstrations, including yer beloved Rory Silver, who was supposed to save the people from all wreckage. Children work within the Triact's houses, families are separated, all for no food for days at a time."

Magnar fell to his knees and bowed his head. "What have I done?" He asked no one in particular.

"Magnar...that army he sold you it was blood money. He rid himself of his guilt for what he did to our people by giving you those men."

Magnar said nothing.

"You must save them."

Magnar stood and paced the room. There was a dull pain in his chest and head as his palms shook. He chose to release this tension with a sudden outburst as he punched through the cabin wall. He turned back to Evander, tears in his eyes.

"How can I protect my family and my people at the same time?"

Evander said nothing.

There was a rustling outside the window as if someone had lost their footing and fallen into straw. Magnar darted out the door, his sword in hand. He then immediately sheathed it and rolled his eyes upon seeing who it was.

"What are you doing here?" he asked irritatedly.

Rose and Jean sat in the bushes with their arms crossed and their lips curling into a pout.

"I was trainin' her and passed by here...and just happened to overhear..." Rose said. "What are you going to do about the Triacts?"

Magnar shrugged, restless about being out in the open while discussing such secretive matters.

"Fight em, I guess."

"With your two thousand men?"

Magnar nodded.

Rose snorted. "I'm coming too!"

Magnar rolled his eyes, "Okay."

"Really?" Rose raised her brows. "You're not gonna fight me?"

"What's the point?" Magnar replied monotonously.

Jean tsked, smoothing the folds of her brown linen dress. "You mean you're gonna fight the Triact Chief with two thousand Triact men?"

"Oh...I suppose not."

Rose slunked back into the straw, pouting as she did. She looked eerily similar to the little seven year-old-girl pouting in the window from so many years ago.

Jean laughed. "Why waste men anyway? There are laws that may be used."

"Laws?"

"Like laws of Scotland."

Magnar stared at her blankly.

Jean rolled her eyes and scurried away with Rose trailing behind her.

"What was that all about?" Evander asked.

Magnar shook his head. "I never know with Rose until it's too late. Jean, I never know, period."

Fergus peered outside the door. "Are we having a party?" he asked. "Because last time I checked, we were trying to save Scotland as we know it."

Magnar rolled his eyes and walked back inside with Evander, who had a smirk glued to his face.

"There's something else," Fergus said, once they had settled again.

"What?" both the boys asked eagerly.

"There was a diplomat or ambassador of some sort. It was a woman. An Outside woman."

Evander and Magnar exchanged glances.

"Are you saying the Outside has allied with the Triact Clan?"

Fergus nodded.

Evander groaned and fell to the floor, holding his hands to his head. "I suppose we're down two thousand men now and are about to need pretty much every man Sluagh na Mara and the Duchannons have to offer."

the Twin's adventure

"They're gone."

Magnar rubbed his eyes open from his position lying in the hay. Only the soft murmur of cicadas could be heard outside. Above him, Evander's hair dangled as he towered in his standing position.

"What?" Magnar asked sleepily.

"They've run." Evander said.

Magnar's eyes widened as he realized what this meant. He rolled to his feet and darted toward the Twins' hut. Their swords, bags, the photo, Eason's memoirs, clothes, bow, and everything that had once been cluttering the tiny room were gone.

"Fergus and Jean are missing as well." Evander said as he caught up to Magnar.

"But where-"

"They left this note." Evander replied, handing the parchment to Magnar.

In Jean's handwriting, it said:

U.S. Article 3, Section 2. We've got Triacts. Go to Fisher Chief.

"What is it with everyone we know and their ridiculously vague notes?" Magnar murmured. He hurried to Laird Gavin's hut. It was larger than those of his people's and bigger than two of Eason's houses put together. Magnar did not care to knock. He opened the door and rushed to the Laird's chambers. The man sat upright in his bed immediately upon Magnar's intrusion.

"United Scotland Article 3, Section 2. What is it?"

The Laird furrowed his brows and bade Magnar to turn so he could fetch a robe. Then he looked toward a shelf adjacent to his bed, dusting off a thick book from it.

"Ah," he said. "It's the one that says that between clans, Kings can be challenged to one on one combat by royal blood of other clans to lessen the deaths of soldiers." He hesitated. "You're not-"

"No, not the Craotic Chief. He's already broken too many Scottish laws to be true to his word," he said. "But the Triact Chief...perhaps."

The Laird sat himself down in an armchair. The man's allegiance, as he had said many times, was no longer with the Triact Chief, but with Magnar for saving the village. The man had been kind enough to provide food and lodging so far, and now, Magnar knew he would provide his silence.

Magnar turned back to Evander, who'd been struggling to keep up with Magnar throughout his discoveries.

"We need to get there before they do," Magnar said and began to run out of the room.

"Wait!" Evander called, his feet glued to the ground.

Magnar stopped in his tracks, rolling back around toward Evander. "What is it?"

"We need to go to Sluagh na Mara."

Magnar narrowed his eyes at Evander. "The Fisherpeople? Did you not hear anything that just happened? Your woman is out there about to foolishly risk her neck!"

"She is wise-" Evander began.

Magnar scoffed.

"She *is* wise! If she deems it wise to risk her neck, I must respect her."

"Hardly the Cheryic clan's way of thinking," Magnar grumbled.

"Tis my way of thinking," Evander said, stepping between the doorway and Magnar. Magnar tried to push through, but Evander would not let him. "Magnar, my friend-"

"You shall address me as Gliocas!" Magnar yelled, his face reddening.

The room was silent. Laird Gavin sat awkwardly in his corner chair, observing the interaction in his night robe.

"Gliocas," Evander said softly. "She is saving all of us."

"How?!" Magnar shouted.

"The Triact Chief may refuse a challenge. If she challenges him and he refuses, he'll look like a coward for refusing a woman, and he will underestimate her, giving her the advantage!"

Magnar shook his head. "I can't let her." He tried to push past Evander again, but Evander pushed him down, unsheathing his sword. He pointed it at Magnar's chin. Magnar's hands shook and tears poured down his face. He stayed on the ground, holding his head between his knees. "How can you understand?" he seethed. "You've never had a family to look after. Your mother is dead. Your father is missing. Stop pretending to understand things that you've not experienced."

There was a slight twinge in Evander's upper right cheekbone, and Magnar could tell his insults hit home.

There was a knock on the door.

Magnar and Evander turned to the door. Jean cracked it open and stuck her pale head inside.

"I see ye realized the Twins left."

Magnar rose to his feet, attempting to regain his composure. "You have returned?"

"No," Jean said. "Well, aye, *I* have. But the twins havena. I just saw them off and thought my use would be better here, where I can help guide ya."

"Guide *me*?" Magnar snorted. "I'll be ok."

"I'm the one who gave them the law and told them to go," Jean said bluntly. "I want to make that clear before ye find out another way."

Magnar's ears turned bright pink and his eyes seemed to brighten into an angered, piercing shade of light green. Evander whistled and took a step back to stand next to Laird Gavin, who was now having a cup of tea and reading a book.

"Why?" Magnar asked.

"Because it was what needed to be done," Jean said. "And you would have stopped them if ye found out."

"Aye, well, you got *one* thing right," Magnar spat on the ground and paced up and down Laird Gavin's chambers for a few moments, until he finally said, "Jean and I will ride to Sluagh na Mara in the morning. Evander, you must take whatever men Laird Gavin allows you and station them along the Triact border. I will send you as many men as I can, but be ready for my call, for when I do, you will attack Cheryic City."

"Shouldna we wait until we know where all of the Outsiders are stationed?"

"We *do* know where they're stationed," Magnar replied.

"Cheryic City?"

"Aye," Magnar nodded, standing up from the floor, wiping his trousers. "Cheryic City."

***

Rose hated Fergus with every ounce of her being. She hated that he knew more information than her of their people and she despised the fact that she needed him to accompany them to Baile Beatha. But there was no choice. She needed a guide to tell her where the people and the Chief were.

She had woken Caiden in the dead of night, who, of course, went with her without question. He was fully healed now and stir-crazy for adventure. They rode hard and fast with Fergus leading the way.

After a day of riding, they set up their camp at Fergus's suggestion on a cliff that overlooked the sea. Caiden built a fire and the children sat idly staring at the flame before going to bed.

After a few minutes of shut-eye, however, Rose was nudged awake by Caiden. "Do ya hear that?" He whispered.

She sat up. The fire had gone out, so it took her a minute for her eyes to adjust.

There was some rustling in the bushes.

Rose jumped to her feet. The bags were already packed in case they needed to run. She put one on her back and picked up her bow, placing an arrow in it. Caiden kicked Fergus awake as well, who jerked up to an upright sitting position, his ears perking.

Rose stared off into the darkness of the forest. She pulled her string back and shot into the abyss.

A startling wail sounded from the trees and there was a big thud. More rustling. Deep voices shouted orders in Gaelic.

"Run." Rose ordered, and then shouted louder. "Run!"

Rose ran and jumped onto her horse from behind, then realized it was still tied to a tree. She pulled out her sword and cut the reigns that bound it. They set off with a sprint.

The three of them rode quickly along the edge of the cliff, but before they knew it, the cloaked figures were gaining on them, nearly riding alongside of her. Rose strung a few arrows in her bow...but there were too many of them. She exchanged glances with Caiden, who was fighting a few with his sword. She threw her pack off of her, and with her sword, bow, and scabbard in hand, she leapt off of the horse.

And she fell.

In her peripheral vision, she saw Caiden falling clumsily beside her. She mumbled a quick prayer to Eason, hoping none of them would smack rocks as they hit the water. Behind her, she could hear Fergus yell, "Och! Why me?!"

And he was off the cliff as well.

Rose hit the water with a thud. She lost herself for a moment, forgetting where she was, who she was...and then she remembered. She swam back to the surface, gasping for air. She wildly looked around her and then gave a sigh of relief. Caiden had surfaced as well...and a bit less lucky for her, Fergus was perfectly fine.

The three swam, avoiding getting too close to the cliff for fear of the waves knocking them against it. They swam around until they found a small rocky shore. The three crawled onto it, breathing heavily and taking a moment to rest their eyes.

As soon as Rose regained her energy, she shoved Fergus back into the water and drew her sword.

"What in the name of Owen Cheryic?!" Fergus asked, struggling to retain his balance in the waves that kept knocking pebbles against his ankles.

Caiden just stared in wide-eyed confusion.

"Do you honestly think I don't suspect you, Fergus? That I don't know you're playing us?" Rose shouted angrily.

Fergus just gaped at her. "What are ye-"

"You think I think it's a coincidence that you were the last one to leave Cheryic City alive, the only one to escape the Triact Chief, and now are leading Craotics to us?"

Fergus held his hands up in self-defense, panting. "Rose ye dinna honestly believe-"

"No." Rose spat, breathing hard, with her hands to her knees. When she regained her composure, she looked back at the red-head kid who had harassed her for all of those years. He seemed so small now, with his wet firey hair sticking awkwardly to his pale freckled cheeks. "But it's hard not to."

The Twins slept for the rest of the night, snuggling together for warmth, for they were wet and cold and no longer had any supplies. Fergus attempted to sleep alone on the other side of the beach, shivering and hugging his knees for warmth.

The next day, it was Caiden's bright idea for them to attempt to climb the cliff. As Rose was nimble, she climbed ahead of the boys and made it up in under an hour. Caiden, however, realized only after he was five feet off the ground, that he was not a fan of heights. He proceeded to whimper the rest of the way and screamed like a small child when he lost his footing. Fergus, who climbed below him, prayed to all the spirits that Caiden would not wet himself. Luckily, as far as Fergus could tell, Caiden did not. And that is when Fergus realized that the spirits were truly real after all.

the Twins don't waste the day

Sluagh na Mara was known as the city of fishermen because, well, it was a city of fishermen. It was a tall and proud island west of the mainland of Scotland. Although technically the Fisher Chief had rights to some of the northern territory of the mainland, they scarcely used it. The Fisher Chief loved to be surrounded by the sea, however uninhabitable the land seemed to other clans.

Magnar remembered Eason's opinions of the Fisherland. Whenever he needed to ride there, he loathed it and was miserable in the hours before. It was a rocky boat ride and the island smelled of nothing but rotting fish and seaweed. It was dark, nearly always rained, and the Fisher Chief was to Eason, "A real pain in the arse." He was a loud, rambunctious man, who had many wives and did not believe in the spirits of the earth. He said exactly what he meant, precisely when he wanted.

And the food, Eason had said, was the worst part of all. It was a wonder that the islanders had not all died of disease, for all of their diets consisted of fish. Perhaps the seaweed was giving them the means to survive, but there was not much else to eat vegetation-wise.

Mara was the clan's capital. It rested on the sea's edge and boats came to and fro. Jean and Magnar hastily boarded a ship in Iasgach. But it was nearly a two day journey to reach the island.

"Do ye miss them?" Jean asked as they watched the reflection of the moon on the water. They had gone to the top deck for air, both slightly seasick from the rocking. Valar had permanently perched herself on the ship's mast and watched over the two intensely.

"Of course." Magnar said. "I'd give my right arm to know they were safe."

Jean smiled. "I'd rip the heart from my chest if I could have my sister back...just for one day."

Magnar looked at her face, which was lit only by the moonlight and the glow of a torch nearby, the warm and cool lighting contrasting each other upon her milky skin.

"Jean, I-"

"Rose has been teachin' me," she said, a smirk forming on her lips. "To fight, I mean."

Magnar gave a sigh of relief for the light-hearted subject change. "Is she a good teacher?"

Jean laughed. "Never been the most patient, I suppose. But she is the best."

Magnar smiled, silently gazing at how large the moon seemed, and suddenly realizing this was the safest he'd felt since the attack on the clan. They were surrounded by nothing but ocean. He'd know if his enemies were near, because, well, he could see them. He envied the Fisherpeople.

"Evander finally told Rose he loves her then, yes?" Jean asked.

"Aye," Magnar replied, still unsure about how he felt about Rose's betrothal.

"And how do ye feel about that?"

"Weird." The word escaped from Magnar's lips faster than he could think it. He liked Evander. He trusted Evander with his life. But not with Rose's.

"Ye'll have to allow it," Jean said, and she took Magnar's coarse hand in her own, gazing into his green eyes, which glowed like a cat's.

"I already did."

"Not them," Jean replied, her eyes not wavering from his own, "allow her to be protected by another...one that's not yerself."

Magnar snorted. "She doesn't need protecting."

Jean shrugged. "But yer protective nonetheless."

Magnar nodded, suddenly getting a flashback to walking Cinnie home after Rose and Caiden had been in the fight with those thugs. *Cinnie.* He hadn't thought of her for so long. His mind had been so conflicted at her death that he had chosen to rid himself of the memory altogether. If he had to do it again, he still would have argued for Rose's honor, but she never deserved to die. He remembered holding her in his arms in her final moments, feeling her suffer as she clung to him. He shuddered to think if that had been Jean. But Jean...she was so different than Cinnie. Less proper. More understanding. She knew things just by looking at people. She could make a valuable queen one day.

"I'll be expected to marry one of the princesses of one of the clans to form an alliance," Magnar said.

Jean said nothing.

"Or...I suppose I could marry a commoner...show the clan I am one of them, earn their respect."

Jean made a small smile. "I think that might be a good idea."

The stars multiplied around their heads, forming bright reflections along the crests of the waves. In one quiet moment, aside from the sound of the waves making their laps against the wood of the ship, Jean rested her head against Magnar's shoulder.

***

Fergus and the Twins finally arrived in Triact City. They trudged inside the gates, weak with hunger. The Triact people all stopped in their tracks and stared at the muddy, beaten, skinny royals. Some laughed. Others exchanged looks, afraid. The rest ran to their homes and barred their doors, concerned about the prospect of an attack, knowing that the clan had much to repent for. The Twins simply marched to The Great Throne, where The Triact Chief looked down upon them with cold beady eyes. He was nestled in his usual vivacious furs, worn regally over his green and blue kilt. His black locks curled wildly around his head, and his beard had thickened since the Twins had last seen him. Many would have called him an attractive young man, had he not been aged by his position.

"Yer people warned yer brother that neither he nor you are to ever return and yet ye dishonor their request after I took yer people in so generously *and* gave ya troops to take yer land back?" The Chief stood up, pacing in front of the throne. "How dare ye return?"

People began to gather around the square, watching in excitement at the conflict that was emerging. Caiden allowed them to settle before speaking.

"Where are our people, Gliocas?" Caiden said, deepening his voice. "We have heard rumors that you have kept them as slaves."

The Triact Chief snorted.

"We *demand* for them to be returned to us."

The Triact Chief did not speak.

"Alright then," Caiden responded. "The Cheryic Clan requests a challenge, Gliocas, between a Cheryic Royal and the Triact Chief."

The Chief looked around the square at the faces peering the situation attentively, then laughed. "Ye dare challenge me?" he asked. He paused for a moment, scanning the crowd again. "No."

"I'm afraid I'm feeling a bit peely wally and cannot fight today," Caiden responded.

Rose stepped up. "I am fighting in his stead."

The Chief could not contain his laughter, nor could the crowd. They looked from the Chief to Rose back to the Chief apprehensively. Some of them shook their friends' arms in excitement, while others just stood with their arms crossed, watching the situation with an intense focus. "Take er down, Gliocas!" One man shouted, while another yelled, "Don't let 'em step on ye this way!" The Chief froze, taking in all of the eager faces and then glared at the twins repugnantly. He grunted.

"Very well," He said, masking his annoyance with a humorous smile. "I accept."

The crowd all laughed and cheered.

"Just a simple request Gliocas," Rose added, seeing how far she could push her luck.

"Yes?" The Chief grumbled.

"May I have a bite to eat before the fight?"

The crowd roared with laughter, as did the Chief.

"Somebody get this lass a final meal!"

***

Magnar marched inside the throne room with Jean trailing behind respectfully. The room was a giant hall with high ceilings and oak walls that towered above Magnar's head. Windows stretched above him as well, with droplets of rain stuck to the glass, reflecting the sea, which was all that could be seen of the world outside. The Fisherlands was essentially one enormous building, with people, poor and smelling like seawater, crowding the rooms. Outside, a few huts managed to perch upon a few high rocks, but they never lasted long. They often were swept away by storms. Most people resided here in the castle or on ships.

Upon seeing the Fisher Chief, Magnar bowed his head. The Fisher Chief was a huge man, just as the tales said he was. He must have been four hundred pounds, towering above the ground like a giant. His great beard was just as magnificent, as it fell down past his immense stomach and was organized in a series of ginger braids and weaves.

"I am Magnar Edom Rankin, heir to the Cheryic throne," Magnar announced.

The Chief nodded dismissively. "Aye, I've heard of yer coming."

Magnar frowned. He remembered how brash the Fisher Chief had been when he last saw him and had often heard his uncle complain about the man's temper. Magnar shuddered. If *Eason* thought that the Fisher Chief had a temper, well, Magnar did not want to rile him up.

"Scotland needs your help, Gliocas."

"Scotland?" the Chief snorted. "What have the clans ever done for me?"

Magnar hesitated. Sluagh na Mara was isolated from the rest of Scotland. Its own island. It had always gone about its own way, separate from the other clans. The other clans neither helped nor needed help from the island, as both were self-sustaining.

"Nothing, Gliocas."

"Damn right."

"But this is about what Scotland can do for you in return for aid."

The Fisher Chief raised a brow. "Conditional love?"

Magnar made a small nod and looked into the eyes of the great man. "Is this not the way diplomacy works?"

The Fisher Chief gave a long hearty laugh, his belly jiggled as he did. His face quickly turned beet red. "I like ya, lad. I do."

Magnar waited until the echoes of the Chief's laughter had ceased, and then he continued. "Gliocas, if you do not help us on the mainland, The Outside will come to your island, and then it will be too late. Scotland, in itself, is a large island. It is more difficult for the Outside to navigate, too many caverns and unknown nooks and crannies. But if the Outside conquers us, they will yearn for more land. And if they have any interest in your land, they can conquer you effortlessly."

The Fisher Chief rose from his throne and approached his window, peering at the gray water thrashing against jagged rocks.

"My people are fighters at sea, young Chief. Our ships can take any one of yers in a fight, with or without the weapons ban."

"I believe that," Magnar said. "But the legends of the Outsiders must ring truth to your ears. With ships made of Iron giants."

The Chief considered this for a moment. "Even if I were to help ya, my people are wasted on land. They're be'er off at sea."

Magnar nodded. "How will rivers do?"

The Fisher Chief chuckled and plopped back onto his throne, which creaked under his weight. "Yer a clever lad, young Chief. I want to help." He turned back to Magnar, examining him for a moment. "Yer much too skinny, though."

"That can be corrected when my people are home safe."

The Fisher Chief chortled some more and tapped his fingers twice against the throne. "I do want to help ya...but I need something in return."

Magnar's heart sunk. "Yes?"

"An alliance. The proper way."

"Through-"

"Marriage, aye." The Fisher Chief gestured toward Jean. "I want your beautiful sister to marry my son."

Magnar's eyes widened as he realized the Chief had mistaken Jean for Rose. He nearly let a laugh slip out, but managed to swallow it back down. "Gliocas that-"

"Is an excellent idea," Jean chimed in. "I would be honored to marry your son, Gliocas."

Magnar whirled around to Jean, who shot him a warning look in return. If he called her out, she would be charged with lying to the Chief, putting them both in danger. He cursed under his breath.

The Chief examined Jean carefully, circling her like a shark.

"What is your name, sister to Magnar?"

"Rosalind Rankin."

The Chief nodded, looking her up and down. "Aye, she'll do nicely for my lad. I have but one son, and many daughters. My son must have an heir when this war is over. You can have your army then, Òganach, but she must stay here."

Magnar bowed his head and thanked the Chief, unsure of whether to laugh or cry.

***

Rose made the first blow to the head.

The Triact Chief deflected it quickly with his sword, his dark curls bouncing as he did. He moved to the offense and attempted to strike the opposite way to her side. She blocked it easily.

The crowd had formed a circle around the two fighters with Caiden standing in the sidelines, praying to Eason and whatever spirits presided with him. He prayed to the Great Mountain, his ancestors, Owen Cheryic, Broden Cheryic, William Wallace, the first horse, the wolf lord, etc. He prayed and prayed and prayed, but could not keep his eyes from the fight.

The swords clashed and both pushed against each other, at first the Chief shove the sword to Rose's throat. Then Rose pushed it back, the Chief whirled under his sword and both hit the ground. The Chief was panting now, reassessing Rose's skill. Of course, word had travelled about a female warrior in training in the Cheryic Clan. But nobody believed that this warrior would prove much of a threat to the other clans. Beads of sweat rolled down the Chief's forehead as his dark eyes met Rose's green.

Rose's eyes were brighter than Caiden had ever seen, practically glowing. Her cheeks were pink, whether it was from the cold or perspiration, Caiden did not know. She swayed from side to side, her eyes never leaving the Chief's. She lunged toward him. He sidestepped and elbowed her rib cage. She let out a yelp of pain. He struck her again in the side of the face.

She fell to the floor, sputtering out small droplets of blood, but her eyes never left his.

He laughed and gave the crowd a chance to take in what he had just accomplished, listening to the chorus of cheers. Then he turned to strike, but she had already run her sword through his gut.

Gasps and whispers raced through the audience as they stared in amazement at their Chief, who fell to his knees, clutching his wound. Rose's eyes were fluorescent, piercing straight through him in the nature her sword had. A teardrop fell from each of his cold, unfeeling eyes, and he dropped lifelessly to the ground.

There was a silence in the crowd that lasted longer than felt comfortable to Caiden as everyone succumbed to their shock. The Chief was dead. Caiden approached Rose slowly, who had fallen to her knees in fatigue. He knelt to her level and put an arm around her. She just stared at the body of the Triact Chief.

"Twenty four." She muttered.

"What?" Caiden asked.

She broke her stare from the Triact Chief's figure for the first time since the beginning of the fight. "He was only four years older than our brother."

Caiden wrapped his arm around her and patted her back. "He was nothing like our brother. Not good. Not feeling. Not a Chief."

"I think," Rose began, "he thought he was doing right by his people. He thought he could play on both sides."

"I don't know much about this world, Rose." Caiden said, "but one thing is for sure. In the end, all must choose a side."

One of the Triact men finally stood inside the circle and yelled, "All welcome Rosalind Tyra Rankin, Chief of the Triact Clan."

The Triact people kneeled, their faces solemn. Rose stood unacknowledging, sheathed her sword and walked inside the former Triact Chief's hut.

Helen's a dreamer

Akir Rowe's hut resembled Laird Gavin's. It was larger than the others, sturdier. It could scarcely be called a hut at all. It reminded Rose of the colonial homes she used to visit as a girl, with sturdy stone walls and doorways lined with white wooden frames. She wanted something that revealed Chief Akir's life to her so she could better honor his death. He had been no Chief to begin with, just a boy with a fancy job. Instead of a trinket, however, she found a forty-year-old woman pointing a knife to her face.

"You." Rose whispered.

"Me." The woman responded.

Caiden barged through the door and unsheathed his sword. His eyes nearly bulged right out of his head.

"Mother?!"

"A family reunion!" Helen said again, giving a nervous, high pitched, screechy laugh. When she sobered up, she dropped her knife and took a step towards Caiden. She placed her hands on his cheeks. "You're alive."

Caiden shoved her hands off of his face and sheathed his sword. He crossed his arms and gave what some of the Cheryic people might call a "pettet-lip".

"Aye, we're alive," he said. "No thanks to you or your people."

Helen laughed again, this time more urgently and she gasped as she did. It was a mangled, fearful laugh. She had grown thin and haggard with age; her curly hair was wildly long. Her bright eyes twitched violently, as she could not retain her attention in one place.

Urgently, she took Caiden in for a giant, awkward, embrace, close and tight enough so her lips were but millimeters from his ear. She breathed very fast and held him there.

"Listen to me. He will not rest until you two and your brother are found. Fake your deaths. Leave Scotland. Hide. I thought you were safe from him here. I was wrong. He will not rest until you are all dead."

Then she kissed both of Caiden's cheeks, headed for the door, and peeked back at the Twins' gaping mouths. "He is coming."

And she was gone.

Caiden started toward the door with a quickened pace and stuck his head out.

"She gone?" Rose asked.

Caiden nodded and shrugged. "See her in another ten years, I guess."

Rose nodded. "Well, I see where you got your laugh from."

Caiden snorted and punched her arm. She punched him back harder until suddenly she was in a headlock. He was giggling so hard that he was shaking Rose under his arm.

The Twins were interrupted by the scream of a woman from outside the hut.

The Twins jerked their heads to the direction of the scream and darted outside. They quickly surveyed the parameter and found a man in a red kilt standing in the square of the recent fight, holding a knife to a woman's throat.

This time, Rose was there to shoot him down quicker than the man could flick his wrist.

The Twins darted toward the whimpering woman, but before they arrived by her side, she yelled, "It's a trap!"

Five men came at them from roofs on all sides. The people all ran screaming toward their homes, slamming their shutters and barring their doors behind them. But the Craotics did not have the people as their target this time. All of them rushed straight toward the Twins.

"We can take 'em, right?" Caiden asked Rose.

She glanced back and spat the remainder of blood that had been sitting in her mouth since her fight with the Triact Chief. "Sure." To the Craotic's shock, the Twins ran straight back at them with full force.

"Aaaaaargh!" Caiden faked a blow to the first Craotic's head and instead side-swept his sword to the Craotic's ribs. His sword hit its mark. The man let out a mangled cry, but did not fall. Caiden used his moment of pain to strike a final blow at his head. His body fell to the ground while his head went flying toward a garden fence.

When he had finished off the other two, Caiden looked toward Rose, whose Craotics were whimpering on the pavement. She plunged her sword through one's heart, silencing him forever.

"I hate you," Caiden heard her whisper, vehemently staring at the corpse.

"I know," Caiden yelled with a grin. Rose looked back at him and turned flush. She punched his arm; Caiden playfully punched hers back. Then he wrapped his arm over her head and noogied her hair.

"Stop! Seriously!" she screamed. Caiden ignored her. "Let me go! They're, they're coming!"

Caiden stopped cold, letting her down and facing the direction she was frantically pointing. About twenty men with red and navy kilts were running toward them from a building corner.

"Oh, pish it," Caiden muttered, suddenly feeling very small.

Rose frantically looked around, climbed a rooftop and left Caiden standing on the ground alone, with the men a mere fifteen meters away. "Oh ok! Ya jessie!" Caiden shouted sarcastically to her, throwing his hands in the air.

"Wheesht!" He heard her reply. Her bow was already in her hands and she reached for an arrow. "I'm evening out the odds!"

She stood upright on the roof's edge. Caiden couldn't help but admire her balance and grace. An arrow whizzed through the air and punctured a Craotic's throat. Another followed, piercing a heart. Then another. And another.

Caiden was glad that Rose was preventing their deaths, but once she shot five or six down, he was beginning to grow restless. "Will you just let a few come to me?!" He shouted up at her. Rose ignored him and managed to kill off ten of the

Craotics before they were on top of him. Caiden grasped his sword in his hands, tossing it back and forth, unable to calm his adrenaline rush.

He blocked the first Craotic's spear and quickly darted closer than the spear's striking range. While the man awkwardly tried to maneuver his spear, Caiden impaled his chest with his sword. Three Craotics surrounded Caiden at once, and it took all of Caiden's focus not to get killed. He blocked and ducked at the same time. An arrow impaled the one to his right, making room for a new Craotic to surround him. Caiden was overwhelmed. He turned his head left to right, right to left, and began getting dizzy, until he felt a sharp pain in his side.

"Jobbyyyy," Caiden said to himself, grasping his side, both trying to stop the pain and the bleeding. Caiden's cold hand stung his wound as he pressed his fingers to the warm, sticky blood between his ribs. He grimaced.

The Craotics closed in now, but they did not stab Caiden. One hoisted Caiden upon his shoulders and began running with the pack surrounding it.

"Not so hasty," a familiar voice said, jumping in front of the pack. A wave of red struck three Craotics in the front of the pack, bringing them to the ground. Suddenly an arrow whizzed so close to Caiden's head that he could feel the breeze it left in its path. It hit the Craotic who carried Caiden, forcing his knees to buckle. Caiden fell headfirst to the dirt.

What is going on? He got on all fours...or all threes, clutching his wound with one hand, and looked around. Rose had caught up to the pack from behind. To Caiden's surprise, Fergus was fighting the Craotics from the front.

Caiden pushed himself up with a grunt, grabbed a Craotic's sword and began fighting again.

"I don't suppose an 'I'm sorry' will suffice?!" Rose shouted to Fergus, fighting two Craotics at the same time.

"I come for our people," Fergus grunted, stabbing a Craotic with his sword. "Not you."

"Can we make it up to you?" Caiden asked. He spun around slicing three Craotics' stomachs, then stabbed them each for good measure. There were only about seven left. Fergus was taking on three; Caiden and Rose were each taking on two.

"Aye, can we talk *after* we kill these guys?" Fergus asked, blocking a Craotic's sword and sidestepping another at the same time.

"Are you sure? I think these guys are willing to wait." Rose replied lightly, her sword dismembering the leg of a Craotic. The second sword scratched her arm. "Why you little…" Rose sneered. She began hitting the man backing quickly to the fence harder and harder until finally his block missed her sword and scratched her other arm. Meanwhile, Rose's sword hit his side harshly. He fell to the ground quickly, clutching his gaping wound.

Rose grabbed his hair.

"Who sent you?"

The man said nothing.

She pressed her sword to his throat.

"Tell me now."

"The Chief!" the man squealed.

"The Craotic Chief?"

"Aye!"

"To attack the Triacts?"

"Naw."

She pressed the sword harder against the man's Adam's Apple.

"To kidnap ya. He knew ye'd be here. To get yer people."

Rose pressed harder, "Why? Why us?"

The man said nothing, but keeled over and died.

The area was quiet, and Rose realized they had pretty much finished the job. She looked over at Caiden, whose two Craotics' accidentally stabbed each other and were keeling over. Caiden grinned, yet still clutched his side. His grin faded as quickly as it came. His eyes rolled back in his head and he fell to the ground.

Fergus raced towards him, but backed away quickly. "I'll find a physician."

Rose nodded, ripping the hem of Caiden's tartan to make a bandage.

***

A physician arrived in no time and informed everyone that Caiden would be fine. He just needed time to regain his blood. They moved him into the Chief's chambers and allowed him to rest. At this point, Rose realized that with all of the commotion since their arrival, she had forgotten the one thing that she had set out to do. Therefore, her first orders as Chief of the Triact Clan were to "Release all Cheryic people."

It was Chelinda Reid who first approached the new Triact Queen, but Rose did not recognize her without all of her glamour. The woman was dressed in haggard gray rags, with her hair covered by a single cloth. Her face was no longer painted in red hues, but had been cleared away to reveal a plain, aging woman.

"I feel absolutely dreadful," she said, "for coming to you in such...distasteful...clothing. But I have heard word that you are the new Triact Chief?"

"Aye," Rose said dryly.

"Then I beg of you...please, oh please...find me something silken to wear!"

Rose spat at her. "You ungrateful witch! I heard you exiled my brother. You?! After all of the times my uncle hired you. You are lucky I do not forever banish you from Scotland!"

Chelinda nodded. "Yes, I suppose I am. And I was wrong. I was frightened. My home was taken from me."

Rose was without pity.

"I...I can give you information! Your aunt was here for a while, as well as your grandfather! I was a slave to former Chief Akir Rowe. I can tell you the going ons. Please, just give me a dress."

Rose sighed and nodded to Fergus, who went in search of a dress.

"Speak." Rose commanded.

"The Cheryic elders were correct. Blayne Rankin, your grandfather, held a meeting with the Triact King, just a few nights' past. He claimed that if they could bring you and your brothers to him, dead or alive, he will leave Scotland, untouched. He wants you gone!"

Rose allowed this to sink in, remembering Helen's words to her. *He will not rest until you all are dead.*

"But why?" Rose asked, in a half-whisper.

Chelinda shook her head. "Before he left, he simply said, 'the bastards shall squander my name no longer'."

Rose squinted her eyes, "...so he wants to kill us...because we're bastards?"

Chelinda said nothing.

They remained that way for a minute, Chelinda bashfully on her knees, avoiding eye contact with Rose. Rose puzzled over her latest family drama, and then chalked it off to madness.

"Are all of the Cheryic people with me?"

"All share similar opinions to me, yes," Chelinda replied. "They know now that Magnar the Honorable is their true Chief, despite his obvious loyalties with his family."

Rose ignored the last bit.

"Then rally them. Today is the last day that the Cheryic and Triact clans are separate entities. From now on, we are one clan and we shall restore our homeland together."

a clan takes leave

In just a few days, an army was marching from Triact City. Magnar sent Valar with a message of his new army's coordinates. He had found a forest cave on the Triact border that seemed safe enough to hide the people, and they were building a fort to surround it. He assured Rose in the letter that the cave had means of escape should they be attacked. But for now, they needed a place to train their new army.

Rose rode ahead of her own army atop of a black mare. She made a mental note to herself that as soon as the war was over, she would hand over her new "Crown" to Magnar and unite the clans for good. She did not like being Chief. She was too stubborn, too free seeking. The responsibilities did not become her.

The first night at camp, armies surrounded giant fires as they gathered close to fight the cold of the night's crisp air. The men began taking swigs of ale and blubbering on about women.

"I once had a love who sang like the gentle breeze that wakes you on the first spring morning, when the birds first bring their songs back," Caiden beamed.

A Triact man with a shaggy beard known as Alec chuckled. "Quite the dreamer, isn't he lads?!" he asked with laughter. His friends joined in. "What happened to her, did she join the stars in their golden dances?"

Caiden stiffened. "I do believe she did." All was quiet. "She was killed by Craotics, I'm afraid. Her name was Gwen. She was the first victim on the day everything changed."

"What was it like?" Alec asked, suddenly pensive.

"Terrible, we tried to get as many people as we could out but-"

"Naw, naw. Not the attacks, Cheryic City. Is it what the tales say of it?"

"Oh," Caiden paused, his face glowing against the warmth of the fire. "I suppose it is. Everything we did was for the people. The spinsters and the soldiers alike. We'd work during the day and tell stories on the eve. My uncle would play the violin as we would wind down from learning and fighting. It was an adventure that I overlooked, my everyday life."

"Is it true there's no pain there, lad?" Alec asked.

Caiden laughed. "It's a city, not heaven. But it's my home nonetheless."

Alec nodded and smiled to himself. He sat for a moment with a funny little smile on his wrinkled face.

"I hope someday," he said through the flames of the fire, "my grandchildren tell the story of their grandfather going to fight alongside the rightful heirs of the Cheryic clan. And I hope they will tell that story from inside the walls of the great Cheryic City."

Rose listened with her head resting on a log, holding her uncle's memoirs to the firelight. She was about halfway through them. She had often read them to put her at peace before she fell asleep. Most had been about the children or the ridiculous encounters he had in the clan. In a particularly funny anecdote, Chelinda Reid had chased him halfway around the city with hot rollers in her hands, claiming neat round curls were going in style. Rose laughed at this, flipped the page and found it was blank. She flipped again.

If you are reading this, you are either Magnar or Rose, and I am dead. (I know Caiden would never have the patience to get this far into any work of literature.)

We returned from the meeting with the five clans today. The Craotics, of course, were stubborn and refused to cast the Outsiders from their clan. I cannot judge them, though. They know not the reason that Blayne Rankin has taken such interest in this land, and they never will if I can help it. It is dangerous for me to be writing this information to you, but it is important for you to know that your life is in danger. It is my fault. I have already stated in these memoirs that I was a young boy, no more than fourteen when I left my mother for Scotland. My father resented me from the moment I was conceived. You see, my father, if defined by any trait, is a wildly ambitious man. His dream in life had been to become pope, but I ended all aspirations of that as he was forced to hurriedly marry my mother. He resented me for ruining his dream, and always made sure I understood this, whether it was through words, fists, or

pipes. The day I ran away, he was searching for me with a gun in his hand. I believe my mother knew that if he did not kill me that day, he would have killed me in the future. So I left my home and lived with my Uncle, Chief William. I was never supposed to be Chief, but William's son was killed in a Craotic battle, and William died of grief shortly after.

This you do not know. Back in America, my father decided to channel his ambitions into his government. He aimed high, as per usual, to be the president of the United States. Although, I expect soon, he will want to upgrade this position to dictator. It was while my father was still a Senator in the process of running for president that Caiden was conceived. Magnar had been born into Helen's unhappy marriage, so she went off and had an affair with another. I do not know if it was my father or Helen, but her husband mysteriously died soon after Caiden's birth. According to her, however, my father had no notion of Caiden's existence. So she took both the boys here, fearing that my father would kill Caiden if he were ever found. I think she wanted the boys to be together and have one another. She loved both of the boys, more than she could handle. There was something wrong inside of her head. I will never know what my father did to her, nor do I want to.

Christine was the rebellious child. She conceived Rose out of wedlock too, some would say with the intentions of a rebellion in mind. During her pregnancy, she wrote a book about everything: my father's abuse, Caiden and Magnar, and me running away. She threatened to publish this book, during which time, Rose's father disappeared. She went into hiding, but the threat of the novel was always in my father's mind. He lost the first election, but this did not deter him.

He kept working to clear his name and appear pristine to the religious leaders of America. When Rose was seven years old, her mother went to work under the alias "Arwen Martelli." She was shot by a masked man three times and killed.

Before this masked man had arrived at Christine's work, Helen snatched Rose from her house, claiming her mother had died in a car accident, and they were to go to Scotland immediately. A few hours later, the masked men arrived in Rose's house, tearing it apart from top to bottom. I say this so the boys may respect their mother, but I still warn them not to trust her. She is not well.

I hope you understand the implications of what I have written. As long as Rose and Caiden are alive, they are a threat to my father's reputation and therefore, power. Magnar is a witness to their existence and relation to him. Blayne Rankin will not stop until the clan and all its witnesses are burnt to the ground.

Rose patted the parchment on her side for a few moments, debating what to do next. She skimmed through the rest of the pages, in search of other hidden notes or letters. Nothing. Just grumblings about the drudgeries of Eason's everyday life.

Rose glanced from the letter to Caiden, back to the letter, folded it up, and stowed it away in her pocket.

***

The moment Magnar saw his brother and sister riding up to camp with what must have been a thousand men marching behind them, his heart seemed to refrain from beating. They were alive. They appeared to be well. Rose's hair was back in an intricately woven braid. She sat upright upon a black mare, her chest sticking out proudly.

Caiden and Rose had always had the exact same smile: wide, with thick lips and large teeth, and crinkles around their eyes. Caiden had that smile right now, but was sitting tiredly with his shoulders slumped forward, as he allowed the horse to sway him with each gallop. His eyes were baggy and his face was pale. He carried a sword but nothing else. As usual, his hair was a rat's nest that somehow had been braided back to keep from his eyes.

Magnar tried to walk toward them as professionally as possible, but it was difficult to slow his eager feet. He practically yanked Rose off of her horse as he pulled her in for an embrace. He held her hair and kissed her head. Caiden had caught up with them also and Magnar did the same with him, letting out a small cry of relief.

As Magnar stepped back to look over the both of them, he realized how mature their looks had quickly become. Caiden was growing a beard, a little fuller than Magnar's stubble. They looked more worn, less youthful in their eyes. Their faces had become thinner and more tired. It saddened him.

"Are you alright?" Magnar asked. "Did you eat well, and stay out of trouble? Were there any more Craotics?"

"Yes, yes, yes and yes," The Twins replied simultaneously.

"What do you mean, yes?" Magnar asked.

They glanced at each other. "The Triact Chief is dead. We ran into a fair amount of Craotics."

"Magnar," Caiden said.

Magnar looked to him with furrowed brows.

"It's Maw. I saw her... she's working for our grandfather, I think. She warned us. He's doing all of this...to get to us."

"What?" Magnar asked, somewhat under his breath. He looked to Rose, whose expression was grave. "My mother cannot be trusted."

"Think about it, Magnar," Rose told him. "We saw her at the Triact clan. Grandfather did not take interest in our land until he knew of our existence! Maybe that's why Helen gave you to the clan, because she wanted you two to go into hiding with Eason!"

Magnar nodded. "Whatever." And he leaned against the table of strategic maps. "Where is she now?"

"She fled." Rose replied, "their base obviously was not in the Triact clan, otherwise there would have been more Craotics, but grandfather clearly had some sort of alliance with the Triact Chief."

"And The Triact Chief is dead?"

"Aye."

Magnar nodded. "Which means…?"

"I am Chief. The clans will be united under your rule."

Magnar grunted, "I suppose we have an army then. But how did Helen slip away? Where did she go? She must have slipped past our borders to get to the base then."

The Twins glanced at each other.

"You know where the base is?!" They both yelled.

Magnar nodded. "Cheryic City, of course. We believe the Americans moved right in there. It's strategically brilliant, with a river, mountain range, and forest. But at the same time, what do they want from there? Right now, they're just sitting. It's like they're waiting."

Evander emerged from a tent and with a full sprint, he darted toward Rose and tackled her to the ground, embracing her and kissing her hair.

"Evander!" Rose shouted in protest. "Look at my queen hair! You cannot mess up my queen hair! It's so...professional!"

Finally, Evander pulled away. "Jean saved us." He said. "She saved you and I."

Rose wrinkled her nose, suddenly realizing Jean was not among them.

"Where is she?"

"She's marrying the Fisher Chief's son to form an alliance." Magnar lowered his voice to a whisper. "If anyone asks, you are my second sister."

He pointed toward a giant muscle of a man with royal armor, surrounded by a crowd of fishermen. He had long curly hair and worn, tan skin.

"*That* is her betrothed."

"And you approve of this marriage?" Rose asked skeptically.

Magnar looked at her warily. "What choice did we have?"

"You *must* send for her now," Rose said, her voice stern.

Magnar narrowed his eyes."Why?"

Evander finally freed his arms from embracing Rose, and hugged Caiden, who let out a small whimper.

Magnar whirled around at the slightest detection of harm.

"Are you hurt?!" he asked.

"The Craotics stabbed him in the side during a fight where Fergus saved our arses."

Magnar grabbed Rose. "Why did you bring him back here then?! It's dangerous at the border! We could be attacked any day! He cannot fight wounded!"

"I'm not twelve, Magnar!" Caiden groaned. "I came of age two years ago! I think I can decide whether or not I want to fight!"

"You act like a twelve-year-old! I will not have you fighting feebly!"

"It's barely a scratch anymore, Magnar, for all of our sakes, stop acting like-"

"Like Uncle? Well, guess what? He's dead; he's not going to take care of you anymore and obviously, someone needs to!"

"STOP!" Rose shouted, jerking in-between the feuding brothers. She turned to Magnar, her olive face crimson with frustration. "You need to stop treating us like children. We are eighteen years old! If you do not think that Caiden is able to fight, then you, as Chief, have every right to stop him from fighting."

"What?!" Caiden yelled.

"But you as Chief must make decisions out of your mind, not your heart. So, watch him fight me and make an educated decision to see if he can fight."

"No...you'll go easy on him!" Magnar replied.

"I care about him too, Magnar. I would only go easy on him if I did not care. Find us two practice swords."

***

The Twins were each presented with a dull training sword. Both tossed them back and forth in their hands while staring at each other with mischievous grins. They reminisced on their younger years when they had ended disputes with one another through sparring. Most of the disputes had been irrelevant to any kind of sword training at all: They fought over who had nicer eyes, who sang better, who was more annoying, and once they even determined who would get eaten in the event of an apocalypse. The winner often varied, but they *did* determine that Caiden would be eaten. This time, Caiden was determined to beat Rose.

Rose struck first, a blow at her brother's head. He successfully ducked, skillfully keeping his balance to strike his sister's leg. She jumped and struck at his back but was deflected with a sword of his own. All of this had happened over the span of a mere second.

Caiden laughed, but grimaced as a jolt of pain went up his side. Rose used this moment of distraction to jump at him with full force, a blow that Caiden managed to deflect, but it cost him his sword. The sword went flying through the air and into the ground, a few meters away. Caiden searched desperately for something to use. He grabbed a mug from a spectating soldier and pegged it at her.

Rose deflected the mug, but this gave Caiden the time he needed to dive toward her, wrestling her to the ground. Rose's sword went flying from her hand as well, just a few inches out of her reach. Rose punched his wound, and he groaned. He punched her in the nose.

"Och!" she yelped.

She kneed his balls, causing him to double over. It was enough time for her to grab her sword again. Realizing her sword was in reach, Caiden dove for his own, and the two were back to sparring again.

It certainly was a fight all of the soldiers would never forget. With a final blow, Rose broke Caiden's cheap sword in half. The blunt side of the other half flew into one speculating soldier's face.

"Back to work on the fort soldiers," Magnar ordered. "Evander, show the new ones how it's done."

Evander nodded once, and led the newest soldiers to the fort, which was currently under construction. They were working fast and steadily on a fort to protect their new training base and people, but not fast enough.

"So, can I fight, brother?" Caiden asked Magnar, his large child-like eyes leading Magnar through memory after memory.

"I suppose we were all given free will. Use it wisely." Magnar gave in.

"I'm fighting." Caiden whispered to Rose.

She giggled.

The dreaded voice came from behind the fort which barely was constructed above their heads. "THEY'RE COMING!"

"GET BEHIND THE FORT!" shouted a voice.

Fergus, who had been watching the fight on the sidelines, tensed. "They must be coming from the west side. That was fast. I thought we'd at least have a few days to rest."

Rose rolled her eyes. "Gee, Fergus. Why don't you go out there and ask for a few extra days so that you can put up your feet?"

Fergus groaned and darted toward the fort.

Rose glanced at Caiden, who stood frozen, staring at the fort as if willing himself to run toward it. "There's no way I'm going in there," Rose said, gesturing toward the meager circular wall of jagged sticks and stone.

Caiden shook his head in agreement.

"To the trees?" Rose asked.

Caiden curled his lip, creased his brows. "What in Owen's name can we do in trees?"

Rose's eyes widened. "Take them by—"

"Surprise…" Caiden finished. The Twins darted toward the fort, racing each other the entirety of the way.

***

"Magnar! Magnar!" Magnar turned toward his sister and brother as they sprinted into the fort. A wave of relief washed over him.

"Thank the spirits. I thought you'd run off!" Magnar sighed. Both of the twins' eyes were bulging out of their skull. "Oh jobby, what is it?"

"How far are the Craotics?"

"About two kilometers. Get ready to defend."

"Why defend when we can attack?" Caiden asked, grinning from ear to ear.

Magnar looked from one to the other. "I'm listening."

"Give us half the men and we'll take them into the woods, hide, and attack from the north." Rose proposed, her chin held high enough to meet Magnar's.

Magnar hesitated. "We haven't time...I-"

"Give me the men I brought with me, for the Craotics may not be expecting them to be here yet."

"Rose-"

"Please...Gliocas." Rose held out her arms to him. Caiden stared at her; his mouth hung open as if he were dead.

Magnar sighed. "Do not treat me like I am above you, for your plan is well beyond my own. Go. Both of you. Be careful."

"ALL TRIACT MEN WITH ME!" Caiden called, for although Rose's voice was exceptionally loud, his voice seemed to be more comprehensible when he yelled. As if the men had been waiting for the order all along, the Triacts clambered along with Rose and Caiden, taking refuge in the shade of the trees. They wiped mud on their faces and placed branches over their heads. At Rose's orders, everyone climbed the trees, avoiding the ground at any cost.

"Wheesht now, men," Caiden ordered, wincing at Rose's annoyed glance toward him. "Men and Rose, I mean. We mustn't be heard in this forest until Rose gives the order."

And so it was, that any man could hear a pin drop, while faithfully watching their commanders from above ground. Rose never flinched, she only watched from her place, perched high in her tree with her bow in hand. Before they could see any trace of Craotics, they heard them: the idle clatter of their marching, the orders shouted to each other, the clanking of their swords and sheaths. Then they saw them: black dots on the horizon. She watched the army of wretched Craotics march right below them. She listened to the daunting sound of the feet of the same monsters which had torn her life apart again and again. But she held her ground, for she thought to herself over and over: *My time will come.*

The wall was about a kilometer from the forest, and by the time the Craotics reached it, they had cleared the forest completely. The Craotics began to yell, wailing and screaming. But nobody popped out of the wall until the Craotics were within shooting range.

The archers alone popped up from the wall, shooting the front lines down. But soon the Craotics were too close and the rest of the men behind the wall jumped from their hidden vantage points, onto the Craotics which screamed at them.

An antsy feeling grew inside of Rose, causing her to squirm in her tree. She did not watch, for she couldn't watch innocent lives be taken without taking action herself. She knew that if she did watch, she would surely jump down from her tree and fight.

When the last Craotics trotted past, Rose stood up in her tree and called the archers to aim. They did so, and soon shot into the backside of the army. The battle blurred before Rose. Flashes of red flickered before her, creating unsettling visions in her head. She aimed for the ones in the farthest back, fearing she would hit her own men. She had lost her usual confidence in her skill with the bow, for she had never been in a full-blown battle before. The chaos was daunting.

She called the archers to shoot again, and arrows flooded the air above the Craotics' heads. Terrified looks etched their faces as they gazed at the pointed object of their demise whizzing down at them. The sight could even have given *Rose* nightmares.

When the blue, gray, and red were blurred together in the distance, she jumped from the tree, leading the Triacts into battle. Her men ran at the Craotics from behind, a look of utter confusion was engraved on each of their faces as they realized the Twins and Magnar had them surrounded.

The battle raged on and on, with flashes of green and blue, brown and pale blue, navy and gray, navy and red. It was a battle of almost all of the clans. *Almost a battle of five armies!* Rose thought to herself and chuckled.

She finally noticed that they were reaching some of Magnar's men. They were killing them off. They were winning.

Suddenly, the Craotics were dropping their weapons, holding their hands atop their heads and kissing the ground: A sign of surrender. It was dusk now, and beads of sweat ran down Rose's forehead. The faint purple tone of the sun behind the mountains barely revealed outlines of men lying everywhere on the ground. Side by side, Cheryics, Triacts, a few Fisherpeople and Craotics lay. It was a strange thing to see enemies next to each other in such a peaceful manner.

Within an hour past dusk, the Craotics had all been taken into Magnar's custody and were being questioned by Fergus and Alec. But there was no sleeping for Rose. She was too giddy with all of the events that had become her lately. She helped men move the bodies to be sent off to the spirits.

She dragged a body along with her to the wreckage that had successfully served as a defense for Magnar's men.

"Rose?"

She turned wide-eyed and smiled.

"Evander!" She shouted.

Evander stood with a bit of a lopsided posture, blood staining his shirt and golden hair. Bags had formed below his eyes, but he still smiled, ecstatic that she was alive.

Rose ran and leapt on top of him. She let out a sigh of relief and felt calm as he squeezed her close.

He laughed and asked if she was hurt. But after the brief wave of happiness, they both turned back to the body she had been dragging. Together they took it to the pyre.

"So you're alright?" Evander asked after they'd swung the man on top of the wooden mound.

"I'm better than that man," she responded, nodding toward the pyre.

"Thank the spirits for that," Evander replied.

Rose winced; her left shoulder was sore from all of the fighting and she stretched it nonchalantly. In addition, she was so hungry, she honestly believed that she could eat an entire stag. And bathe...there wasn't much she wouldn't give for a warm bath to wash off all of the grime and blood that had molded onto her since she left Triact City.

"Any sign of my brothers?"

Evander nodded. "Caiden and Magnar are behind the fort. I'm sure they'd want to see ya."

Rose smiled. "And you thought you could have me for yourself?"

Evander casually placed his hands in the folds of his tartan and looked her over, clicking his tongue as he did. "Dinna say anything stupid. Especially to Magnar. Ye ken he's afeart for ya."

Rose nodded, "Aye sir."

She started toward the fort, but immediately was jerked backward when Evander grabbed her arm.

"I dinna ken when I'll see ya next," Evander began, his voice low, "because...well, who kens what your next wreckless plan will be. But will ye see me tonight? By the burn[29] below the elm in the forest. In an hour's time?"

Rose hesitated, but nodded.

Evander let out a sigh of relief. "Okay, go!"

Rose sprinted toward the back end of the fort.

---

[29] Creek

a make-believe world

"There you are!" Magnar yelled when he saw Rose approach him. He began to run up to her, but before he could reach her, she was wiped out and knocked to the ground by a bloody, messy, fur ball called Caiden.

"Caiden for goodness sake," she heard Magnar say. The next thing she knew, drool was descending onto her right cheekbone.

"EW! THIS IS WHAT I GET FOR BEING ALIVE?" She whined and shoved him off her.

"Glad to see you too, cousin," Caiden laughed.

Magnar offered her a hand and hoisted her off the ground. But even after she was standing, Magnar's hand continued to hold hers with a firm grip as he looked her in the eye. "The spirits must truly love us, for they have answered my prayers: You are alive," he said, his expression first being sincere, but then soon turning into a teary laugh as he embraced Rose. Caiden, of course, unable to stand being without attention, joined them in a long group hug.

"The spirits have been so good to our family." Magnar whispered.

Rose stepped away.

"They have?" she asked.

Magnar smiled, putting his arm around his little brother. "We are alive and well, are we not?" he asked innocently.

"Look where we're standing, Magnar!" Rose protested, unable to believe they were having this conversation. "Look at all who've died because our home, our Uncle, was taken away from us."

"Uncle made a choice, Rose," Magnar replied, tears welling up in his eyes.

"Yeah, and so did we. But we got out alive," Rose said.

"And we are blessed because of it. The spirits saved us," Magnar replied.

"No, we saved us."

"Are you saying Uncle was not skilled because-"

"Of course not, but spirits didn't save him, and the spirits didn't save my family," Rose said.

Pause.

Caiden stepped up this time, his face contorted with worry.

"Rose, we are your family," Caiden said quietly.

Rose shook her head. "You don't know the half of it."

The brothers said nothing, but waited for an explanation. She reached into the folds of her loose breeks and pulled out an old piece of parchment, shoving it into Magnar's chest.

Magnar hastily opened it, cutting his finger in the process and shaking it. He skimmed over it, his brows furrowing as he reached the end. He looked to Caiden, bewildered.

"We're half-brothers."

Caiden laughed. "You're hilarious."

Magnar held out the parchment for Caiden to snatch. "Don't read it out loud."

Caiden was a slow reader and struggled with putting letters together. So while Caiden attempted to decipher the words on the page, Magnar looked to Rose.

"What does this mean for us?"

Rose shrugged. "Perhaps we should leave the Highlands. At least then we can draw our grandfather away from our people."

Magnar shook his head. "No."

"Magnar don't be selfish, there are a lot of people-"

"Who will end up like McCaig and Cinnie if we leave," Magnar interrupted. "Our grandfather does not care about these people. He'll get rid of them anyway, with or without us. They're all witnesses to our existence, Rose. Leaving them won't protect them."

Rose was silent for a few minutes.

"So you've known too?" she asked.

"Known what?!" Magnar asked impatiently.

"McCaig." Rose played with the folds of her tunic. "The Outsiders killed him."

"Aye." Magnar said, "I'm not a fool."

Caiden looked wildly from Magnar to Rose to Magnar again, his eyes nearly bulging out of his head. "WHAT!?" Caiden shouted. "YOU'VE BOTH KNOWN WHAT AND YOU DIDN'T THINK TO TELL ME?!"

"It was similar to Cinnie, don't you think?" Magnar ignored Caiden. "The Outside does not care for our people. They kill for fun. In fact, when we're gone, they will probably kill them all to get this land anyway. Our grandfather is after us, but rest of their nation is after our land."

"So…" Caiden said.

"So I suppose all we can do is resume as planned. And if we run into Blayne Rankin, we kill him."

"I suppose."

Magnar gestured toward a nearby tent, ducking under it. The Twins followed.

"He obviously hadn't expected us to successfully unite the clans, judging from today's battle. His plan is backfiring."

Caiden finally finished reading the letter. "And his plan is…?"

"For the clans to destroy one another. That way he has no ties to us. He's backing the Craotics to kill us." There was a long silence as everyone digested this information, their minds buzzing with speculations and plans. "So," Magnar said, "do you think he's here?"

"In Scotland?" Rose shook her head, "I don't know. But if what you say is true, I know who is."

"Mother." Caiden replied, his face in a dream-like state.

"Aye," Rose said, "she can get us into contact with him."

"No," Magnar's voice rose, "Uncle's letter specifically says not to trust her."

"But she saved us, Magnar," Caiden argued. "She can help us!"

"Caiden, we have had this conversation since we were five years old. She doesn't love us. She is twisted, crazy, and evil. She will not save us."

"According to this," Caiden held up the letter, shaking it wildly. "She *does* love us."

Magnar snagged the letter back before Caiden could pull it away. "It's out of the question."

Rose, who had steadily grown angrier as she watched this interaction, groaned. "I can't just sit here, as this man who has killed my parents, taken my home twice, is now trying to kill everyone I love!"

"That is what war is for, Rose! For destroying him once and for all."

Rose pounded her fists on a table. "You are so daft, Magnar! War is for the Americans to watch on a television screen as they pit us against each other. Our grandfather will not lose anything from losing this war! He will simply come in with his own army and kill us while we're weak."

Magnar said nothing. He just stormed out of the tent.

Silence.

Fergus opened the flap and ducked inside.

"Well, that was insufferable. What's the plan?" He asked.

Rose smirked.

"We save our people. But first...I have a boy to see."

Rose knows passion

Eason used to tell the children stories of the enchanted forests of Scotland: The spirits that resided there had the power to create any being or entity or emotion. They determined who lived and who died. The very air they breathed was a product of the forest's mercy.

That night, Rose removed her boots, feeling the relief of the soft moss between her blistered toes. A cool breeze gently brushed her hair and she saw Evander, sitting under the elm by the creek, whittling a figurine under the light of a torch he brought along.

"A torch in the forest," Rose remarked. "Not very smart."

Evander did not jump at the sound of her voice, which surprised Rose, because she thought she had come quite quietly.

"Hence the burn[30]," Evander said, and dug the end of the torch deep into the creek so that it would stand up. He took

---

30 Creek

her hand and knelt to the ground, bringing her down with him. "I wanna marry ya, Rose."

"Me too," Rose said. "When the war is over, I promise I will be yours."

Evander shrugged, "Aye, but," he hesitated, unsure of the words to use, "I wanna marry you today. Right now."

Rose, for once in her life, was at a loss for words.

"Think about it." He said, "You are always the spontaneous one who does the unexpected. Me? Well, the only unexpected things I have done in my life have been with you and yer family. So I just thought, why canna I be a little spontaneous tonight? I mean, who kens whether we'll both still be here tomorrow, that battle today made me realize just how...how easy it is for us to die."

Rose hesitated again. Only the cicadas and crickets could be heard, buzzing in the bushes.

"You're right." She said finally, and kissed his lips. Just like that. "But we cannot marry now."

When she pulled away, his face had turned a deep shade of purple, detectable even in the dim torch lighting.

"I promise you, Evander, before all the stars below the ben, that I will marry you when this war is finished," she said.

Evander snorted. "Well…let's live somewhere quiet…like a farm, outside of the city."

"What?!" Rose said, "so I'm risking my life to save a city I will never live in?"

Evander rolled his eyes. "Well with all the commotion of the war, I just thought we'd-"

"Och! You just thought, did ya?" Rose smirked. "I suppose you think we're gonna have a dozen blond bairns scrambling around the place too?"

Evander hunched over and pouted, drawing in the dirt with his forefinger. Rose couldn't handle it anymore. What started out as a small giggle, grew into endless laughter.

"What is it?" Evander asked.

"Magnar," Rose said. "He'll kill you."

Evander whistled. "Maybe we can wait until after we have retaken our home to tell him we are betrothed? After all...he's under a lot of stress…"

Rose nodded.

"Perfect."

***

After the fire died down, the troops slept on the ground, huddling with each other for warmth. Magnar withdrew to the tent with Caiden, Evander, Rose and Fergus. A torch lit the middle, where they placed a map of the kingdoms on the grass.

"We are so close to home, it's as if I can feel the Outside's presence among us," Magnar muttered, staring at the map.

"What do you propose?" Evander asked.

"I-" Magnar hesitated, and he looked over at Evander's grin, which seemed permanently etched upon his face. "Evander, did the sun bite you? Your face is the color of a cherry!"

Rose giggled and her face darkened as well. "He just looks so funny. Sorry I can't stop laughing."

Evander punched her playfully and she rolled onto the floor, wriggling like a worm with laughter.

"Um...we have a war to fight, if you please," Magnar cleared his throat, unsure if he actually cared to know what was going on between the two of them. "Wheesht!"

Rose stopped giggling suddenly and shot Magnar a warning look. “You’re the Chief. Figure it out,” she said.

So she still was angry with him after the day’s conversation, Magnar realized with a sinking feeling. He didn’t know why he had expected anything different. The girl had always been as stubborn as a mule.

“I haven’t been blessed on the mountain yet,” Magnar snapped back. “I’m still an heir, equal to you.”

She scowled.

“Wooooah,” Caiden interjected. “Magnar’s right, let’s think of what to do together.”

“We send scouts to search out the numbers and strength of whoever may be occupying the city.” Rose said.

Of course. Why didn’t I think of that? Magnar thought.

“I’ll send one of the men-”

“No.” Rose replied. “I only trust most (she shot a glance toward Fergus) of the people in this tent. Caiden and I will go.”

Caiden nodded.

Magnar sighed. “You’ve already done this once, I don’t want you to be separated from me again. We’ll send someone else. Evander and Fergus?”

“No,” Rose replied. “Evander is much more eloquent with the people. Caiden and I are awkward and cannot take care of the people like him.”

“Thanks,” Caiden replied defensively.

“Anytime,” Rose smirked, but her face hardened as she returned her gaze to Magnar. “Let us go. We are no use to you here.”

“What about me?” Fergus asked.

"You are neither good with the people nor can you be trusted as a spy," Rose replied coldly.

"Because we had issues with each other as bairns? That's ridiculous. I'm coming."

Magnar groaned. "Can we please just get along?"

"Aye, we can get along fine, if he doesn't go." Rose replied, her gaze burning through Fergus.

"All three of you go," Magnar insisted. "He's saved you before and will again."

Rose groaned. "Fine."

"It's time you learn to trust, Rose," Magnar said softly. "We have gotten through this war only by trust."

Rose grunted. "A bit hypocritical, don't you think?"

Magnar glared at her, but nodded in agreement. Caiden said nothing, tracing his fingers absentmindedly through the dirt. Magnar thought about threatening Fergus, instructing him to keep his siblings safe, but he realized it would get him nowhere. They would go and leave him behind to lead once again.

Rose knows pain

It was a day's journey toward home. They rode horseback until they reached the forest. Rose was oddly upbeat, so she joined in with Caiden as they hummed nonchalantly—well aware that it annoyed Fergus. They arrived at where the woods drew closest to the city with an hour or two left until nightfall. They waited, collected a few berries from spots that sent waves of nostalgia through the Twins, but avoided the river and its crawfish.

After a bit, Caiden wandered off to find a good place to take a poo, so Rose and Fergus were left alone, munching on mulberries.

"I envy you, ye ken," Fergus said, his teeth stained red from the juice.

"Of course you do," Rose said. "I'm strong, a good fighter, fun, kind and heroic. Everything you are not."

Fergus rolled his eyes. "Nope...actually...that's not it."

"Wow, there's more?"

Fergus groaned. "Forget it."

He stood up from his position perched on the forest floor, kicking over a pebble violently as he did. Then he whirled around at her. "You ken, ye dinna need to be so stubborn all the time. I disliked you as a bairn because ye made my life completely miserable!"

"What?!" Rose stood, with her hands held in fists at her sides. "Are you kidding me?"

"No!" Fergus yelled.

"WHEESHT," Rose said. "The Craotics could be anywhere!"

"Fine!" Fergus said, in a loud, obnoxious whisper, "I blamed ya for killing my brother, Rose, and even before that, I blamed ya for having him banished. He was the one thing that stood between my lousy father and me. Not to mention, he was my brother, and aye, he wasna the best person in the world, but I canna emphasize this enough, *he was my brother*! And I had to watch you and your brothers get along every single day and ken that because you wanted to be a warrior, my brother was gone."

"Oh, whatever!" Rose scoffed. "It's not my fault your brother was an ass!"

"I ken that," Fergus said, much more calmly now. "I understand that now, which is why I'm asking for your forgiveness."

Rose felt a chill run down her spine as she looked over at Fergus, who was staring at her intensely, his eyes almost shimmering with the faintest traces of teardrops.

She opened her mouth to speak, when Caiden bounded over from a faraway bush. "Well, I feel much better now, shall we be off?"

She nodded and shot Fergus a glance as if to say, *to be continued.*

As the sun disappeared behind the mountain, the Twins ventured outside the line that hid them in the woods. It was almost pitch-black by the time they arrived at the gate, only this time, the moon was not on their side. They had to crouch beneath the grass, hoping it would cover their bodies from the sights of any guards.

There were guards at the front gates: both bony Craotics with rotting teeth and bloodshot eyes.

The children decided to crawl around, still unsure of how many Craotics stood inside the fence, until they came upon the old tree that they had always climbed as children. They often would hide there and wait for friends to find them in a game of hide-and-seek...but many of those friends were gone now. Those hide-and-seek skills, however, were still quite useful. Rose climbed to the highest stable branch and looked right over the wall. Caiden climbed below her and Fergus stayed at the lowest branch.

"What do you see?" Caiden whispered.

She shook her head. "Too many buildings are in the way for me to get a good look."

Caiden sat silently in his branch, dreading what would come next.

"I'm going over there."

Oh boy.

"Rose, it's suicide if there are Craotics down there!"

"I'll be quieter if I'm alone. Wait for me here. If I'm not back by daylight, go home...or wait until sundown and then go home…so just wait about 24 hours."

"That's a lot of waiting." Fergus replied reluctantly. "Let me go with ya."

Caiden could feel the heat of her glare as it passed through him and landed on Fergus.

"No." And she jumped off the branch, landing on the other side of the fence.

All the boys could do was wait.

***

Rose clung to the knife at her side, her boots treading carefully on the mud beneath her dark cloak. So far, she heard nothing but a soft whirring sound. She counted her steps, taking about two per minute until after a few hours of the whirring noise growing louder and louder, she determined the source. Upon her arrival at the town square, she realized that the whirring noise was the snoring coming from a mouth-dropping number of Craotics camped in the square. All were crowded together, sleeping peacefully, right in front of her house...her house! She looked up to find a light in the window. She glanced around at all the other houses. None held a light, except her own.

I need to go back, she thought, but something about the light drew her. Who was in her house…? Why hers of all the houses? The Chief's house wasn't known to be the most luxurious, but not the poorest either, so why?

More quickly this time, she took the back way to the house, weaving in between buildings and through alleyways. When she arrived, she stood on an old crate, peering through her old bedroom window. She heard two familiar voices inside.

"Why are we still here, father?" A woman screeched. "This is pointless. We must go home. Your own people are suffering there without your presence. We're getting a bad reputation."

"We will get a worse one if any of those children are found," a low voice with a monotonous drawl responded.

"They won't be! I don't think these kids are ever gonna leave this place!"

"Oh please," the old man responded. "Of course they would. *I* would have if I thought my father was president...or my grandfather."

"This is insane," the woman responded. "And for what? You're never going to have legitimate grandchildren. Your name will never be carried on. So who cares?"

"Helen, please!" the old man said. "You're the one who got us into this wretched mess in the first place! You and your idiot sister. I won't have you ruin this for me. I don't trust you to fix it on your own."

"So why don't you go attack them then?" The woman asked drily. "Why are we just sitting here?"

"Helen, Helen, Helen. Eason is smart. I know my son. He will know why I'm here and he will give them to me himself. He values his people above all, and understands that the only way to end this is for the two brats to have never existed in the first place."

Rose's breath caught in her throat as she realized that the two of them believed Eason was still alive. Not only this, but their conclusion troubled her. He wouldn't have handed them over to their grandfather, would he?

Rose fell so quiet listening, she almost forgot to breathe. In realizing her fault, she took a slight breath, yet perhaps it was enough to bust apart the entire crate on which she stood.

The crate fell in with a snap. With a rush of adrenaline, she realized that it was stuck on her leg.

"What was that?"

She briefly recalled a word her mom used to say when she was still alive.

Shit.

She pushed the crate with her right foot and pulled on the left to try to remove it.

Creeeeeeaaaaaak.

She gasped as she heard the nostalgic creak of her own front door. She struggled hard, blood streaming down her leg as the wood splintered it. She tried to get up and run with the crate attached. Nothing worked. She fell on her face once more and turned only to see a man standing above her with his sword.

The Craotic Chief...what was his name…

BAM.

Fergus sits by the window

Fergus had gone off for a little bit, supposedly to scavenge for food. Caiden sat perched in a tree, carving out Gwen's name into a thick branch.

BONG. BONG.

His ears perked up as he recognized the sound of the old warning bell. His breath stopped.

"Something's wrong," he muttered to himself. "They've found her."

He looked below him, searching for Fergus in the brush below. It didn't take him long to pop into view.

"Did ya hear that?" he mouthed.

Caiden nodded. He tried to stare into the city as he began to hear metal clanking in the distance and incoherent shouts of Craotics. He didn't realize it, but tears were streaming down his face.

"We have to go get her," Caiden choked, staring in the distance.

"Naw," Fergus was already his unsheathing his sword. "We have to tell yer brother."

Caiden didn't listen. He moved to leap over the fence, similarly to Rose. However, he was not so graceful. He quickly lost his footing, smacked his chin against the top of the fence and fell to the ground, groaning.

Fergus stood above him.

"Wheesht," Fergus said. "Listen."

All he heard was the clanking of metal and shouts.

"There are too many of them," he told Caiden, his face expressionless. Caiden said nothing. "We have to go now. The sooner we leave, the sooner we can come back and get your sister."

"She may not have that long! She may be dead already for all we know." Caiden breathed deeply and closed his eyes.

But she wasn't dead. He knew in his soul that she wasn't.

"Caiden," Fergus said.

Caiden looked over at Fergus, whose eyes were beginning to grow teary as well.

"The only way to save her is to go back."

***

Rose awoke in her bed. It was the oddest feeling, staring at her old rusty ceiling, seeing her medieval wardrobe and crickety bedside stand once more in her old room. For a moment, she was happy again. She felt the simple warmth of being in her own home and half-expected to hear Eason yell at her to do her chores. But as she lifted her head, an immense pain shot through it, and her memories came flooding back. She struggled to get up, only to find her hands were bound to the bedpost.

Her knife.

Where was it? She had to get out of here.

Rose froze, as a loud cackle sounded from the other room. She looked wildly around her, searching and searching for the knife she had held. It was gone.

When the door opened, Helen and the Craotic Chief led two men into the room. One of them held a whip, the other held a knife.

"Hello dearie," Helen said. "You know, I didn't recognize you at first, but when the Craotic Chief told me you were part of the once royal family, I realized who you were immediately. Oh well, my bad. Remember me?"

Rose didn't answer. She was confused. According to Eason's letter, this woman had saved Rose from being murdered. Of course, she had also allowed her own sister to be slaughtered. Now, Rose wanted to trust her, but it was nearly impossible, as she was bound by the hands to her bed and Helen was looming above her.

"So," she continued, "your friends are in the other room."

Rose tried to force her face to remain expressionless, but she couldn't resist her mouth from dropping slightly. They were here? She told them to stay in the tree! How could they be so foolish? They could've gone back for help.

"Now, in a short time, Eason will come looking for you," She interrogated. "How will he do so? You know him. Will he bring his army? Will he send a spy? Who will he send?"

Rose remained silent. She could hear her uncle telling her, "if you have nothing to say, don't say anything at all," as he grumbled over biscuits at the breakfast table. Well, now Rose didn't know what to say. She certainly did not want Caiden and Fergus...well, Caiden to die. But her people: Magnar, Evander, all those who had welcomed her to the clan, she could see their faces by the fire once again the first night that she arrived. She could see them celebrating L'anaman. She could see them dancing by the fire, happy and peaceful, thankful that the spirits had brought them such bounty in life. And right now, she could see her grandfather willing to take away every single Cheryic person's happiness, simply for power. Surely Caiden would understand this. Even Fergus would understand this.

I will go with you, my friends. Rose vowed to them.

"Let's try this again," Helen continued. "Tell us Eason's plans and we won't kill your friends."

Rose bit her tongue, but at the mention of Eason's name, she couldn't help but to tear up.

The Craotic Chief nodded slowly. "It is as I suspected," his voice boomed. "Eason would not live to see his clan defeated. He is dead."

Helen turned pale and looked to Rose for confirmation. She said nothing. Helen backed slowly away and turned to the men.

"Kill the first one."

Rose closed her eyes tightly, wondering which one that may be, hoping it was Fergus.

***

Magnar had moved the people closer to Ben Nevis, within the forest where they could be hidden safely from sight. It was dangerous at night, with wolves lurking about, but it was worth the risk. They could afford no more open attacks from Craotics or Outsiders, not before they attacked Cheryic City.

Magnar left his tent to find Caiden and Fergus sprinting directly into him, knocking him to the ground.

He cursed.

"What happened? What did you see?" Magnar asked. He looked from one to the other, then scanned the premises. "Where's Rose?"

Both of the boy's eyes were red with tear stains. Magnar's heart sunk.

"Where is she?" He choked again.

"They took her," Fergus replied. "She might be dead, but more likely they're grilling her for information. She was scouting the city."

Magnar swore, desperately searching for something to punch, but finding nothing. Caiden and Fergus just stared up at him with eager eyes.

He pushed Caiden. "You fool! Why did you let her go alone!"

"It wasna Caiden's fault!" Fergus intervened. "She just left!

Magnar stopped, his eyes fixed on Fergus. "She's never been captured before, how did she get taken this time?"

Fergus shrugged. "She probably was just too reckless; there were so many of them."

Magnar looked to Caiden. "Were you with him the whole time when Rose ran ahead?"

"Aye," Caiden nodded, "I mean at one point he went to look for food, he-"

Caiden's eyes bulged so wide, Magnar was afraid they would leave their sockets. Caiden turned to Fergus.

"Are you a spy?" Caiden asked, his voice cracking slightly.

"What? No! Of course not!" Fergus said quickly, his face turning from Magnar to Caiden to Magnar again. "No,

Gliocas, I would never. There was no way I could have-. Well, I ken it looks bad, but I swear upon Owen Cheryic's-."

"My sister never once trusted you." Magnar said through his teeth. "I thought that was just because you were a punk of a child. But now, perhaps she had good reason."

"Gliocas, please, my allegience is with your family."

"Isn't it a little suspicious that you got away from the Craotics on the day of the attack? That they found our fort as soon as you arrived? That everywhere you are, things seem to go wrong?"

Fergus shook his head too fast, nearly giving himself whiplash in the process.

Magnar scanned the camp looking for the closest soldiers he knew the names of. "Evander! Alec!" he called to them. "Tie Fergus and question him."

Alec did as he said without hesitation, but Evander raised a brow. "Gliocas, are you sure-"

"Do it."

***

"Your friend is dead."

Dread overtook Rose's body as she felt herself grow weak inside, and a tear fell down her cheek.

"All you have to do is tell us where the people are, and the other will live. Even you will live."

She knew it in her heart now, if either Fergus or Caiden truly died because of her, she would never let their death be in vain. She would never ever give this woman information.

Rose said nothing.

The Craotic Chief came inside, holding Rose's bow out in his palms.

"This," he said, "is what you are so famous for throughout the clans. Even *my people* say you can shoot the eye of an eagle."

With some effort, he snapped it in half and threw it on the bed.

"Kill the other."

Rose closed her eyes. Caiden would soon be dead if he wasn't already. It would be Rose's fault.

She examined the remains of the bow and finally took the time to translate the Gaelic that Eason had had engraved on the wood: *Tha goal agam ort.*

***

The whip cracked on Fergus's bareback, and he let out a cry of pain, straining against the ropes that tied him to a Scots pine. Evander, Magnar, and Alec had taken him deep within the forest, where they could be sure no one would hear his cries.

Fergus leaned against the trees, his right leg desperately moving to keep the other upright. But he was struggling, with his pale back covered in the scars of the whip.

"That's enough." Magnar ordered, and he approached Fergus, who shook uncontrollably as he heard his footsteps. "Tell me what you did. Where are they keeping my sister?"

"I swear to ya," Fergus's voice shook. "I may not love yer family, but above all else, I am a loyal Cheryic. I am loyal to my people."

Evander stood at a distance, upright, his face unmoving.

"You will never be welcome among your people again," Magnar fumed. "You are no Cheryic to your Chief."

Fergus said nothing, but sank to his knees. Magnar could only hear the sound of Fergus's wheezing breath as he heaved in and out.

Alec readied his whip again, snapping it into the palm of his hand.

"No." Magnar held a hand out to Alec, restraining him. "He's not worth your strength."

Alec backed away, putting his fist to his chest in respect. Magnar continued to stare at the mangled body that was Fergus's.

"We leave him for the wolves to dine on," Magnar said.

"Gliocas!" Magnar whirled around to find Gilbert Stowe wheezing with his palms held to his knees. He had grown thinner and grayer in the past few months. Dark bags sagged below his eyes, in several shades of purple. "Caiden," he wheezed. "He has run away to Cheryic City."

Magnar cursed and kicked Fergus in the shin, who howled in pain. "Without Rose, Caiden is nothing. He will get himself killed."

Magnar raced away, with Alec close behind him, leaving Fergus crumpled on the forest floor.

Evander remained as still and upright as a statue throughout all of this. Everyone pretty much had forgotten he was there. There was no telling Evander's thoughts unless he let on to them, so nobody attempted to decipher them in vain. When their footsteps disappeared, Evander hurried to Fergus's side and unsheathed his sword.

"Kill me quickly." Fergus whispered.

"Haud yer wheesht, ya fanny." Evander said and cut the ropes which tied Fergus.

Fergus remained in a fetal position on the floor.

"Why? I am a traitor."

Evander snorted, "we both ken that's not true. I've known ya my whole life Fergus, and I ken two things about you: One, yer a bit of a jessie and couldna last two minutes of torture without caving."

Fergus grimaced at this and let out a small, sarcastic, "Thanks."

"And two: ye love yer clan more than anything in this life and would never betray yer people. You are loyal, despite all yer shortcomings."

A few tears ran down Fergus's cheeks, cleaning lines of dirt away from his face.

Evander patted his shoulder and handed him his sword.

"Make it right."

And Evander was gone.

Rose sees rain

"Your friends are dead," Helen said again, but this time Rose felt nothing. She was past the feeling of grief and saw only the wooden planks of the ceiling above her. She didn't know why she could not grieve. She couldn't cry or sob like she had done for Eason. Something about it hadn't settled inside of her. It wasn't as if it was impossible to believe they had been killed, but it wasn't supposed to have happened this way. She could not picture Caiden getting thrown out and...beheaded or stabbed...alone. Something about it did not fit the story.

"Where is Magnar now?" Helen asked, her voice hardened.

She continued staring, barely hearing her, her voice was so distant.

"Fine," Helen replied. She bent over next to Rose, her lips almost touching her ear. "I know your type," she whispered, "You are convinced you will die like a martyr, with a noble and graceful death. Well, let me kill that fantasy right now. Your death will be painful, long-lasting, and humiliating. And I shall make sure no one ever hears of it. Mark my words, your tale will be laughed at as one of the most pathetic stories to ever go down in history."

Rose didn't listen. She refused. She drowned every word Helen said out of her mind and closed her eyes.

"Perhaps we should torture her," Helen said excitedly.

"With respect, my lady," the Craotic Chief interrupted from his position looming in the background. "This lassie is of Scottish blood. Torture is useless on our kind."

"We'll try anyway."

The two men that Rose had seen earlier, grabbed Rose, then cut her ropes, threw her off the bed and onto the ground. She struggled to stand up, her muscles tight from hours of laying in the same position. They grabbed her by the hair and forced her up, sending a stream of pain through her head. They dragged her back to what used to be their living room-kitchen. She looked toward Eason's chair for comfort, but it was gone. There was nothing there but the dirt floor, a fireplace with a pot in it and a small table.

It wasn't the table itself that scared her speechless. It was what lay on it. There was an assortment of knives, a rope, a whip, and something that looked like tongs.

The Craotics ripped her shirt down the back, ensuring that the front was still covered, then lifted her hands to the ceiling, tying her so that her feet barely touched the floor.

Rose looked wildly around her, wondering what they were going to do. She couldn't take the anticipation. In fact, she was sure they were making her wait on purpose, torturing her. She faced the window, which looked out onto the square. She tried to imagine the shops all lined up as they had been just a few months ago. It was enough to distract her.

She couldn't think; she couldn't breathe. The first snap of the whip knocked the wind out of her as she felt its sting on her back. It was so overwhelming that Rose let out a surprised yelp as it came in contact with her skin.

For the first time, Rose closed her eyes and prayed to the spirits.

After sixty cracks, she could feel the hot sticky blood dripping down her back, and even a few drops streaming down her legs. When the whipping stopped, she was surprised. She had gotten used to it at last, and now they were giving up? Her vision faded in and out of darkness, and perhaps they realized it too, for she felt a cool mug of water being pressed to her lips. She accepted it willingly. She half-hoped that the water was poisoned, meant to trick her into dying. But on the contrary, it was given to keep her alive.

"You should see how *noble* you look now," Helen laughed. "Just tell us where your people are and we shall not harm them. We simply want them to return to their kingdom."

Rose had felt what *not harming people* looked like. Helen was a fool. Little did she know that the more they hurt Rose, the more she wanted the people to stay as far away from Helen as possible.

Rose said nothing.

"Your mother thought she was noble too," Helen continued. "She thought it was noble to force me to separate from my sons. All she had to do was keep her trap shut, and we could've been a family."

The men removed the pot from the fire, now boiling and steaming. Rose braced as they winded it back and launched its water at her. She screamed again. The pain was unfathomable now. Every part of her body was burning red. She wiggled and squirmed, doing everything she could to move away, change her position, or best of all, die. The torture wasn't only the boiling water or the whip; it was the helpless feeling brought with it. For the first time in her life, Rose felt powerless to stop any force from coming upon her.

"Do ya see?" She heard the Craotic Chief in the distance. "It is useless on our people. Ye should just kill her and be done with it. I will find yer father…"

Rose heard footsteps fading away, a door shut, and she was left alone to slip out of consciousness.

***

Magnar strapped his leather armor together, securing his sheath to his waste. He slipped his sword inside it, satisfied with the sound of metal brushing metal and the final clink as it fastened.

Magnar turned to find Evander standing at the tent entrance.

"I want to go. I want to save her," Magnar choked.

"She isna some lass that awaits us on the top of a tower," Evander replied matter-of-factly.

"But she needs me now. I want to go."

"The people need someone reliable to stay with them. They need their Chief. After all, Caiden is already going after her."

Magnar scoffed. "Caiden...and what will *he* do? *Talk* my grandfather to death?"

Evander shrugged. "Perhaps."

Magnar shook his head. "No, you think they're invincible, you always have, but this time feels different! It feels real."

Evander paused. "I ken that." He fell silent for a moment, then his hands began shaking so hard, they clenched the fold of his kilt. "I hope they kill her. That lass is not one to be in a cage...and tortured. I hope they allow her to die honorably."

"There's no honor among evil," Magnar murmured to himself.

"I will go to them," Evander said. "At least then ye will ken someone you trust is looking out for them."

Magnar shook his head. "You're the best commander I have. And the man I trust the most here. I cannot lose you now. Not when I've lost Jean and Rose and Caiden." Magnar placed a hand on his old friend's shoulder, then pulled it away. Magnar stepped outside of the tent, with Evander trailing behind him.

"Gliocas!" A small voice said.

Magnar whirled around to see the little girl, Eara, holding up a small pendant.

"My da taught me to carve. Here. Yer our new Chief, so ya need one. For protection."

She placed the pendant in his hand. He studied it, forgetting the Twins for a moment. A tiny deer with great branching antlers had been engraved on the wood. He traced his finger over it.

"Thank you." He let out a breathy laugh. "It's beautiful."

Eara put her hand to her chest and scampered back to her father.

For the first time since the Craotic attacks, Magnar studied his people.

Children were weaving in and out of tents, chasing one another with wooden horses. A mother was sitting on a rock, breastfeeding her newborn son. She had travelled all this way with-child, and given birth in a tent just a few days ago. Gilbert was stroking Valar and feeding her bits of fresh meat as she perched on his shoulder. A group of women in their thirties, many the mothers of young children, were sitting in a circle, singing a Cheryic lullaby as they weaved baskets.

Magnar had come to know Eara and Wallace's father as William. He now sat with his children, telling them the legends of Owen Cheryic under the Mountain. Eason had always been impressed with the versatility of children. He once said that they could adapt to any situation.

Now, as Magnar looked to his people, he could see that it wasn't just children who amazed him. He realized that in his heart, he loved all these people, every one of them. He understood Eason better now and for the first time, he realized why Eason left them on that final day of his life.

Magnar turned back to Evander.

"The Twins will have to do on their own for now. We have an army to lead." He gestured to the infant the woman fed. "That bairn has yet to see his homeland."

He looked to Evander, who stood with his mouth hung open, shocked that he would not need to put up with another fight against Magnar.

"Call the captains. We move tonight. We must plan now."

***

The Cheryic Clan, as well as all the five clans, traditionally had a tight-knit circle of military leaders called "captains," which the Chief appointed. Just about all of the Captains that

Eason had appointed were dead, so it had been left up to Magnar to appoint a new group.

Magnar appointed Evander right away as the first-in-command, which seemed to anger the other qualifiers. Nobody had ever heard of a baker's son being a captain, not to mention the first-in-command.

Among the other captains were Alec, who previously had been first-in-command of the Triact clan; William, whom had served under his uncle; Evander's father Andrew, who had fought gallantly in the last battle; and a few others who also had proven themselves worthy. Magnar had intended to give The Twins positions, but they were never actually around to accept them. He would never, ever allow either to be first-in-command, he had decided. They were too compulsive.

The men filed into the tent and sat in a circle on the ground.

"You all know why we are here," Magnar began, attempting to make his voice deep like Eason's had been. This had always been difficult for him. He had a soft, high-pitched voice for a man. "We need to reclaim our home from the Outside."

"Aye," Alec said bluntly. "but how?"

"We canna meet them in open-field," William chimed in. "Their numbers are too great, even with the clans united. And the Fisherpeople havena sent their full army yet, and even when they do, they claim they'll only use it to block off the river."

Magnar spread a map of their city before them. Above the city, Ben Nevis towered in the background, shadowing over the houses and buildings. "When they attacked us," he began, "they attacked us from the South. They didn't know the forest as we do, and they had numbers, so once they were on the farmland, they weren't afraid of being seen."

He paused, his gloved hand brushing over his beard absentmindedly.

"Well," he began, "we don't have their numbers. So we can't meet them from the South."

He reached over and crossed a line through the south with a piece of black coal.

"The West is out of the question," Evander chimed in. "It would take days to reach the other side of the valley without being seen."

Magnar nodded and crossed out the west as well. This left only the East. Or…

"What about the North?" Magnar asked, creases forming above his eyebrows.

Alec laughed.

William cleared his throat. "Forgive me, Gliocas, but that is suicide. They ken the North passage now. Rose closed it off to us anyway."

The room stiffened at the mention of the princess's name. Andrew studied his son nervously, but Evander's face did not twitch. All other eyes studied Magnar for even the slightest reaction, but he gave none.

"Our people," Magnar began, "survived inside that mountain for hundreds of years. The Twins stumbled upon that entrance at fifteen-years-old. You are telling me that there are no other ways to enter that mountain?"

"Well," Evander replied, "there's the main gate which the miners used on the north side, but I'd be shocked if it wasna guarded or closed off. And the little door on the south side, surely they closed that off as well."

Magnar clinked his fingers against his knees.

"Send the fastest rider to the Fisher Chief and tell him that if his army does not block off the river on the East side, the wedding is off." He looked to Evander. "As for my decision: we ride to the north side tonight. You and I will go ahead with a few miners and scouts." He turned his eyes to the rest of the group, who appeared to be silent, but uneasy. "I expect my army to be on the Northside in three days' time."

He stood up and exited the tent, then popped his head back in the door. "You must learn to trust your Chief."

The men cleared out of the tent behind Magnar. Before Evander could leave, however, Andrew grabbed his shoulder.

The two remained silent in the tent for a few moments, listening to only the clinks of ale mugs outside.

"Well?" Evander asked.

"How are ya?"

"Fine." Evander said quickly. He turned to leave.

"Yer no fine, son." Andrew replied. "Perhaps ye willna show it on yer face, but it doesna take a genius to guess."

Evander said nothing.

"I'm proud of ya," Andrew said, "I ken it's a wee bit late to say so, but ye've kept yer head. Even with yer lassie gone."

"She's no my lassie!" Evander spat. "She's my betrothed! And she's no gone!"

Outside, someone won a game of poker. There was a chorus of cheers and groans, followed by, 'Feast yer eyes ye bloody bastards!'

When the choruses subsided, Andrew said awkwardly, "Congratulations!"

Evander nodded.

"Shame I wasna the first to ken." Andrew joked.

Evander rolled his eyes. "No one kens."

"Yer not alone, lad," Andrew said, his face sobering. "Losing your woman…it's a terrible thing."

"I'll no lose her!" Evander shouted. He opened his mouth as if to say something else, but could only storm out of the tent.

a final adventure

It was a night's journey to find their way behind Ben Nevis with the small group that Magnar had taken with him. He was shaking with anticipation. There were a million things that could have gone wrong: The Fishpeople might not come on time; the army might be found before it reached the mountain; the Craotics could be swarming inside of the mountain; or worst of all, Caiden and Rose might be dead by the time the army arrived. But this plan was all Magnar had and he prayed Eason would get him through the rest of it.

When Magnar's expedition arrived upon the mountain's base, they found the tunnel which Rose, Caiden, and Fergus had successfully blocked. Magnar dismounted his horse and stared at the entrance for about five minutes. Evander, noticing the awkward cessation in accomplishing anything, rode up beside him.

"Shall we dig through it, Gliocas?"

Magnar shook his head. "They know it's there. They followed us, remember?" Magnar looked below Evander's horse's shoe, and stomped on the ground.

"Our people lived below this mountain once. Do you remember the stories?"

"Aye," Evander said. "There was an entire city below our feet."

Magnar nodded. "We dig here."

***

The knife was touching Rose's ear, its cold metal pressing hard, her blood drizzling down her neck. She closed her eyes tightly.

"Where has Magnar hidden your people?" Helen whispered.

"Nowhere."

The knife sliced through the skin. Rose could not hear the commotion from the outside over her screams, but something drew the woman away from her as she hurried outside.

"Maw." Caiden stood in the doorway, his arms at his side looking like a little kid again. He could see something stir in Helen's cold, unfeeling eyes. "What have you done?" he asked.

Helen's voice wavered. "How did you get inside...past the guard…? I'll call them now."

"You won't though," Caiden said. "There are two things that you have avoided your whole life, Maw. I believe it is because these two things make you human. Magnar and myself. Me. I am your son."

It was all Caiden could do to keep his eyes from Rose's crippled remains. Caiden had never seen her so...broken. He focused on his mother. She looked so much like him...but with Magnar's eyes. Her hair was wild, dark and frizzy. Her skin pale. What had his father looked like? Caiden had always imagined him with blond hair like Magnar, since Magnar looked so different from him and Eason. But he supposed Magnar's father was different than his own.

"You should leave here," Helen whispered, wiping her bloody knife on her pants. "He wants you. He'll recognize me in you, in an instant. He says he wants your land, but it's you and Rose he wants. He's always wanted you."

"If you care so much, why did you do that to your own sister's daughter?" Caiden asked, pointing at Rose.

A tear fell down Helen's cheek. "Don't you see? *She* kept us apart. *Her mother* forced us to be apart the day she wrote of your existence in that book. I needed to find you. Please, it's been you, it's always been you. You need to hide. Forever. Or he will find you. And kill you and your brother."

Caiden nodded. "That's why you sent us here all those years ago, isn't it mother? You wanted to hide us. You wanted no one to know we existed. Especially grandfather. And then...you wanted to forget that we ever existed."

"Please leave," she choked. "Stop this war or you all will die."

"Correct," A deep voice boomed. "You will all die."

Helen screamed.

***

The army had arrived, and the men were not given the courtesy of a fire, for fear that they would be seen in the darkness. Only the soft sounds of dirt being drawn up from the ground could be heard. Magnar chewed on a piece of dried deer meat as he watched the mud pile before him grow larger and taller, and the hole below become deeper.

What if this doesn't work? We are wasting time.

He could rely on it, the steady rhythm of the earth being lifted, and he murmured an apology to the spirits of the earth under his breath.

CLANG.

Magnar turned and heard murmurs of the men digging.

He looked below the ground. Already, they needed to form a ladder in the side of the hole to crawl up and down.

"What did you find?"

"Stone, Gliocas," a man, caked with dirt from head to toe, responded. "An ancient ceiling!"

"Break it," Magnar ordered.

They tied a rope to the man and held him dangling above the stone as he mined it for what seemed like hours until finally the stone crashed down about ten feet below.

"Bring the ladder," Magnar ordered.

They did. The soldiers filed down the hole into a dark room, one by one.

While the men were still clambering down, Evander took the risk of lighting a torch. The room was piled with dust. He coughed as the men's feet kicked it up. There were old desks and shelves everywhere, many with wood chipped off the sides, eaten by termites and bugs of the ground. To the men's relief, there were no people inside.

"This was a library." Evander said to no one, "who knows how large this place is."

"Scout it," Magnar ordered. "Take Andrew with you."

Evander protested with a glare, but then gave a quick nod. He and Andrew headed out the library door, torch in hand. They both looked below the balcony and saw nothing but rooms, floors and floors below.

"There must be a hundred floors down there," Andrew remarked.

Evander pursed his lips, hoping to keep the small talk to a minimum, "And two hundred above...this will be difficult."

They continued down the narrow path, peeking into room after room. "Do ye even mind going through here? Everything from that day was such a blur."

"I mind ye leavin', without questioning where yer son is." Evander said. He normally wasn't afraid of heights, but his stomach lurched when he looked below him. He didn't remember feeling like this. "We were lower. We have to find a way down."

"I did look for ya."

Evander snorted.

They continued down the path, extremely aware of the steep drop to the right of the railing.

"It's sooo dark," Andrew said. "Perhaps that's why your lassie gets so tan and we stay pale. She didna have ancestors who lived in darkness for hundreds of years."

"Dinna talk of my betrothed." The floors towered above them and the air felt damp. He traced his hands along the wall to his left, careful not to fall in the narrow space between the path and the wall. It was strange; the path was attached by segments of stone as opposed to being completely held to the mountain. The wall felt damp and filled with deep grooves.

Andrew grabbed Evander's arm. "One thing that shall be clear from this day on. I looked for ya and found the Chief. He said ye were back in the house with yer lassie. I looked in the house. Ye werena there. Then I heard that ye had made yer way to the ben, so I followed. That's all."

Evander yanked himself from his father's grip. For a moment, his eyes scanned the premise.

"I'm sorry." Evander finally said.

Andrew nodded, and they continued walking. "This is odd," Andrew changed the subject. "Ye would think that if a civilization lived here, they would have need for lots of stairs. We havena come across a single staircase yet."

Evander stopped in his tracks and held his torch up to the wall.

"Of course." He murmured under his breath. He held one segment of the wall in his hand, placed his foot in a foothold, and then down he went. Andrew gave a breathy laugh and followed closely behind.

"Like the grooves on our own walls," Andrew said. "I miss those walls."

"Aye, me too." Evander froze for a moment upon reaching the bottom and looked to his left. They could barely see past their torches, but Evander continued to his left anyhow, surefooted.

"Careful," Andrew warned. "Yer not giving yourself time to look around."

"No, no," Evander murmured. "It's this way."

Andrew wrinkled his brows. "How do ye ken that?"

"It's warmer."

"That's yer torch."

"Naw!"

Evander halted. To his side was the bridge that the Cheryic people had used to flee their city. He bolted across, remembering how brutally endless the walk had originally been.

Suddenly they were there, standing below the little door hatch, which had provided their escape in the first place. He could easily have lifted it...peeked his head through...but then they would know.

Hadn't they thought to explore this place? Perhaps they just thought it was useless. Just a bridge to the other side of the mountain. It could be used for travel, but what need did the Americans have to go to northern Scotland?

"There has to be another door," Evander said. "I mean, think about it, this place is huge! How else would our people have gotten out for trade? They had carts and produce!"

Andrew shrugged. "You dinna think *that* door had anything to do with it, do ya?"

Evander whirled around to where Andrew's finger was pointing to see that the giant, wooden wall was not a wall at all...but had a handle.

"Um...aye…"

"How do we open it?"

"Ehhh we leave that to Magnar."

***

They stood at the base of the gate, eyes wide.

"Wow." Magnar said, "So...this leads-"

"I assume so."

Magnar turned and looked at the army flooding the interior of the mountain, waiting patiently behind him. They had been as quiet as they could, but there were a thousand men. It was impossible to be silent. Still, they were inside a mountain. How could they be heard?

Magnar faced the gate again with his chest heaving in a deep breath of air. "So, when we open it...that's it. Right? They know we're here."

Evander shrugged. "I assume."

Magnar sucked in his cheeks. *What if they've heard us and are waiting for us right outside this gate?* Magnar thought, but then again, *How could they know it's there?* Nobody in the clan had ever seen this door from the outside. It probably looked exactly like the mountainside.

Then suddenly, Magnar realized why the plan was too easy: If they broke down this heavy door, surely an alarm would sound before they got through. They needed to open it as quickly and quietly as possible.

"How do we do this, Evander?" Magnar asked. "How do we get through? Och, Rose was always so good at-"

"We could try opening it," Evander said plainly.

"Haud yer wheesht." Magnar rolled his eyes.

Evander impatiently bounded to the door, and with minimum struggle, opened it.

The entire room gasped, for on the other side of the door was a big wall of dirt.

Magnar spat on the floor. "This was a horrible idea." He turned back to the men, who held their small bits of laughter tightly in their stomachs.

"You." He pointed at a random group of four in the back of the room. "Scout for more doors. The rest of us...shall dig."

***

The Twins had been tied up and the guards left the room, leaving Helen, Blayne, and the Twins to host an overdue family reunion.

"So," Blayne Rankin began. "These are my grandchildren."

Helen sat frozen in her chair, staring at her feet.

"Both yours?"

"No." She whispered.

He grunted and strode over to the tied Twins. "Amazing, the likeness between them. Both from my side no doubt."

"Please, daddy," was all that Helen could squeeze out of her mouth.

Blayne slapped her in the face.

"What a mess you and your sister have made of this family." Blayne cleared his throat and approached Rose.

She spat in his face.

He snorted. "Arrogant…like your mother."

He called the guards back inside.

"Hang them." He ordered, and two giants of men took the Twins by their ears and dragged them out the door.

"No daddy, please!" Helen screamed, yanking his arm back. "He's my son!"

Blayne narrowed his eyes at her. "And Eason was mine. I'm over it and so shall you be soon."

Helen lay in a fetal position on the ground as Blayne left.

Rose did not respond. She let the guards drag her, with her mouth dangling limply, gazing directly into the sun. Caiden squealed.

"Rose!" He whispered loudly. "Rose!"

She said nothing. Secretly, she hoped it would be over soon. She missed Eason. She missed her mother.

"Rose!" Caiden shouted desperately.

"Silence!" One of the thugs shouted.

"DAMMIT WOMAN IF YOU DON'T PULL YOURSELF OUT OF THIS, MAGNAR WILL DIE."

"Quiet, savage!" The thug holding Rose ordered, and he kicked Caiden in the gut.

As soon as he turned away, Rose was on top of him, holding his neck with the very rope that tied her hands. He gagged on it, and the man holding Caiden had no choice but to watch, for fear of loosening his grip on Caiden and then having two escapees. Finally, the thug's face was a dark purple, and his eyes bulged red. He fell to his knees and then gradually the floor. Rose took the weapon which had been strapped to his back: a medium axe, sharp enough to cut her hair with, and she chopped the other thug in the chest.

With a wild look in her eyes, Rose held the axe over her head in anger. Caiden screeched. She let the axe down on the ropes that bound him.

"You talk to me like that again and I'll cut yer arms off," she said.

Caiden nodded dramatically.

what lies on the field

"We've broken through Gliocas!"

Magnar stared at the fist-sized peephole of cool air coming from the outside. He peeked outside: Nothing but the backs of stone homes in the distance.

He looked behind him. "When this door is opened, we must all get through this door as soon as possible and charge the city. We cannot be narrowed by this pathway. And no war cries. We move quickly and quietly."

The men nodded.

"Dig a hole in the bottom." Magnar said. "Everyone back up."

Two men dug at the base of the doorway until suddenly they leapt as the dirt from the door fell to the ground, filling the room with crumbles of rolling stone. Everyone but Magnar covered their eyes as beams of light blinded them. Magnar looked straight into it. Home. It would be different without Eason. He would be reminded every day that he was gone now that he was back where he'd been raised. But he didn't care. This was his one chance to take back what was rightfully his. He would not waste it.

He ran full speed to the city, his men rallying behind him.

A bell sounded. They had been seen, but it was too late. They were all nearing it, their swords unsheathed, their hair whipping behind them in the breeze. These men knew the terrain better than any Outsiders. Their boots trotted the grass skillfully as they understood the placement of every pebble, divot, and stone.

A few men, Craotics, appeared in between the houses, shouting at them in gargled tones. Magnar ducked one's jab and stabbed his gut. He could hear Evander beside him slicing another.

They ran a few more feet and then suddenly, they were hit with a wave of Craotics.

***

The Twins weaved between houses, jumping through windows to hide in stone corners when a Craotic or Outsider passed by. They finally stopped to rest in an empty cellar. Rose looked so pale, Caiden swore she would topple over. They scoured the cellar for any sort of remnants of food and managed to find a few rotten apples which they settled for. They slumped to the floor, enjoying the coolness of the underground.

Rose was quiet. She had barely put two words together since they had escaped execution. Part of it was out of fear that they would be heard, but another part, Caiden sensed, was from something broken inside of her. He drew his brows together. There was a bit of dried blood masking the side of his face. She was unsure if it was his own or someone else's, but she didn't ask.

"Hey," he said, nudging her with his foot. "Remember when we were sixteen and there was that baltic winter? Like the coldest one I've ever seen and there was so much snow, I thought it would go over our house. But you wanted to hunt food for the people even though Uncle told you not to go outside? So we snuck out and you got hypothermia and I had to drag you back and I thought you were going to die and I was gonna be in so much trouble, but you were okay after a few weeks?"

Rose rolled her eyes. "If you're going to say this is exactly like that you're-"

"Well, this is *exactly* like that," Caiden said. "I mean, come on. I thought you were gonna die, because you did something really good for the people, but now, I will get you home safe...and after a few weeks, you'll be okay."

Tears welled up in Rose's eyes as she hugged her knees close to her chest. "This isn't the same, Caiden." She sobbed. "The world will not stop until I am alone. First my mother, then Eason, and now you and Magnar's lives are in danger too. They told me you were dead. I was alone."

Caiden shook his head. "You and I, Rose, will never be alone. We're just not good at it. I mean, look what happened when you went off to spy on your own, or when I went off to get you!"

Rose laughed a little and nodded, wiping the waterfall of tears from her cheek. Caiden could hardly look at her without wondering how she was still alive. Her back, which he had covered with his cloak, was caked with blood. The skin that was not covered in blood was red and blistered. An entire ear was missing from her head, which Caiden had managed to bandage using shreds of his tunic. He knew she was right when she said this time was different. He believed it when he saw her. But when he looked away, he could convince himself she would be alright again.

"From now on," Caiden said, "we stay together."

Rose nodded as he took her hand and squeezed it.

The Twins froze. Men were shouting in the distance. Swords were clanking. Chaos was ensuing. They stood up slowly with their ears pressed against the cellar hatch, trying to make out the commotion. They exchanged looks of hope.

"Magnar!" They chimed in unison.

***

The men were closing in on them now. Magnar barely had time to think as he blocked and jabbed and slashed, sometimes fighting two at once. He had lost sight of Evander and was now in the midst of a blood bath. Sweat glazed his face and he felt that this was one of the hottest days he could remember.

The Cheryic-Triact army hadn't even made it to the edge of the city yet, and they were being pushed back, bit by bit. Where had all of these Craotics come from? The city had been so quiet.

Magnar blocked a blade and drove it to the ground, bringing it up quickly to stab a man's neck.

Out of the corner of his eye, he saw his men falling, one by one. Was this what Eason had felt in his last moments? He was not tired, nor hurt, but wounded by his complete sense of failure. How many lives had been ruined on his account? How many more would be ruined?

He began contemplating a form of retreat when he realized his siblings were still somewhere in the city. They were alive; he could feel it. But where were they? Retreating would be signing their death warrant. And where would the clan go? Retreating, Magnar realized, would be the end of the Cheryic people as he knew it.

Magnar took in a breath and continued to fight forward, gaining a second wind as he slashed and jabbed and ducked.

Suddenly, the fighting paused a beat and Magnar turned his head to the West. A horn was sounding near the West gate. A million questions whirled through Magnar's head: Who were these people? Whose side were they on? The horn represented a clan, but it would be impossible for any Cheryic or Triacts to get behind the mountain so quickly without being seen.

The Craotics seemed equally perplexed, for their full forces had been on the attackers from the north. Those in the back of the lines quickly darted to the West gate, but it was too late. Ladders were being thrown against the wall and someone was pounding against the gate.

The wooden gate broke after only a few pounds of a large tree trunk, forming a splintered hole, which the Craotics shot their arrows through. A few men from the other side were hit, falling back into the men's arms behind them. But soon, the door was opened and streams of garnet men and women filed inside, sporting pitchforks and axes—the Farmerpeople. Leading them rode a flaming haired Cheryic man, dashing gallantly into the Craotics.

Magnar could not make out the man's face, but he was grateful to him. Whoever it was, he was a hero. With the Farmerpeople hitting the city from the West, and the Cheryic-Triacts from the North, the Craotics were rapidly being pushed Southeast, toward the town's square.

***

"I need a helicopter near Ben Nevis. Now."

The Twins remained in the cellar, silent, their backs to the wall.

"What do you mean you can't get that close to the mountain? This is your Commander in Chief speaking!"

Rose climbed the cellar ladder slightly, and creaked open the door, peeking out. Sure enough, her grandfather stood right in her view, surrounded by six thugs. He was so close, she could…

And before she could consider what she was doing, she lurched out the door with nothing but a small kitchen knife in hand. She could feel Caiden right behind her, and she leaped on top of the first thug, stabbing him in the neck. Caiden had no such luxury of a knife and managed to punch the first thug's face, but it wasn't long after that he was getting kicked and beaten by two others.

Rose, meanwhile, was facing two thugs at once. She flipped her knife over and under her fingers skillfully. She spat at one's face and stabbed the other's leg, but suddenly, she felt a sharp pain in her calf and she looked at it, horrified. An arrow ran through the calf, shot by an American a few feet away. He smiled beneath dark glasses and put his crossbow back by his side.

Rose cried out in pain, but continued thrashing wildly at the two thugs she fought. It was in vain.

no more tomorrow

Magnar and his army pushed forward for hours, finding it was much easier now that the Craotic army was being thinned. They had broken into the city, weaving between the streets that they had grown up on, slaughtering all Outsiders and Craotics in sight.

The sun was setting when they finally reached the square. The sky had a deep orange and purple hue, complimenting the red leaves growing on the few trees in the middle of the square. One of them looked particularly beautiful: An old oak with great thick arms branching out vastly. Attached to these arms were leaves of all colors: tints of yellows, oranges, and reds. Also attached to these thick branches were two nooses.

The Twins were only standing on their tippy toes on makeshift chairs, their necks bound by these nooses. An arrow still protruded from Rose's leg. Her face was so pale, for a second, Magnar thought she had already died.

"Magnar!" The old man's voice boomed above the crowd. The Twins stood in the center of the square, held by the four thugs. Caiden squirmed, his face was covered in blood and dirt. Rose's head sagged and blood dripped from a hole that had once been her ear. Magnar stopped dead in his tracks, his eyes wide with horror as they met Rose's for a brief moment.

"What are you doing?" His grandfather asked from his position next to the tree. He wore a tight black suit and red tie, the same outfit he had worn to his meeting with the clans so many years ago. "Why do you insist on hurting those around you with this...war? Eason would have been so...disappointed."

"No Magnar, that's not true, you know that's not true," Caiden yelled quickly. "Eason wanted to fight him since he first-" Caiden groaned as he was kicked in the ribs by one of the thugs holding him. He struggled to stay on top of the chair, his hands bound together behind his back.

"Don't touch him!" Magnar shouted and started after his grandfather, sword ready.

"Nah-ah" Blayne tsked. "If you come here, it will be with your sword on the ground in surrender and only then will I let your brother and cousin live. Understand?"

For the first time, Rose picked up her head. "No," was all she said.

"Yeah, what she said!" Caiden added intelligently.

Magnar turned behind him to his people. All had stopped fighting and were watching Magnar with eager eyes. He could hear Eason's voice in the back of his head: *This is what they do, they slowly take over, and pretend that it's temporary, just a little more, until suddenly they have killed all around you.* But then he looked back at the Twins with desperation in his eyes. He remembered how little they had once been, with chubby cheeks, and giant curls. He could not kill those children. His people would understand. This was his fault for choosing them over his brother and sister before. He should have come after them in the first place and left Evander to lead. They would have been okay without him. This was his fault for not choosing his family over his people.

He turned back to his soldiers and motioned for them to lower their weapons.

The old man laughed.

"*Tha gaol agam ort!*" A voice choked.

Magnar's breath caught in the back of his throat as he turned back to Rose, who shouted it again: Tha gaol agam ort. *I love you.* A bead of sweat fell down the side of Magnar's head as he looked his cousin in the eyes. His hands shook. He knew what she said, but he did not want to believe he knew why she said it.

"Lead," she mouthed. Her eyes were brighter than ever now, as Eason's used to be when he was passionate.

she kicked over the chair.

She did not struggle. She just hung.

Caiden glanced over, saw what she had done, gave one last half-smile at Magnar, and kicked his chair over as well.

"NO!" Magnar shouted as the walls closed in around him. He couldn't breathe. He couldn't think. He saw nothing but his grandfather, surrounded by red, and he charged. His sword ready to kill. Four thugs were ready for him, and he smashed his sword into the first one, and dodged the second one's blade. But the other two came at him from behind, one slashing his side, and the other jamming his head with his hilt.

Magnar gasped for air and fell to his knees, sputtering. The thugs grabbed his arms, holding him tightly. Out of the corner of his eye he could see the lifeless bodies of his siblings, their eyes staring unseeing at the clearest sky Ben Nevis had ever seen.

Then he glared at the pale-blue eyes of his grandfather and spat.

His grandfather smiled.

"Your people," he whispered, "will die too."

"Why?" Magnar asked. "because I am your grandchild? Because *they* were your illegitimate grandchildren?" Magnar nodded to The Twins, who still dangled from the tree.

He could feel the thugs' grips loosen, not enough for him to break free, but enough to make him realize that this was news to them. Magnar turned to them.

"He is not killing us for our land," Magnar seethed. "He is killing us because we are a taint to his bloodline and he will kill you for knowing. Mark my words. Escape while you can-"

Blayne punched him in the mouth. It was hard for a man of his age, hard enough for Magnar to spit up blood. The thug's grips still did not loosen more, and they seemed unconvinced of any truth to Magnar's words. *It was worth a try*, Magnar thought.

Suddenly, the sun was blocked by a pair of golden wings. One of the thugs behind Magnar screamed and released Magnar completely from his grip.

Magnar whirled around. Valar was pecking the eyes of the thug. The man blindly swatted at the bird, his eyes bleeding profusely.

Magnar seized the opportunity and plunged his blade into the second thug.

He turned to his grandfather, his sword ready.

The old man opened his mouth as if to say one final word to his grandchild, but a knife slit his throat from behind, before noise could even leave his mouth. The blood sprayed onto Magnar's blond hair. His grandfather toppled to the ground, his face quickly turning a deep violet.

Above him stood Helen, panting with red eyes. For a moment, she met Magnar's frazzled gaze, but then she dove to Caiden's side. Magnar fell to Rose's side as well.

The fighting continued as the Cheryic-Triacts and Farmers chased the remaining Outsiders and Craotics to the East. Magnar was soon left behind, but he was not needed. He heard another horn as the Craotics arrived at the river.

The Fisher people have arrived. He thought. *We have won.*

The Craotics and Outsiders would have no choice but to attempt to flee south. The land was too vast there, too open. They would surrender. When the shouting quieted, Magnar realized they had surrendered and he felt the whole world take a breath.

Helen took Caiden's head in her arms and cried out to the spirits. Magnar only stared at Rose, pushing a piece of hair behind her ears. He didn't want to close her eyes, her beautiful green eyes, because that would be the end of her, and Eason, and Christine, and all of those who had suffered under this one man. Those green, pained eyes which had been forced from place to place could not be at rest this way. This could not be the end of them.

Corpses of people were sprawled out all over the ground. They made Magnar wonder, were they going to the same place? The earth had gained so many spirits on this day. How was it big enough to contain them?

A few Cheryic men lowered the Twins' corpses to the ground. Magnar observed them with a heavy heart, wanting to preserve every detail of their faces in his mind. Both of their leather boots were worn and the souls were beginning to peel off. Their breeks had tiny holes throughout them. Rose's had a large hole at the knees, filled with the blood of scraped skin.

He looked into her green eyes one more time, wiping the blood from his fingers. As he closed them, her long lashes touched the top of her cheekbones.

Rose's dark hair reached her waste by now, with strands hardened by dry blood. She was so thin...he never had noticed how flat her stomach and sunken her cheeks had become. She was so strong when they had started, but now her body had begun to cave after so many days of hunger. Her rosebud lips were chapped, tiny cuts had formed around them.

Magnar took her hand. It was calloused inside the knuckles and almost completely covered in mud and dried blood. The nails were broken with chunks of blood inside as well.

Helen did not let go of Caiden. Her sobs were beginning to quiet as she swallowed a lump in her chest.

"I haven't told you the reason why I took you here."

Magnar did not look at her. She had saved him, but she had killed Rose. He wholeheartedly believed that. He did not respond. She continued anyway.

"You know what your grandfather did to us...he was...he was mad. He was insane. I lived with him the longest. Eason broke free as a teenager and Christine ran away with a boy. It was me who stood by him. He was my father. How could I not?"

Magnar brushed his fingers through Rose's hair. He still could not look at this woman, but he couldn't help but realize her tone sounded less strangled than he remembered it. Her voice shrieked less and now was soft and free. *How could that be?* Magnar thought. *Her son is dead.*

"Eason said you were protecting us from our grandfather," Magnar interrupted, hoping to end the conversation.

"No," she said softly, "that is why I took *Caiden* to this land. But you and I, Magnar, we had such good times. Those were the best two years of my life when I had you. But- I could feel myself changing, becoming like him."

She began to sob harder, tears rolling to the ground in rivers, much like Rose's had when she cried.

"Oh Magnar, he would hurt me so much. I was becoming like him. It was all he taught me to do, to hurt." She nodded to Rose as she said it, referring to her mangled body. "I couldn't bring you up like that. I couldn't make you like him, like me. I had to break the cycle."

For the first time, Magnar studied his mother and saw so much of Rose, Caiden and Eason in her. If Rose had grown to her forties, he supposed she would have ended up looking like Helen. Her eyes had the Rankin mark: bright green with long lashes. Her face was pale, with small lips like Eason's, and a round profound forehead. Magnar was jealous. Only his eyes had ever resembled his uncle's.

Magnar allowed himself to give her a slight nod, for that's all his courage could amount to.

He turned to Caiden, taking him from her. She stood up and backed slowly away.

"I will tell everyone the truth," she said. "I will make sure no one goes near this place again. I swear on my life."

Magnar still said nothing.

Helen ran away.

That was the last time he ever saw her.

Magnar studied his little brother.

His mouth was slightly wider than Rose's, yet still possessed the same thick lips. He hadn't shaved his face in a while, an uneven stubble had formed all across it. His hair was down to his chest now, nearly in dreads it was so dirty. He had done his hair partly in braids before battle, but those were barely recognizable now. The corners of his mouth were crimson with dried blood. In fact, everything was dampened with blood. Their faces, their clothing, everything.

Magnar shook Caiden, urging him to wake up. He didn't move. Magnar hoisted himself up and began jumping in a similar manner to the way Caiden would jump on his bed in the morning.

"CAIDEN!" Magnar shouted, over and over. Then, with a small glimmer of hope, he turned to Rose and shook her as well. She was so limp, her head flailed as he shook her. Her skin felt as if she had just come out of a cold rain.

Magnar turned to find Evander standing helplessly behind him, unmoving, his eyes and nose red.

Magnar shook Rose harder, but Evander grabbed his shoulder aggressively.

"Be careful." Evander choked out the words.

Magnar ignored him and started slapping her face, unable to see through tears.

"Be careful with her!"

Magnar couldn't help it, she needed to wake up right now. But then he was yanked off of her and thrown onto the ground.

"They're gone, Magnar."

Magnar sobbed on the floor for a minute and then turned to a nearby soldier. "Send word to the women and children that the city is free and safe to return."

He felt a cold hand on the back of his neck and jumped.

"I will." A woman's voice said.

Magnar whirled around to find a tall, thin woman with pale hair and high cheekbones looking down at him with teary eyes.

"You have done it," Jean said. "You all have saved our people."

Magnar still held Rose's hand in his. "It doesn't feel like saving."

"But still," Jean said. "At the price of a few brave souls, you have saved countless. Songs will be written about ya."

Magnar sucked in a breath, trying to regain his composure. "What about them?"

Jean closed Caiden's eyes and whispered a prayer to his spirit. "Songs will be written about them too. Just as they always wanted."

She held a hand to Magnar and hoisted him to his feet again.

"How are you here?" Magnar asked. "Are you married?"

Jean looked bashfully at her clothes. "I requested to come here to dress the wounds of those in battle. Alas, I couldna save my husband-to-be from a Craotic arrow piercing his heart. And the Fisher Chief has no more sons. When he was killed, I had the funniest feeling The Twins were dead too."

Jean gave a hearty laugh through sniffles and tears.

Magnar scrunched his brows. "What would the Twins' death ever have to do with the death of your husband-to-be?"

Jean gave a sideways smile. “Because only the spirits of The Twins would have that cruel sense of humor.”

Magnar snorted, gazing at the Twins’ bodies on the ground. His eyes were glued to them, even when Jean reached out and took his hand in hers.

“The Fisher Chief will request payment,” Magnar warned.

“Aye,” Jean said. “Perhaps a few ships, once we land back on our feet?”

“Aye, you may make a good queen yet.” Magnar nodded.

Jean glanced around the field, her eyes passing over the bodies. “I should get back to work. Have ye seen Fergus?”

“Fergus is dead.”

Jean gasped. “What?”

“We tied him to a tree and left him to die.”

Jean smacked him in the back of the head. “Fergus led the Farmerpeople into battle, ya eejit. Yer alive thanks to his timing.”

Magnar’s eyes widened. “Then where?”

“Here.” Fergus said, behind the tree. His eyes were glossy beneath his dirt-caked face. “I saw it all happen...may I?”

Magnar did not apologize for what he had done, but instead did the hardest thing he could: backed away from Rose.

Fergus fell to his knees, his face unchanging at first, and he grazed his hand across a few peelings of dried blood on her temple.

“Ye closed her eyes.” He said.

“Aye.”

Fergus nodded, his eyes beginning to redden, but his face still unchanging. “Please forgive me, Rose,” he began to whimper. "please." Then he bowed his face to the ground and left, leaving Magnar standing alone with his chin to his chest.

"Magnar."

Magnar whirled around to find the Farmer Chief looming awkwardly behind him. He clearly had been waiting for the perfect moment to interject and had found one. Now he seemed quite uncomfortable.

"I am sorry about yer family," he said. "Their spirits are with us now."

Magnar held his fist to his heart in thanks. "Thank you for your aid, Gliocas. Scotland is safe thanks to you."

The Chief nodded. "It is safe thanks to *us*."

Magnar turned back to the Twins, but the Chief stopped him before he could get too close.

"My men will get them ready for the ben," he said. "But for now, there is another matter that needs yer attention. By the Pit."

***

The Craotic Chief was bound from head to toe. The men had made sure he couldn't move, couldn't speak, couldn't think. The Farmer Chief and Magnar watched him struggle to maintain his balance on the pit's edge for a few minutes.

Finally, the Farmer Chief spoke.

"Chief Stuart Craotic, ye are here being tried for breaking The Treaty of *Còig Cinnidhean,* and compromising the unity of Scotland. Do ya have anything to say for yerself?"

The Chief tried to say something through his gag, but only managed to let a few lines of drool escape.

The Farmer Chief grunted. "Nothing? Well I hereby condemn this man as guilty. Chief Rankin?"

Magnar watched the man struggle through tired eyes. He had seen too much war today.

"This man is not the enemy," Magnar said quietly to himself. "He was betrayed into thinking that wealth surpasses unity."

Magnar stared at the Craotic Chief's broken desheveled form. "You have killed my uncle, cousin and brother. But I forgive ya."

The Farmer Chief sighed. "Aye, Magnar, ye are noble...and wise beyond yer years."

The Farmer Chief began backing away from the pit. "Unfortunately, his clan has killed so many of my people and caused them to relocate from their homes. I am *not* a noble man. I am a Chief."

With that, the Farmer Chief kicked the Craotic Chief over the edge, and the man fell into the pit, landing with a harsh crack.

"They say this pit swallowed the Outsiders," The Farmer Chief murmured. "Let's hope it swallows traitors as well."

the changes are Magnar's to make

The Twins were taken to the top of Ben Nevis and burnt on a pyre to join the spirits. That afternoon, the clan realized that they had not celebrated L'anaman this year and they owed it to the spirits to renew their thanks. On the way back down the mountain, Magnar took an apple and bit into it. It was especially sweet this year and the juice ran down his chin as he entered the city.

A fire was made to celebrate the spirits, and all gathered around it. Chelinda had sewn Magnar a new tartan, and he wore it inside his house now, as he awaited his time to join the people by the fire. His hair had been neatly brushed and braided. It was now a soft, golden color after months of neglect. Jean stood beside him, her hair equally golden as it fell to her waist along with the long white gown she wore. She took his hand.

"You are ready for this."

Magnar nervously patted down his tunic, searching compulsively for wrinkles or traces of dirt. He admired Jean. She seemed fit for this role, as she stood with a regal posture. She returned his gaze with a smile, her delicate cheekbones rising to her eyes.

"Ye ken," she said, "Rose never did finish teachin' me to fight."

He took her arm and patted her shoulder.

"That can be remedied," he said with a wink.

They opened the door and walked outside together.

Evander stood next to Andrew, wearing his army kilt, cleaned and plated, with a perfectly white shirt and cloak. He was the new head of the Cheryic army, dedicating his life to the clan. Even Fergus was there, but in brown breeks and braids of a simple fisherman, for he wanted to live out the rest of his days in peace. The clan held out their arms to Magnar as he bowed to them. When he rose again, he made this speech:

"In the Outside, my sister once told me that they believe that their God is looking down upon them, watching from above. I never was one to understand the views of the Outside. To me, he or she or they are all with us, connecting us all to each other. Our ancestors are guiding us here on earth. But none are above us. My family is with me herc, in the eyes of every one of my people. If I look hard enough in the meadow, I can see them as children, getting a good old-fashioned hiding from my uncle." This earned a series of laughter and humorous murmurs. Magnar allowed the silence to settle back in, his eyes off in the distance. "I do not feel grief, but gratefulness, because without them, I am nothing. It is a cruel irony, but without their sacrifice and the sacrifice of all our loved ones, in this war and the wars before, our clan as we know it would cease to exist. That is the miracle of Scotland. We know that the spirits exist, because every piece of suffering we experience connects to create love. I am Chief because my grandfather abused my mother. Our clan is safe because the Twins are dead. I will be a good Chief because the Twins taught me to see through my fear. I know that they will be with me today and forevermore, to protect, guide, and celebrate the world with you."

It was a short speech, but later would be made into a song, entitled, *Mìorbhail Crìochnachaidhean Briste* or in English:

The Miracle of Broken Endings.

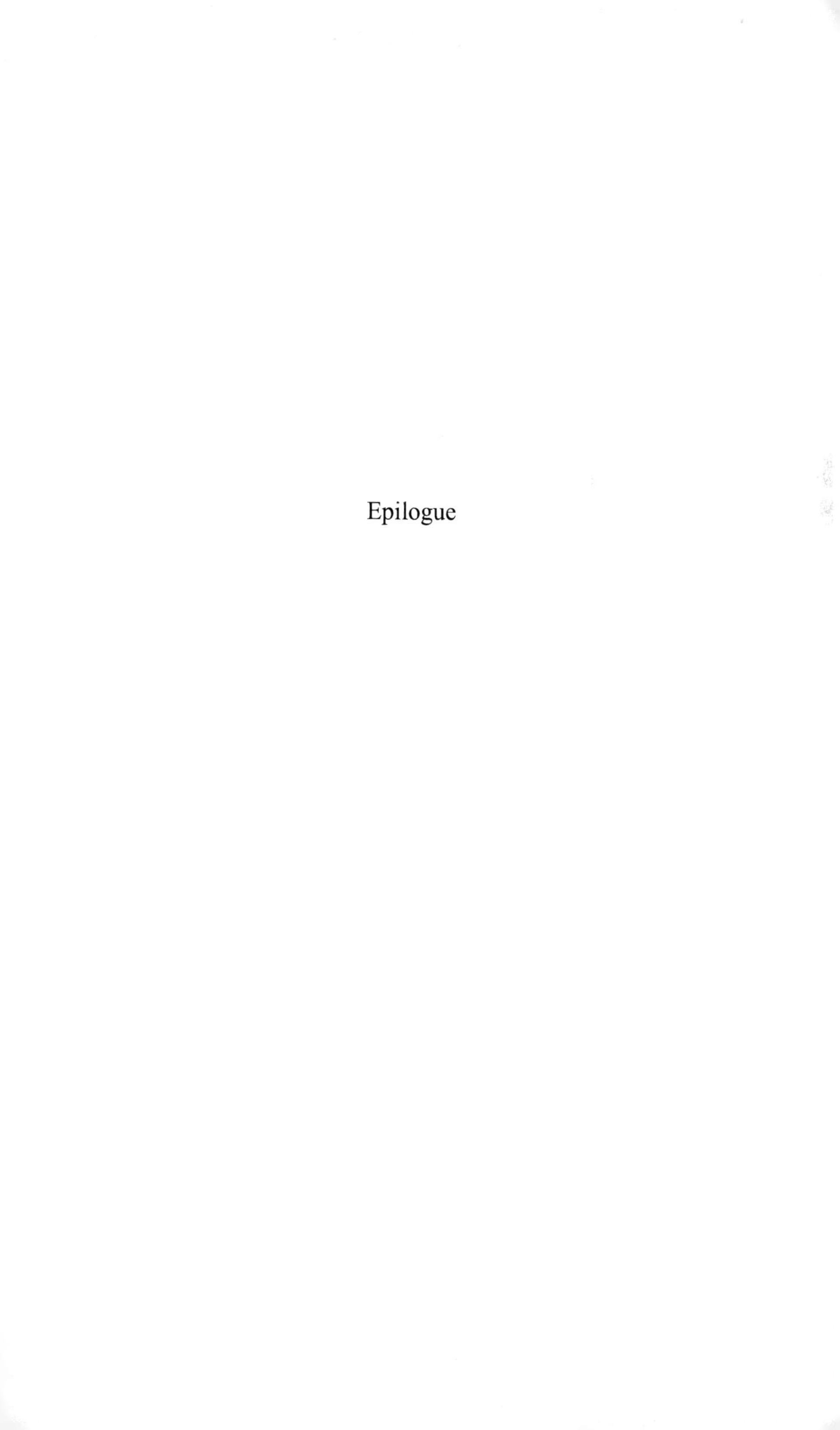

Epilogue

the broken mold

An old man, a shriveled dying Chief lay in the golden folds of his bed. Outside, his people awaited with candles illuminating their faces, shining with tears upon each cheek. Some of the people went to bed, refusing to believe that the man would ever leave them, thinking him to be immortal. But the elderly remained outside of his door, remembering just how mortal the rest of his family had been.

In his room was the man's adopted son: a sweet Triact orphan, who they said he had found years ago during the war. Now the boy was graying and bearded. The son stood with a wife and daughter by his side, a fiery girl who had taken to fighting and scrutinized each detail of the adventures of the long lost Twins. The dying man's wife stood by his side as well, her long pale hair now white as the snow forming on the ground outside. She grazed his palm with her frail fingers.

She let solemn tears fall atop his chest, as she held her head above him, taking in the details of his face. The man himself was peaceful, with one hand resting in his wife's and the other on his sword.

"It is time," he said softly. "I have lived too long without them."

The thought of two children, a boy and a girl playing in a meadow together possessed his mind. How mischievous those children were! Hiding, stealing, daring, and fighting in good spirit. He left his wife and family behind, waking in a bright new world.

***

"I am proud of you, my son."

The Great Chief turned around to see a majestic, stout man with dark braids and a fresh kilt walking toward him in bare feet.

"Magnar's here! Let's go!"

Caiden leaped on top of Magnar, taking him in for a long embrace. Rose joined. Both were innocent once more, their hair flowing past their shoulders and skin glowing with youth.

Eason smiled. "They've been waiting for you for sixty years."

"Can we go? Can we go, Uncle? Mother?" Rose asked.

I gestured toward what Magnar suddenly noticed to be never-ending stairs.

"Where does that lead?" Magnar asked.

The Twins smiled mischievously.

"Our greatest adventure."

Acknowledgments

Dad, although you never actually finished reading me The Hobbit, thank you for getting me obsessed with Lord of the Rings so that I could develop an imagination. Mom, thank you for always being a role model to look up to in my writing endeavors. Jonald and Carly, thanks for being the sources of inspiration for this story. Ben, I couldn't have done this without you getting me motivated to finish this damn thing.

About The Author

Talia Martini is a Psychology major at Villanova University. She began writing this book at fourteen-years-old, inspired by The Lord of the Rings. (Talia thought her mother was half Scottish at the time. A total lie.) This story was based on a dream that Talia had in 8th grade about the dwarves from The Hobbit, which of course, just had to be made into a book. Although Talia made Rose's appearance like her own, she based the character Magnar off of her own constantly worried nature.

Made in the USA
Monee, IL
07 September 2020